All That Glitters

To a
Fellow Square
Dancer

All That Glitters

Lisa J. Flickinger

All That Glitters

ISBN: 978-1-62020-548-8
eISBN: 978-1-62020-468-9

Scripture quotations taken from The King James Version, The Authorized Version.

Cover Design and Page Layout by Hannah Nichols
eBook Conversion by Anna Riebe Raats
Author Photo by Photo Magic

AE Books
411 University Ridge, Suite B14
Greenville, SC 29601
www.ambassador-international.com

AMBASSADOR BOOKS
The Mount
2 Woodstock Link
Belfast, BT6 8DD, Northern Ireland, UK
www.ambassadormedia.co.uk

The colophon is a trademark of AE Books

To the love of my life, Matty, thanks for your encouragement.

CHAPTER 1

"VIVIAN, ARE YOU IN THERE?"

The bedroom door opened; Vivian Connor clutched her embroidery hoop tighter, and her needle paused in midair, the indigo blue floss dangling.

Her younger sister Virginia stomped into the room and threw herself onto the bed. "I think . . . I think I'll suffocate if I have to stay in this house one more minute." She kicked her feet and hit the coverlet with clenched fists.

Not again. The pockmarks in the rose-colored wallpaper across the room were a reminder of the last "unfortunate incident" as Mother called it. Was it just a week ago? Father had replaced her brush, comb, and mirror with the sterling silver set arranged on the chiffonier. They must have cost dearly—too dearly for a family without any wages. Tucking a ringlet behind one ear, Vivian stood and crossed the room hiding the gift from Virginia's view. "All right, Virginia, what is it now?"

"Father decided I couldn't go to the Fireman's Ball on Saturday. I asked him a week ago when Logan asked me. He said he doesn't know Logan Harris well enough to trust his daughter with him, but I've known him for a whole month."

"Ginny," The soothing tone masked the exasperation bubbling in her stomach. "You know Father can't abide one of your fits right now. And furthermore, he's right. No one knows anything about your so-called hero, Logan."

"I know everything I need to know."

"Well then, has he told you where the money he flashes around town comes from?" No, and he wouldn't, either. His kind had been seen before: arrogant, pushy, and good-looking enough to get away with it.

Ginny sat up and pinned Vivian with bright blue eyes. Her chin lifted, and a slight smirk appeared on her lips. "I didn't think discussing where either of our fortunes came from was important."

"Fortunes? What fortune? Our family's situation is worse now than ever before with Father so sick. Oh, Ginny, you didn't!" As Vivian's fingernails pierced the palms of her clenched fists, the pain was a reminder to be civil. *One must always be civil.*

Ginny fussed with the pearl button on the edge of her wrist cuff and gave an exaggerated huff.

One ... two ... three ... deep breaths. "Ginny, did you lead Logan to believe Aunt Margaret's home was our own?"

"Not exactly."

"Not exactly?" It was hopeless to keep her voice from rising. "You mean you neglected to tell him we were living here only until Mother and Father decided what to do?"

"I didn't think it was important, and frankly, he didn't ask. All that really matters is that we have each other," Ginny lay back on the bed once more and spread her arms out with her dainty fingers extended and sighed. "You'll understand some day when you're in love, like Logan and I are."

Maybe a sharp smack to the side of Ginny's face would matter, and perhaps even wipe that smug grin off her face, too. How could she be so mean? It wasn't fair; Vivian was twenty years old, two years Ginny's senior, and almost an old maid. The longing to be in love filled many daydreams, like linking an arm through another strong and protective one for a stroll through town or clasping a sturdy and supportive hand to step up into a carriage. But how would it ever happen when Ginny kept Vivian busy tidying up ridiculous messes? Between that and Father's illness, there was no time to meet a fellow—let alone court one.

"So if money doesn't matter, why did Logan ask you to join him as he followed the men up North looking for gold?" Vivian asked. How could her sister be so naïve? The only things Logan cared about were money and finding the easiest way to get it. The gold rush was just the current prospect. Lots of folks had been saying they expected '98 to produce more fortunes than the last two years put together. Every second man was heading up North to the Klondike seeking the elusive gold; Logan Harris was only one more fool.

"Well, Logan feels one should never lose an opportunity. He says the men need all kinds of supplies and services in the Klondike. He aims to meet the demand. I could be rich!" she said extending her arms above her head.

"Shush, they might hear you downstairs. Ginny, promise me you won't go." Why bother asking for a promise? She'd never kept them anyway. And she'd never listened to reason, either. But her family deserved an attempt. "We don't know anything about Logan, and you've only just met him. And even worse, you've misled him! What happens when he realizes you have no family money?" The grooves between the boards of the hardwood floor dug into her knees as she knelt on the floor beside the bed and took Ginny's hand within her own. "I love you too much to let you do this. We all love you. Please, don't go."

"Really, Viv, aren't you being a bit dramatic? I'm sure you will all get along fine without me." She pulled her hand from Vivian's and adjusted the collar of her dress. "You're always saying I'm such a bother anyway."

The breath caught in Vivian's throat. It was true, Vivian thought Ginny a bother, but Ginny had no idea how high the resentment had built up incident by incident, brick by brick, until it was difficult to see over the top.

"And you wouldn't believe what it's like up North. Every second man is a millionaire. There are thousands of opportunities to make a fortune. In Dawson City there are fancy dance halls and splendid theatres. The women wear clothes as fashionable as those in Paris."

"I am not concerned about what they wear. I am concerned about you."

"Logan is going to buy a hotel. I can't wait to live out my dream and walk down the staircase in a satin and velvet gown embroidered with tiny golden flowers," Ginny's finger traced a flower in the air, "and the train flowing behind me on the stairs, my suede gloves on the banister. Everyone will turn and look at me."

And it still won't be enough. It will never be enough. Does Logan have any idea? But if Ginny leaves right now, it might kill Father. "Don't go! I beg you, Ginny, don't go!"

"Settle down. I promise you I won't go until I am sure of both Logan and his intentions."

"What will happen if Father— "

"Well, if you don't think Father can bear the news right now, keep this conversation between the two of us." Ginny grabbed her shawl from the bed and wrapped it around her petite shoulders. "I think I will make my way down to Lady Annabelle's and see if she needs any errands run." She stood and walked toward the door.

Lady Annabelle was a wealthy neighbour confined to a wheel-chair. Ginny liked to make a habit of helping the elderly woman during the day and reading the Bible to her in the evenings; it was one of the few things to be admired about her sister. But it still wasn't fair. All the endless hours of taking care of their two siblings, running errands for the family, and doing household tasks fell on Vivian's shoulders with no appreciation. Yet, Ginny received constant praise from her mother, father, and aunt for her kindness to a stranger.

"Maybe . . . you should go," Vivian whispered to Ginny's back.

Ginny paused and looked back over her shoulder; tilting her head to one side, she raised an eyebrow. "Go? Where?"

The question hung between them, unanswered.

Ginny turned, grabbed fistfuls of her dress, and stormed out the door.

Turning to lean against the bed, Vivian covered her face with her hands. The bedrail pressed into the flesh on her side, and her legs prickled down into her toes. Why did Ginny make life so difficult? Why was she so hard to love?

Dear Jesus, I don't even understand who Ginny is any more. She's done so many horrible things. I am so afraid she will do

something I can't fix. My family needs Your help, Lord. Please give
me Your guidance. Amen.

Taking a deep breath, Vivian pushed errant wisps of hair back from her forehead with her fingertips and tucked them into her coiffure. A wave of peace entered her heart. Standing, she smoothed the skirt of her yellow cotton dress. Ginny must be told she was about to make a terrible mistake.

The grandfather clock in the vestibule chimed eleven. Where were Jeremy and Sarah? Vivian had agreed to take the two for a walk during Father's midday rest. They were likely in the backyard working on their fort. Poor Aunt Margaret—her beautifully manicured lawn and elegant gardens would not survive the constant digging and climbing of the two younger siblings.

Vivian closed the bedroom door and descended the staircase to the main entrance hall, the even grain of the cherry wood banister cool beneath her fingers. The hushed tones of Mother and Aunt Margaret echoed from the parlor—they must be having tea. But why did Mother sound so upset? Upon reaching the landing, Vivian paused. Mother and Aunt Margaret sat on two velvet cushioned chairs in front of the floor-to-ceiling bookshelves in the parlor. The silver tea set sat on a small table between them. It was odd; they usually took their tea in the kitchen where the large windows let in more sunlight.

Mother dabbed her eyes with a lace hankie. Auntie reached over to pat Mother's hand murmuring as she shook her head from side to side.

Mother looked up and startled when her eyes met Vivian's. She brought the hankie down to her lap, and a tiny smile came to her lips before she spoke. "Why, Vivian, I didn't know you were here. Your Aunt Margaret and I were . . . we were having a nice chat," she said.

"What about, Mother? Why are you crying?"

Her mother lifted the hankie and covered her eyes; her shoulders quaked.

"Don't worry, Vivian," Aunt Margaret replied. "Sometimes we women need to talk things out. You'll understand in time."

Mother sat crying as Aunt Margaret stood and picked up the teacups to place them on the silver tray.

Descending three stairs, Vivian walked over to stand beside her mother. She reached a hand out and placed it on her mother's shoulder. Mother shrugged, and Vivian's hand fell to her side. The gesture stung, and tears gathered behind her eyes. Her voice carried a hitch as she spoke, "Mother, what's wrong? Is it Father? Is he worse?"

Aunt Margaret moved the cups and saucers around on the tray, a small tremble to her fingers.

"Mother?"

"Vivian, please, you're not helping. Let your mother be."

"Mother, please. I need to know."

Mother didn't say a word as she stared off into the corner and wound a hankie around her fingers.

Aunt Margaret straightened her slender back and turned to speak to Vivian. "I think it would be best if you took the children for their walk. Your mother is exhausted and mustn't be bothered."

"Aunt Margaret, why don't you tell me? What is going on?"

"It's not my place to tell you. Your parents will tell you when it is necessary. Please, go for your walk." The dismissal was unmistakable.

"Mother, Aunt Margaret, if you will excuse me," Vivian curtsied, "I will be taking a walk with the children now." She turned on her heel, marched to the front door, and closed it with a firm thump.

They will tell her when it is necessary? Would they ever understand how all the secrets twisted in her stomach at night, how she curled up in the window seat in the bedroom for hours upon hours staring at the moon and wondering what would become of them? How long would they try to protect her from the truth? When would they realize she was a grown-up, an adult only a few months from her twenty-first birthday? The need to know if her father's health had worsened burned in her chest; if they wouldn't tell her, she would find someone who would.

Vivian clomped down the front walk. Jeremy and Sarah peered out of the apple tree on the front boulevard as they plucked blossoms off the branches and sprinkled them on the ground. Their cheeks flushed with exertion, and their eyes sparkled with mischief.

"Vivvy," Jeremy said, "we're making snow!"

Vivian laughed and walked over to the tree; she reached through the thick leaves to help the children climb down. "Come on, you two. I think Aunt Margaret might want some apples this summer."

Sarah, five years old, favored Ginny's looks with jet black hair and vivid blue eyes. Her chubby arms circled Vivian's neck. Vivian gave her a quick squeeze before bending over to set her on the grass.

Jeremy grabbed an upper branch with one fist and swung to a lower one. He curled his legs around the next and released his hands to swing back and then dropped to the grass on his bare feet. At seven years old, he'd grown three inches in the last year. He took after their mother's family with long, bony limbs and large joints. She envied his golden brown curls.

Since their father's illness and the move to Aunt Margaret's home, most of their care had fallen on Vivian's shoulders. Ginny considered herself much too important to spend her time with "mere children," and Mother and Aunt Margaret were kept busy taking care of Father.

"But we weren't picking apples—just silly old flowers," Jeremy said.

"In that case, I think we have something to talk about on our walk. And I might even have a couple of pennies for some candy from the general store on Main Street."

"Oh, could we, Vivvy? Could we get some of my favorites?" Sarah asked.

Vivian brushed the leaves and sticks from Sarah's brown pinafore and wiped the smudges of dirt from her sister's cheeks. Sarah licked each palm and ran them along her forehead and down each braid. She looked up at Vivian, a grin stretching across her tiny face.

"That looks better," Vivian reached out to pluck one last stray leaf from Sarah's blouse. What would she do without the distraction of her younger brother and sister? She stretched her hand out to tidy Jeremy's collar.

"Ah, cut that out, Vivvy. I can brush my own self," he squirmed away and straightened his jacket.

He was growing up so fast, like a little man of the house.

The trio sauntered down the lane of the sleepy town. The family's move three months ago had brought them East across the country to Aunt Margaret's hometown of Brentwood. Vivian missed back home where everyone knew her by name, but the Brentwood residents were friendly and had welcomed them with open arms. Several waved from their gardens and front lawns as the trio walked by.

The intoxicating scent of the spring blossoms filled her nostrils as the warmth of the sun spread across her back releasing some of the tension between her shoulder blades.

Two houses down from Lady Annabelle's sprawling lawn, Vivian noticed Ginny's blue skirt protruding from the corner of Lady Annabelle's summer kitchen several yards from the main house. What was Ginny doing out there? Perhaps this was an opportunity to take a moment and apologize for her earlier rudeness. Then she could convince Ginny not to make a decision she might regret the rest of her life. She grasped the hands of her siblings and quickened their pace.

As they neared the house, the reason for Ginny's location became apparent. Ginny and Logan stood face-to-face in the shadow of the summer kitchen with Ginny's back against the brick wall and Logan's left hand leaning on the wall next to her shoulder. They appeared deep in conversation and completely oblivious to the trio's advance. Logan handed Ginny a small leather pouch. She clasped it in both hands and held it to her chest, staring up into Logan's face. He leaned forward and kissed her on the lips, and then his entire body pressed Ginny against the wall, his hands now holding either side of her face.

Vivian gasped, and Jeremy and Sarah turned their faces toward her.

"Uh . . . " Raising a hand to her mouth, she pointed to a bumble-bee in a flowerbed a few steps away.

"Are you afraid of a stupid old bee, Vivvy? It won't hurt you if you don't bother him." Jeremy stepped over, nudged the flower with his boot, and the bee buzzed away.

What was Ginny thinking? If Jeremy and Sarah saw what had transpired across the street, how would she ever explain it to them? Ginny's plan had gone so much farther than the family suspected. Glancing up toward the summerhouse, Vivian exhaled as Ginny headed toward the manor, and Logan was nowhere to be seen.

"What beautiful violets," Vivian bent over next to the flower bed and brought her nose to the tiny petals, inhaling their sweet aroma. *Lord, what should I do?*

Sarah knelt on the grass, leaned over, and took a big sniff. "That tickles." She giggled and rubbed the end of her nose.

Jeremy stood and watched his sisters, a smirk on his face and arms folded across his chest.

Vivian straightened and dusted the front of her skirt. "All right. Let's go." She clasped Sarah's hand, pulling her to her feet. The three continued walking toward Main Street.

All the talk about helping Lady Annabelle and going on about ministering to the lonely, all the times Ginny excused herself from chores at home so she could help someone who "really needed her," were all lies. She'd pretended to be unselfish when all along it was a ruse to meet Logan. Of course her kindness had never been real. Why would Ginny change? And it had been stupid, so stupid, to believe her. Maybe Mother wouldn't think so highly of her little dear when she heard the truth. Perhaps Ginny had finally gone too far. Regardless, knowing the condition of Father's health was more urgent than her sister's shenanigans, and Sarah and Jeremy deserved her attention.

As Vivian and the children walked along, she took the opportunity to explain why they shouldn't pluck the blossoms from Aunt Margaret's tree, as it needed the flowers to produce the apples they both loved to eat. She also peppered the children with questions about their bug collection, which was kept in small jars in the backyard.

"Maybe we should let some of our bees go in the tree to make sure we didn't kill all the apples?" Jeremy's eyes met hers.

"I suppose that might work. I'll bet the bees would love to spend some time in that beautiful tree, anyway. Do you think you could do it without getting stung?"

"Ah, sure. I'm not afraid of bees. Not like you girls," Jeremy hitched up his trousers and strutted down the street, his small fists jabbing the air. "I'll bet I could even take a round out of that fellow who was kissing Ginny. He wasn't supposed to, was he, Vivvy?"

Her heart thudded in her chest. "Uh, pardon, Jeremy? I don't think I understand."

"You know, that tall fellow mucking all over Ginny's face over at Lady Annabelle's. I don't think Father would be too happy to find out, either."

"Why do you think that, Jeremy?"

"I heard him talking to Ginny the other day about not making decisions she would regret. Do you suppose that's what he was talking about, kissing that guy and such?"

How long had Jeremy been concerned about Ginny? He was much too young to be troubled over his older sister. Ginny needed to realize her choices affected the whole family. "I'm sure Ginny's fine, Jeremy. Please don't worry about her. She knows right from wrong. And you know Father is not feeling well. I think he's being overly cautious. How did you overhear them anyway?"

"I was sneaking cookies for Sarah and me from the pantry when Father and Ginny were talking in the kitchen." He stopped for a moment and reached out to touch the sleeve of her dress. "You won't tell him I was doing that, will ya? I wasn't meaning to listen in."

Hand extended, she brushed the curls back from his forehead and clasped his chin with her fingers. "I think he would understand,

Jeremy, and if you talked to him about stealing cookies, you would feel better, too. As for Ginny, I'm not quite sure what she's up to or what Father was talking to her about, but I do aim to find out. There are too many secrets in this family."

"Will you tell us when you know?" The trust and innocence on Jeremy's and Sarah's face both melted her heart and fueled her anger toward Ginny.

"I promise you two, I won't keep any secrets." Unless, of course, it would do more harm than good to tell them. "And I would like you to promise me, too. If you know something important, share it with me before it's too late."

"I promise, Viv," Jeremy said with the sincerity of a solemn pledge.

"Me too, Vivvy."

The three of them clasped hands and ambled further down the street.

"All right, let's see what we can do about getting you two some of those peppermint sticks you love so much from the general store."

CHAPTER 2

TWENTY MINUTES LATER THEY ARRIVED at the end of Main Street. Tall and short, brick and clapboard, the buildings lined either side of the bustling plank sidewalks. Benches for patrons' convenience sat outside several of the establishments, and flower boxes filled with spring flowers hung under the windows of many shops. Large black lettering painted against a grey backdrop read, "Willy's General Store" on a sign above the door of a two-story brick building across the street. Vivian removed two pennies for each of the children from her drawstring purse and shooed them over to buy their peppermints. They begged for time to visit Misty, the store cat and playmate of the town's children. Vivian agreed and instructed them not to leave the store. It wouldn't take long to finish her errands.

The sidewalk creaked under her boots as she proceeded to Dr. Mason's halfway down the street to inquire about Father's health and learn whether or not it had taken a turn for the worse. And no wonder if it had. Father must have some idea of what Ginny had been up to if he'd been giving her warnings.

"Ahh!" Vivian lost her balance and tumbled to the dusty sidewalk. Pushing herself upright, Vivian felt a sharp pain shoot up from her ankle and through her knee. Doubling over, she gripped her left ankle with both hands. The pain throbbed as her jaw clamped together. Giving a small tug on her ankle, Vivian winced as the pain spiked up her leg once more. The foot was firmly wedged in a hole made by a broken board. Several of the buttons from her boot lay scattered in the dust.

Oh, not now. How could she have been so clumsy?

She tried once more to remove her ankle from the sidewalk. The jagged edge of the board cut into her ankle, and she bit her lip to keep from crying out.

"Are you all right, missy?"

She looked up. The voice belonged to an older gentleman sitting on the bench in front of the blacksmith shop.

"Could you use some help?" He stood and hobbled her way.

"I'll be fine, sir. I need a moment to collect myself, thank you." Sucking in a breath, she held her fingers up in a wave. He shrugged and returned to his bench.

How embarrassing. She needed a moment to collect herself, all right, and to figure out how to remove her ankle from the sidewalk. Could the day get any worse?

A young boy stepped out of the bakery and nearly toppled over her.

With a quick movement, and ignoring the pain, she gave a twist to the ankle. It didn't budge.

"It looks like maybe you could use some help," a deep voice said as large hands appeared and pried the splintered board from the side-walk. The nails released with a harsh screech.

Only one tear escaped her eye as the same large hands gently turned her foot and removed it from the hole. The material of her skirt bunched against his chest as he scooped her up from the planks like a small child.

"What are you doing? Put me down!"

The arms tightened. "Let me know where to, ma'am. I saw the whole thing from across the street, and I know you are in no condition to walk by yourself."

"I said, put me— " Vivian looked into such deep brown eyes that the protest left her lips.

A chuckle vibrated through his chest. "McCormack. Ben McCormack, ma'am. It's a pleasure to make your acquaintance."

A warm flush crept up her cheeks as reason returned. She dropped her gaze and squirmed in his embrace. If Mother saw the situation she'd gotten herself into, she'd never be allowed out of the house again.

"Mr. McCormack, this is most improper. Please, put me down."

"If you say so," Ben placed Vivian on her feet and removed his grip.

"Ouch." The ankle gave way, and she stumbled forward.

He reached out and grasped her elbow to steady her; then he effortlessly lifted her into his arms once more.

She swallowed, "I—" The words stuck in her throat again as she looked back at his face. He had high cheek bones, a firm jaw, and a shock of chestnut hair fell on his forehead. When she met those eyes again, her heart gave a tiny flutter. "Sir, would you mind if I lean on your arm? I'm going to Dr. Mason's; I'll have him take a look at my ankle."

"Yup, I mind. I don't want you to do any more damage to that ankle than has already been done." He carried her several doors down to the doctor's office. The solid muscles in his chest pressed against her arm as he bent to twist the knob on the door.

"Doc, I've got another patient here for you."

"Is that you, Ben?" A muffled voice emerged from the back of the office. "I'll be with you in a couple of minutes. Have a seat."

Ben stepped over to the row of wooden chairs under the window in the waiting room. He bent over and placed Vivian on one of the chairs. Her own shaking fingers tidied her hair and smoothed her skirt.

"We should get that boot off. Your ankle is probably beginning to swell."

"Um . . . no, really, I'll be fine. I so appreciate your help. Thank you." She arranged her skirt to cover her boots. How did one get out of a predicament like this? He was probably very busy, and she'd taken enough of his time. If she'd been paying attention, this never would have happened, although those few moments in his arms had been heavenly.

"Would you mind giving a name to that pretty face of yours? I don't believe we've ever met, and I've been around these parts forever."

"We're new; we moved here about three months ago. My father is not well, and we have come to live with my elderly aunt until he feels well enough to preach again."

"Oh, a parson's daughter with a penchant for daydreaming," he said. "And your name, ma'am?"

Who was he to cast judgement so quickly? Vivian straightened her shoulders and reached out her hand. "Connor, Miss Vivian Connor, and I'm pleased to make your acquaintance. However, I don't wish to keep you any longer. I'll be fine." Warmth tingled in her fingers; he still held her hand. She pulled it from his grasp as her eyes glanced about for somewhere to land, anywhere but on his wide, even smile.

"Really? And how do you intend to get yourself home? Looks to me like you might be laid up for a while with that ankle. Do you have a carriage nearby?"

Could he hear the pounding in her chest as she looked over at the tall, broad-shouldered stranger? "No, I don't. We walked; it was such a lovely day."

"How about if I come back with my wagon in about half an hour and give you a lift home?"

They did need a ride home; her ankle wouldn't bear walking. And he was offering, even if it was out of politeness. But was it proper to take the offer unescorted? Although, Jeremy and Sarah would be with them; surely Mother and Father would understand the necessity. "Thank you, that sounds fine. I mean, if you don't mind. I have two small children with me as well."

He gave her another one of his toe-tingling smiles. "What do you take me for, a child hater?"

"I'm sorry, no. I—"

"Look, don't worry. I'm not trying to sweep you off your feet, even if it seems like I did."

A low chuckle rolled from his throat. "I simply want to give you a ride home."

Not trying to sweep her off her feet? Why not? He said she was pretty. Was there something wrong with her? Was he already married? He hadn't mentioned it if he was. It was probably of no matter anyway. "That sounds fine, Mr. McCormack. I will be here when you return."

"I'm at your service." He removed his black Stetson and swept his arm in a wide arc as he bowed in front of her.

Despite the discomfort of the situation, a giggle escaped her lips, and her hand rose to cover her mouth. "Thank you, sir. It will be greatly appreciated."

He returned his hat to his head and spun on one boot heel to leave the doctor's office.

Vivian thought she caught the words "foolish pride" as he closed the door, and the latch clicked shut. Shoulders slumped, she leaned back and held her breath for a moment. Severe throbbing pulsed inside her boot. Lifting the edge of her skirt, she poked at the swelling around her ankle.

"Ugh," her eyes squeezed shut. That hurt. Why today, of all days, did she have to hurt herself?

The clinic's inner door opened. Dr. Mason appeared and was followed by a middle-aged woman. Deep lines fanned out from the corners of her eyes, and her homespun dress was patched and re-patched. Three young boys followed, jostling each other with their elbows as they tried to pass through the doorway at the same time. The tallest sported a white bandage across his forearm.

"Now you boys, you need to listen to your ma and stop fighting. I can't be fixing one of you up every week. I don't want to see you in here for a good long while, you hear?"

The three cut their antics and answered in unison, "Yes, sir," their expressions the picture of earnestness.

Dr. Mason wagged his finger in their faces. "I'm going to hold you to it. Now, go on."

"Thank you again, Doc. I don't know what I'd do without your help, what with their pa off chasin' gold and all. I've had to take in a whole lot more laundry." The woman's brow furrowed as she lifted her shoulder and let it drop. "I'm too busy to watch them every minute."

"You're doing a fine job raising those boys alone, Susan. I knew you had it in you. You all take care now." Dr. Mason walked them to the door and tousled each boy's hair as they passed. "Those boys, they're a challenge for sure," he said as he closed the door behind them and turned toward Vivian.

"Now, young lady, what can I do for you?"

Tell me my father's fine. Make my sister behave. Fix my ankle. Tell me more about Ben. "Hello, Dr. Mason, I think I've injured my ankle. I wasn't paying attention and stepped in a hole in the sidewalk. I fell and twisted it; I hope it's not serious."

"You know, I asked old Isaac to make sure he got that hole fixed last week before someone got hurt. Let's take a look."

Vivian lifted her skirt and rested her ankle in the doctor's out-stretched hand.

"It's swelling up all right. Why haven't you taken your boot off? The restriction must be causing you some considerable pain."

Undoing what remained of the lacing, the doctor slid the boot from her foot and asked her to remove her cotton stocking. He probed the area around the joint indicating that she move it from side to side and up and down.

Biting the side of her lip, she could move her foot a little in each direction.

"Well, it's not broken; however, it does appear sprained. It's hard to tell how badly at this point; could be a couple of days or maybe several weeks to recover. We'll know more by later today, I suspect." He pulled another chair from the wall and rested her heel on it. "I'll have my assistant bring a bandage out here, and we'll loan you a cane as long as you need it. I've got a patient waiting in the inner room, so if you will excuse me." The doctor turned to scurry through the same door he'd come in.

The adjacent chair thumped on the floor as she smacked the arm rest with a clenched fist. Leaning forward, her elbow put pressure on her knee and a sharp splinter of pain coursed up through her calf. She snapped upright. How could she have been so stupid? She would be completely useless at home. Arms covering her face, a sob escaped her lips.

"Here, here, no need to cry. It's a sprained ankle; it will heal."

Vivian's hands dropped into her lap. A tall, lanky young man stood with a handkerchief in his outstretched hand and a rolled bandage in the other. He handed her the handkerchief, and she dabbed at her eyes. Then the young man tilted his head to the side as though studying her.

Vivian raised her eyebrows and leaned forward as his silence became uncomfortable. "Do I know you from somewhere?" she asked.

"I don't think so."

"You don't think so?"

"You remind me of someone, though. As a matter of fact, you look a lot like her; only, she is dark where you are fair."

Dark where I am fair? Virginia? No one had ever compared the two of them before. Virginia was the family beauty. Vivian wasn't even in the running.

"Could you possibly mean Virginia Connor?"

"Yes, do you know of her? Are you related? She never mentioned having a sister."

"You've met Virginia?"

"Yes, we are well acquainted. But I've actually come to wrap your ankle, if you would allow me. I'm working with my uncle for the summer until I decide where I want to practice." He extended his hand to shake hers. "My name is Dr. Alistair Williams."

Vivian reached out and shook his hand. How does he know Virginia? She's never talked about anyone named Alistair. It was something else to ask her about when Vivian arrived home. There were more significant matters to attend to at the moment. "I need to talk to Dr. Mason; it's very important. It's about my father." Vivian searched his eyes; maybe he could give her the answers she was looking for.

"Don't you worry. He hasn't gone far, but Dr. Mason is a very busy man. Now, let me see that ankle."

Vivian held her breath to keep from crying out as Alistair deftly bound her ankle with the bandage and pinned the loose end on the top of her foot.

"Thank you for being so careful, Dr. Williams. I appreciate it." She slowly brought her foot to the floor and brushed the upturned ruffle of her skirt. "But I really must speak with Dr. Mason. It's about my father; he's a patient of the doctor. I need to know what's going on, and no one will tell me. They keep whispering behind my back." She sniffled. "I don't know what's happening, but I need to know." The tears welled up and overflowed. Why did everything have to be so secretive? She couldn't help if she didn't know what was wrong. The handkerchief in her fingers dampened as her tears fell to her lap.

Alistair's light hand patted her shoulder. "There, there. I know this is a very difficult time for your family. Your sister has often shared her concerns with me about your father's health."

"She has?" Ginny had shared her concerns? What concerns? She cares only about herself. And when does she share all these concerns—on her visits up the street to the poor widow? "I'm sorry for getting so upset, but could you please tell me what's happening with my Father?"

Alistair opened his mouth, paused, and closed it. Then he sat in the chair beside Vivian without saying a word.

"What is it? What's wrong? You must know him. Have you attended him with Dr. Mason?" When she saw the look on Alistair's face, desperation welled up in her chest. "Answer me. Please answer my questions."

He spoke, his voice slow and even, "Miss Connor, you know your father is in very serious condition, don't you?"

She nodded.

"And he has been sick for, what—a year now?"

"About that, yes."

"Miss Connor," Alistair looked down at the floor and scuffed the toe of his boot forward and back. "It would appear he is getting much worse. Dr. Mason doesn't think he has much time left." He looked up. "Haven't you noticed? He's deteriorated rapidly in the last couple months."

"Not much time left? What do you mean? He's getting better. That's why we're here." She clutched his wrist with her fingers and leaned toward him. "He's been smiling lately and spending more time with my younger brother and sister. What are you saying?" He's dying. Father is dying. Her stomach heaved. "He's been pretending? He can't die; we need him. He has to get better!"

The room was closing in. Alistair's face grew fuzzy as Vivian fought to keep her head up. Her forehead hit the crook of his shoulder as everything went black.

* * *

Whose arms encircled her? Where was she? The doctor's office. Alistair said Father was dying. Tears flowed from her eyes; there was no point in trying to stop them.

The door creaked open.

"Vivian, are you in that much pain?"

She lifted her face from Alistair's shoulder. The tears ran freely down her cheeks. Alistair pulled away and propped her up in the seat.

Ben McCormack stood in the doorway with one dark eyebrow raised.

"I don't know, maybe . . ." Her eyes closed. A hand gripped her elbow, and she opened her eyes again. "I need a moment." She ran Alistair's handkerchief across her face and tucked loose hair strands over her ears.

"I'll fetch you a cane," Alistair said as he released her elbow and left the room.

Ben removed his hat, brushed his hand back through his thick hair, and sat down in the chair next to Vivian's. "It looks like I made the young doc a bit nervous."

Fog filled her brain; numbness shrouded her limbs. "I want to go home, if the offer still stands?"

"This wasn't quite what I expected to see. I leave to get my wagon and come back to find you in the arms of another man." He laughed.

The man wasn't humorous, and she didn't deserve the accusation. She stared at Dr. Mason's degree hanging on the wall at an angle across the room. "Please, take me home. I've been given some disturbing news."

He cleared his throat and tugged at the red bandana fastened around his neck with a bent finger. "I'm sorry, Miss Connor, please forgive me for assuming the worst."

Her eyes flitted to his. Was he telling the truth or continuing to mock her? "Thank you for the apology." *Father, what will we do without you?* The world had become a bottomless pit, and she was falling into it.

"How about I carry you out to the wagon, and we'll get you home like you asked."

Keep your head, Vivian; you have to live in this town. "Dr. Williams is bringing me a cane; I might as well get used to it. If you could kindly wait a moment."

Alistair returned to the waiting room with a shiny wooden cane and handed it to Vivian.

"I must be getting back to work. So, Ben, if you would give her your arm, I'm sure the two of you can manage." He paused. "Miss Connor, I'm sorry to have been the one to break the news about your father. I pray the Lord will be with your family in the coming days. Good day," he gave a slight bow and left through the inner door.

"Your father? Is something wrong with your father?"

"It's a private family matter; I don't wish to talk about it. If we could go now it would be greatly appreciated."

"Certainly." Ben bent over to grab Vivian's boot, and then he handed her the stocking. Taking the cane from her grip, he gathered her up into his arms.

"I thought I said it wasn't necessary for you to carry me." The man was so persistent. "Could I please walk?"

"You'll have plenty of time to practice with the cane, but I don't have all day." He crossed the wooden floor and stooped to turn the doorknob. There was no point in fighting him.

Along the hitching rail a wagon sat with two young sorrels impatiently stamping their hooves. Ben walked around and lifted Vivian onto the front bench, depositing her boot and cane by her feet. As he went back to close the door, Alistair stood in the doorway watching them. Ben gave a slight nod, and Alistair nodded in return. Ben stepped to the wagon and jumped up to sit beside Vivian. Grabbing the reigns, he gave them a jerk, and the wagon rumbled down the dusty street.

"Whoa, girls, take it easy. We've got us an injured lady on board. No need to rush." The horses calmed at the sound of his voice and slowed their pace.

Vivian's body rocked with the motion of the wagon.

"Didn't you say you had some kids with you? Where would we find them?"

"They're at the general store. I'm sure by now they're wondering what's become of me."

"I imagine so."

The wagon rolled down the street until Ben pulled it to a stop across from Willy's General.

"If you wouldn't mind, would you go in and get them? Their names are Jeremy and Sarah; they are five and seven years old. I usually find them in back of the store with Misty the cat."

"Sure thing." Ben jumped down from the wagon and tied the horses to the rail; he then crossed the street and disappeared into the store.

Weariness engulfed her entire body. If she could only climb under the covers of her bed, she would wake up tomorrow and father would be well. It must be a dream. If he were really dying, she would have known, wouldn't she? The whispered conversations, the doctor's visits, her mother's crying—they hadn't come to Brentwood so Father could recover. They had come so he could die. She clutched her stomach and bent forward.

That was why he had been happier here; he knew Aunt Margaret had made the family welcome in her beautiful home. But it wasn't fair; they should have told her. What would she do without her Father? Who would manage Ginny and her impetuous behavior? Who would teach Sarah and Jeremy about Jesus? Who would keep her mother happy?

The door opened across the street; Jeremy and Sarah raced out with their fists full of peppermint sticks and their cheeks covered with red and white smudges.

CHAPTER 3

"VIVIAN! WHERE HAVE YOU BEEN? We have been waiting and waiting." Jeremy arrived at the wagon first and ran around to hop up on the step. "Hey, what happened to your foot? Why do you have a bandage on? Whose wagon is this? Is it the nice man's who bought us some more candy?"

"So many questions at once. Hop in the back, and I'll tell you what happened. And yes, it's the nice man's wagon, and he's going to give us a ride home."

Ben smiled as he helped the children scramble into the back of the empty wagon.

"Mr. Ben McCormack, how nice to see you in town this fine day. Why, if I had known ahead of time, I would have arranged for you to come to dinner today instead of Saturday."

The syrupy sweet voice scraped across Ben's nerves. Ben turned to face Mary Beth Hastings. She looked like she was dressed for church; she wore a fancy dress and twirled a silly umbrella over her shoulder. There wasn't a cloud in sight.

Leaning toward him, she placed her gloved hand on his forearm. His skin twitched under his shirt. How did she always manage to find him? It seemed like he couldn't come to town without running into her for some reason or another. And what was she talking about? They had no supper plans for Saturday. The sooner he heard what was on her mind the sooner he could take poor Miss Connor home. "Hello, Miss Hastings, imagine running into you."

Mary Beth's eyes narrowed. She let go of his arm and swished to the front of the wagon. "And who might this sweet little thing be?" she asked, her hand clutching the edge of the wagon, the corners of her mouth turned up in a tight smile. "I don't believe we've met before. Mr. McCormack, are you just going to stand there? Or are you going to introduce me to this lovely lady?"

Mary Beth was always a force to be reckoned with. "Pardon me, Miss Hastings, this is Miss Connor. She is new in town and is staying with her aunt. Vivian, Mary Beth Hastings."

"A pleasure to meet you, Miss Connor." Mary Beth nodded her head, and the corner of her mouth twitched a little.

"Miss Hastings is an assistant in the milliner's shop at the end of Main Street. I know how important work is to you; we mustn't keep you from it."

"You know, it's really just a hobby of mine until I have something more long-term to occupy my time," she batted her eyes and twirled her parasol again.

Heat crept up Ben's neck at the insinuation. The sun was shining particularly hot. He removed his hat and studied the brim. The sooner he got Vivian home, the better. She appeared way too innocent to defend herself against Mary Beth's manipulations.

"It's so very nice to meet you, too, Mary Beth. However, we really must be going. I've sprained my ankle, and Mr. McCormack has offered to give me and my brother and sister a ride home."

"Perhaps you all have time for a tea? There's a lovely shop—"

"I'm very sorry. I would love to stay and visit; however, I find I'm not feeling very well." Maybe she could manage Mary Beth after all.

"I could visit you while you convalesce and help you pass the lonely hours." Mary Beth's eyes slid over to Ben's. If she wanted a reaction, she wasn't going to get one. He bent over and pretended to be occupied with straightening the horse's harnesses.

"What is your aunt's name?" Mary Beth inquired.

"It's Margaret Vickrey, on Oak Street."

"How wonderful! I know where she lives. She taught me piano lessons when I was a young girl. I've always admired her beautiful home."

"I look forward to your visit, Miss Hastings. Mr. McCormack, could we please go?" Her voice sounded bone tired; it was time to get Miss Connor home.

"Sure thing, Miss Connor."

"Mr. McCormack, if you wouldn't mind. I find I've used all my lunch hour and must get back to work. Could you give me a ride, too?" Mary Beth asked.

"I thought you said you would like to have tea? How could you if your lunch time is over?"

Mary Beth covered her mouth with her hand and inclined her head to one side. "Silly old me; I lost track of time."

"And you'd like a ride to the end of the street? Why, it'd take less time to walk there than to get in my wagon."

Stubborn as always, Mary Beth sauntered her way around the wagon to his side and held her hand out as a cue to be helped up. Vivian scooted over on the bench and muttered a soft "ouch" as her foot bumped against the side of the wagon. After Ben gave Mary Beth a hand up, she plunked herself down on the bench and spread her full gown over Vivian's lap. Vivian didn't even seem to notice.

When Ben sat down, his arm and thigh sensed more of Mary Beth's presence than entirely necessary. He gave the reigns an extra quick flick with his wrist, and the horses trotted down the road.

Jeremy's voice piped up from behind them. "Vivian, you said you'd tell us what happened to your foot."

"You're right; I hurt it on my way to the doctor's office."

"You hurt it on your way to the doctor's? Why'd you do that?"

"Do what, Jeremy?"

"Hurt your foot so you could go and see the doctor. It was fine when we were walking here."

Ben stifled the laugh in his throat.

Mary Beth sniggered beside him.

"I didn't try to hurt myself, Jeremy; I fell on the sidewalk in front of the bakery. Then the doctor's nephew kindly wrapped it up in this bandage," Vivian turned to look at her brother. "But I'm afraid I may be off my feet for a few days."

Ben could hear the exhaustion in her voice.

"Oh, so you've met Dr. Alistair. Isn't he the gentleman? And imagine, a doctor already at his age. What did you think?" Mary Beth asked.

Here we go, Mary Beth at her finest. Couldn't she leave the poor girl alone?

"I thought he was very good at his job," Vivian answered.

"That's not what I meant. I mean, what did you think of him as a man? Didn't you find him good looking, what with his gorgeous blond hair and sparkling blue eyes? And his teeth—have you ever seen teeth that white?"

Judging a man's looks wasn't really his area of expertise, but it sounded to Ben like Mary Beth was exaggerating the boy's attributes a wee bit. Alistair always looked a bit uncomfortable in his skin.

"I suppose. I didn't really notice," Vivian considered a moment. Her soft response dissipated into the air.

"Here we are, Mary Beth," Ben said as he pulled on the reigns. The wagon rolled to a stop. "I'm sure you don't want to be late." He jumped out and reached out a hand to help Mary Beth down.

Holding his gaze, she took her time stepping down from the wagon, squeezing his hand with hers. Back up went the parasol twirling over her shoulder as she spoke to Vivian, "So nice meeting you, Miss Connor."

Time to bolt. He leapt into the wagon and urged the horses on. Who knew what else Mary Beth might have to say? He gave her a quick salute with two fingers as the wagon pulled away.

She stomped her foot, and a cloud of dust billowed up around her dress.

"Sorry about that; the woman tends to speak her mind. I have no doubt she'll make good on her promise to visit you. Mary Beth hates for anything to be going on without her knowing about it." And if something wasn't going on, she would tell you about it anyway.

"I look forward to it. We haven't met many people in town yet."

Ben looked over to see if Vivian was being serious or not. She stared straight ahead. Her face had grown pale, and dark circles had formed under her eyes.

"I didn't like that girl," Sarah said and wrapped her chubby arms around Vivian's shoulders from the back. "She smelled funny."

"She was wearing perfume, Sarah. Sometimes ladies wear it to smell nice."

"Well, she didn't smell nice to me, nuh-uh. You smell way better." Sarah sniffed the back of Vivian's neck by pressing her tiny nose against her skin again and again.

"Now you're being silly. Come and sit in the front here with Mr. McCormack and me." Vivian patted the bench between them.

Sarah climbed over the back of the seat and snuggled in next to Vivian. "Does your foot hurt much, Vivvy?"

"It sure does; look at how swollen it is," She lifted her skirt to show her ankle.

Ben glanced over. It was twice its size under the bandage.

The foursome continued on down the street with the warmth of the sun across their backs. Ben visited with Jeremy and Sarah. He tossed his head back and laughed at Jeremy's silly jokes and then shared a few of his own stories to keep them occupied.

He glanced over at Vivian a few times, and her solemn profile continued to stare off into nothing. A finer looking woman he hadn't seen in quite a while; she was willowy, with such fine features, and had a pile of golden hair. It sure was nice having company sitting beside him in the wagon.

She finally broke her silence. "I see your wagon is still empty; what did you come to town for today?"

"I came for supplies to fix some of our wagons and other equipment. But there isn't anything to be had."

"You couldn't find what you needed?"

"It seems all this clamouring for gold up North is drawing most of our supplies that way. But I guess if they can make double, or even triple the money, why would they bother to sell the stuff here?"

"I am sorry to hear that. It seems like the Klondike gold rush has affected a lot of people's lives."

He caught sight of her out of the corner of his eye; she was feeling more than she was saying. But there was no way she was going to hear the real reason that brought him to town every third day or even more often if he could wrangle it. He couldn't tell anybody. Some days he swore he was like a man possessed; the need was so strong he couldn't think straight.

Six months ago he'd written a response to an ad in the local paper that read:

> Wanted: Fine, upstanding, young to middle-aged man who loves farming to correspond with lonely female in her late teens. Must be God-fearing and not afraid of hard work. Please send picture. A return picture will be forwarded to the applicant of choice. Submit your reply to Lonely, C/O Klondike Star, Box 40, Dyea, Alaska, USA.

By now, he'd have thought his sister-in-law, Julie, would have put two and two together and started asking questions. But so far she hadn't said a thing; she just gave him this strange look when he said he was off to town. Perhaps it helped that he picked up the things she needed for baking and such when Amos couldn't do it. Or maybe she was sticking by the rules they had agreed upon when they decided to farm Ma and Pa's land together. Amos and Julie had agreed to give him space and not interfere in his life unless invited to, and he'd do the same for them.

Since his first response to the advertisement, Audrey's letters had arrived every two or sometimes three weeks. He wasn't much of a writer, and with all the spring farm work, he'd replied only three times.

The picture she'd sent rested safe in his pocket, handy for taking out if he found a spare moment. She looked cute as a button with her dark hair and dark eyes. He'd been told the picture was about three years old and must have been taken before they'd left for up North. She stood with her hand on her mother's shoulder. Her mother sat in a big armchair, and another girl and young boy stood in front of their father next to the arm chair. No one was smiling.

Audrey sure had a way with words. The letters overflowed with details of life in a bustling gold rush town. But those weren't his favorite parts. The inside of his heart almost melted as she shared her yearning to be a farmer's wife and raise her own chickens and pigs. She talked about growing a huge garden and perhaps a few fruit trees to put up some preserves for the winter. She appeared to have a deep relationship with the Lord, which was something very important to Ben. Growing up, both of his parents had demonstrated a genuine relationship with Jesus that showed up in their everyday life. Ben tried to follow their example, and he wanted a wife with the same values.

He should have received another letter from Audrey in the last day or so; this was why he couldn't keep himself from coming to town every day. His thoughts seemed to all jumble together when he worked, preventing anything from getting done. The trip to the post office always calmed him and settled his stomach. By now old Hannah Mae, the postmistress, didn't even wait for him to speak; she nodded her head one way or another when she saw him coming. Said she was saving him some steps, trying to keep his strength up; it was a good thing she was a woman who didn't like to jaw.

Audrey's last letter had been different; he could hear the desperation in her words. What had changed? She'd asked if they could come out East and meet him this spring instead of after the year's harvest. If things worked as they planned, they would marry soon after the arrival. The family would continue to stay on until they found a place of their own, maybe in the area. Wouldn't folks around here be surprised? He hadn't told a soul about the relationship. The way everyone had been pestering him for years about finding a good woman made his blood boil at times. He'd had enough of the interfering.

Mary Beth Hastings was another story. She would be madder than a hornet. His sister-in-law Julie was her best friend, and Mary Beth planned on them becoming family. But one thing was for certain: he'd never led her on. In fact, he'd done everything he could to discourage her. However, she was one determined woman, which hadn't helped. But why borrow trouble from tomorrow on such a beautiful day like this?

He peeked over at the young woman sitting by his side on the wagon. Tired as she looked, hers were some of the prettiest blonde ringlets he'd ever seen. How would Audrey feel about him driving Vivian and the children home? She'd probably be happy about such an act of Christian charity. She didn't sound like one to get jealous and often wrote about doing her Christian duty as though she were some sort of church matron instead of a young, single woman.

Vivian had pretty green eyes and a cute little upturned nose. She was quite a looker, even if she didn't have the "raven hair" and "ocean eyes" like Audrey described herself. Audrey might approve of his good works, but she probably wouldn't approve of where his thoughts were going. Ben forced his gaze on the road ahead as the wagon rolled down the street.

"Mr. McCormack, where do you live?" Vivian asked.

"My brother and I farm the home place about five miles east of town. Ma and Pa passed on about six years ago."

"I'm sorry to hear that."

"I appreciate it. Since then, my two sisters went off and got married. It's just my brother Amos and his wife Julie and I on the place now."

"Do you all live together in the same house?"

"No, Amos and Julie live in the family home. I've been building my own place for about three years now."

"Sounds like quite an endeavor to do that on your own."

"Sure is. Sometimes I think I'll be an old man before I finish."

Vivian laughed.

What a sweet sound. Maybe her world wasn't looking as bleak as it had a bit ago. "It has a roof and four walls, thank goodness; but it's all the inside work that seems to take up the time. I haven't finished the kitchen yet, so Julie takes pity on me and feeds me supper."

Vivian directed Ben to turn at the next street on the right.

"It's a good thing she does. I'm not much of a cook, and the farm keeps both Amos and I pretty busy. He's always wanting to try new-fangled ideas."

Within minutes they pulled up in front of the house. Ben looked up at the three-story brick home and gave a low whistle.

"Wow, this is some place you folks have here."

Vivian grabbed the front of the wagon and pulled herself upright. Ben jumped out and tied the horses to the post. "If you give me a moment, I'll come around to help you."

Sarah and Jeremy crawled from the back of the wagon and scampered up to where Vivian was sitting.

"As I said, it's not my family's home; it's my Aunt's. We're staying here while my father . . . my father is sick." Vivian's face turned white as a sheet, and she looked like she was going to lose her balance.

Ben ran around and reached his arm out to steady her.

"What is it, Viv? Is your foot hurting again?" Jeremy asked.

Ben helped her out of the wagon as she answered.

"I'm sorry, don't worry. It's been a long day, and I need to have some rest. Now you two go on in and let Mother and Auntie know not to be alarmed. I saw the curtains move when we got here. Tell them it's a sprain, and I'll be fine."

They turned and ran up the sidewalk. Jeremy stopped about halfway and called back to Ben, "If you're thinking of picking some of those pretty white flowers on the tree and giving them to my sister, don't, 'cause the tree needs them to make apples. My whole family loves apples."

Scrunching his eyebrows together, Ben looked at Jeremy. What was the boy talking about?

"There are some awfully pretty pink ones around the other side of the house; we pick them all the time." Jeremy and Sarah ran into the house calling for their mother.

Ben handed Vivian the cane and grabbed her spare boot.

"It looks like that boy's been doing some figuring. Would you like some nice flowers, Vivian? Would they put a smile back on that pretty face of yours?" He looked straight into her troubled eyes. "If I thought it would make you happy, I'd go back down town and get you some from the flower shop. I wouldn't rob your aunt's flower bed."

Vivian didn't say anything; she just stared back at him from her beautiful eyes. She was so close that the heat from her body jumped to his, and sweat trickled down his back.

She dropped her head and wiped something out of her eye with Alistair's handkerchief still clutched in her fist. "I'm so tired, and my foot really hurts." He bent his head to catch the whisper. "Could you please carry me into the house?"

Tongue clinging to the roof of his mouth, he tried to swallow. Parched, he needed something cool to drink mighty soon. But it must have taken a lot for her to ask; maybe she was too tired to put up a fight. He handed her the boot and grabbed the cane with his right hand. He bent and gently lifted her from the ground. As he carried her up the sidewalk, Vivian's mother rushed out of the house to meet them.

* * *

"Vivian, are you all right? The children told me you couldn't walk anymore, and I should come out and help you. And who are you?"

"Ben McCormack, ma'am. If I could come inside and put Vivian down, I'm sure she can fill you in on the details."

"Oh my. Yes, of course, do come in." Vivian's mother held the door as Ben carried Vivian into the house. Jeremy and Sarah had already hurried off to play in the backyard. "If you'll take her in the parlor, that would be fine." She motioned toward the archway.

Aunt Margaret entered through the door from the dining room. "Vivian! Oh, dear. Here, let me take those," she took the boot and cane and motioned to the settee in front of the window. "Why don't you put her down over there? Vivian, whatever has happened?"

In three strides, Ben crossed the room and bent to place her on the stuffed seat. As he stepped back, his tall frame filled the room, a contrast to the delicate Queen Anne furnishings and fancy china bric-a-brac. "Aunty, this is Ben McCormack. Ben, my Aunt Margaret."

He removed his hat and nodded, once more running his hand through his thick hair. "Nice to meet you, ma'am."

"And very nice to meet you, young man. Thank you for helping our Vivian."

Vivian lifted her foot to rest it on the settee, the throbbing in the joint pounding like a hammer. The folds of her skirt fell back to reveal the swelling under the bandage.

Her mother gasped as she raised a hand to her mouth. She stepped to Vivian's side and took her hand, patting it over and over.

"Oh my, Vivian, what happened? Margaret, do you see her poor ankle? Vivian, sweetie, are you in a lot of pain? Can I get you something? A cold glass of lemonade or some hot tea, perhaps?"

Vivian pulled her hand from her mother's. "Lemonade would be lovely, Mother. Mr. McCormack, would you care for some too?"

"I could sure use a glass."

Aunt Margaret pointed to the largest chair in the room. "Please, have a seat."

As Mother bustled out of the parlor to fetch their drinks, Aunt Margaret took a pillow and gently placed it beneath Vivian's ankle before sitting down in the rocking chair beside the settee.

Vivian's eyes strayed to Ben's. Could the circumstances of their meeting be any more embarrassing or difficult? He looked uneasy as he perched on the edge of the chair. Maybe he would appreciate the opportunity to leave rather than stay out of politeness. "Mr. McCormack, we would hate to keep you any longer than we already have. If you have more pressing matters, we understand."

The chair creaked beneath him as he shifted. He met her eyes. "I am happy to stay, if it's no bother."

Oh it's no bother, no bother at all. "We're happy to have you."

"Vivian, please tell me what happened," Aunt Margaret said.

Vivian gave her aunt a brief description of the events that transpired when she went to Dr. Mason's office.

"Oh, I see. I'm so sorry you were injured. But were you satisfied?" Aunt Margaret asked.

"Satisfied? With what?"

"With the news of your father."

How could she be satisfied? The news had turned her world upside down and shaken it. Father was dying, and the rest of them were simply waiting for it to happen. "I want to know why you all kept it a secret."

"What did the doctor say, Vivian?"

Should Ben be a part of this conversation? He wasn't family, but he'd been so helpful when she hurt her ankle. He seemed kind and understanding; he was someone they could trust. "The doctor said his heart was deteriorating, and he might not have long."

Mother stepped into the parlor as the words left Vivian's mouth. The glasses of lemonade wobbled on the tray, and Mother gave a strangled cry. Ben jumped up and steadied her elbow as Aunt Margaret reached in to take the tray from her hands and place it on the table. Mother collapsed into Ben's chair and pressed her fists against her eyes.

"I'm sorry, Mother. I know . . . "

Ben backed toward the door. "This looks to be a difficult time for your family. I'll see myself out."

Yes, the family needed time to be alone—time to talk. He should go, but Vivian wanted him to stay. Would she ever see him again, her Good Samaritan, now that he knew their circumstances?

"Thank you so much for your help this afternoon. I would see you out the door, but—"

"I understand. Good-bye, Miss Connor; I hope your ankle heals well in the coming days. And I'm very sorry about your father. Perhaps I could stop by in a day or two, if you don't mind?"

Stop by? He wanted to stop by and see how she was doing? He wasn't afraid of the chaos in their home or her father's prognosis? Maybe he was trying to be kind. He seemed like the type that would go the extra mile. Her stomach fluttered as she replied, "If you find the time, we would appreciate a visit, thank you."

Running the brim of his cowboy hat between his fingers, Ben tipped his head to Mother and Aunt Margaret. Aunt Margaret retuned the nod as she rubbed her hand back and forth across Mother's shoulders.

Ben left the house, the door hinge squeaking as he departed.

CHAPTER 4

GINNY LIFTED A HAND FROM the horse's reigns and brushed at the stray wisps of hair clinging to the moisture on her brow. It was good to be on the road. Over the last week, whenever she could sneak away, she'd met Logan at the warehouse where he was packaging the supplies for their journey. They'd wrapped pounds and pounds of rice, beans, cornmeal, flour, and other extras into square, fifty pound bundles and stacked them snuggly in the wagons. Logan had covered the stacks with canvas and bound them with rope. The most precious part of the cargo, hidden deep inside some of the bundles, was gallon jugs of whiskey. They could fetch as much as one ounce of gold a piece up North.

Logan figured they should head out West about twenty miles to the town of Little Springs before boarding the train. He was right; there was no way they wouldn't be noticed loading the freight car in Brentwood.

She'd taken particular care with one of the bundles, her nest egg, as the items could be easily damaged on the long journey. It was filled with medical supplies a suffering miner might be in need of and be willing to pay raw gold for.

Finding out what to buy had been the easy part. She'd instigated evening strolls with Alistair, the Doctor's nephew, and he'd shared his love of medicine as they'd walked through the boring town. She'd also plied him with questions about common ailments or injuries. What a fool he'd been to never once question her interest in him. His proposal, though, had come as a complete surprise. How would he feel when he learned she had left town with Logan?

"You doing all right back there, honey?" The drawl of Logan's voice tingled down her spine.

"I'm fine, Logan. It's warm out here, that's all." She pulled the reins to the left so the team would head down the center of the dusty road.

"I don't want you falling asleep; you've got a heap of supplies on that wagon—enough to make our dreams come true, sweetheart." Logan smiled with that beguiling mouth of his.

Dreams, all right. The waiting would soon be over. He'd promised she'd be Mrs. Logan Harris before they reached Dawson City. Imagine the envy in other girls' eyes as she paraded around as the wife of one of the richest, most handsome men in the whole country. If only Logan would've made arrangements for the wedding before they left on the train. It wouldn't have been too difficult to find a preacher in town. She was eighteen and didn't need her parents' consent.

Two dusty hours later, they arrived at the Little Springs train station and pulled the wagons to a stop out back where they could be unloaded onto a freight car when the train arrived. The train was due in about half an hour, and Ginny couldn't wait to get cleaned up and be on their way.

"Logan, if you don't mind, I'd like to go and use the restroom to freshen up."

"Fine. Make sure you're on that train when it gets here." He swatted at a fly buzzing around his ear. "I don't want to have to look for

you. I'm going to find someone to handle the transfer of the freight."
He jumped down and strode away without even a backward glance.

"Thanks for the help," she said to his back as she grabbed her reticule and gathered her dusty skirt in one hand. Holding on to the edge of the wagon, her foot sought the step. As her other boot went over the edge of the wagon, a rip sounded in the air. The ruffle of her skirt remained pinched in a splinter on the rough wagon side as her feet touched the ground.

"Look at that. Drat, I don't even know where my sewing kit is." She tugged her dress from the splinter and overlapped the two pieces of material hoping to hide the long tear down the front of her calico skirt—more correctly, Vivian's skirt.

A man sitting in the ticket office gave directions to the restroom on the far end of the building. The cool water splashing on her face refreshed her spirits. Looking in the mirror, she combed her hair and reset her stylish touring hat. The vibration of the train moved up through her feet as it pulled into the station. She quickly glanced around the loading platform to find Logan as she exited the restroom. Where was that man? She stepped back inside the station. He wasn't there, either. The edge of her lip folded between her teeth.

Would he board the train without her? She crossed the platform and stood behind a woman with two children being helped by a porter up the stairs into the train. Her eyes searched the length of windows. Where could he have gone?

"Ma'am," the porter held his hand out to give assistance.

"Oh, thank you, sir." Taking his hand, she ascended the stairs and stepped into the car. No Logan. What if there'd been a difficulty with the freight? She didn't even have her ticket. He must be here somewhere. Through five passenger cars she bumped and jostled her way as the others stowed their belongings.

As she entered the dining car, Logan's deep laughter rose above the din. He stood with his back to her beside a table halfway down the car. Two women dressed in colourful silk gowns with low-cut necklines and sparkling jewelry laughed along with him. Ginny walked up to the trio. The women looked at her, and their mouths pulled into prim smiles.

Logan turned around. "Ginny, I'm so glad I found you. I was beginning to worry, darlin'."

Both women raised a gloved hand to their mouths, suppressing a giggle. She met both sets of eyes as her teeth clamped against one another.

Logan reached out and squeezed her elbow between his thumb and forefinger. "Ladies, I'd like you to meet my wife, Ginny Harris. Ginny this is—"

"Star," one woman said as she extended her hand to shake Ginny's.

"And Buttercup," the other woman giggled and extended her hand as well.

"How very lovely to meet you," Ginny replied, "now if you will please excuse us," she pulled her elbow from Logan's tight grasp and slipped her arm through his. She turned, attempting to tug him with her, but he resisted.

"Sweetheart, we just met these lovely ladies; must we leave so soon?" He raised an eyebrow.

"Logan, I need to talk to you; it's important."

He turned to the women and bowed, rolling his hand out in front of him. "Ladies, I am pleased to make your acquaintance, and I hope our paths will cross again."

Ginny followed Logan back through the crowded passenger cars. When he found an empty bench, he sat down and pulled her down beside him. She rubbed where his fingers had bruised the flesh around her elbow. The whistle blew for the second time, and the doors to the cars were closed by the porters. The train rumbled forward.

"Logan, who were those women? They didn't look very respectable."

"Ah, darlin', I was being friendly, that's all. Their beauty doesn't hold a candle to yours." He rubbed his smooth thumb across her cheek.

Heat crept up her neck. Turning away, she couldn't help the smile that rose to her lips. Logan reached over and grasped her chin between his fingers. Turning her face back toward his, he pulled her forward and planted a hungry kiss on her lips.

Ginny pulled back, "Logan, please, we're in public." Her hat had been pushed askew. She removed the hatpins and placed them on the bench beside her as Logan laughed.

"What? Isn't a man allowed to show appreciation for his new wife?"

"But I'm not your new wife; why did you introduce me to those women as such?"

He reached into his pocket and removed a smooth gold band. "Oh, that's right, before I forget—here, take this." He dropped the ring into her hand.

"What is this? Why are you giving me a wedding band?" Ginny looked up at Logan.

"If you're supposed to be my wife, you need a ring, don't you? Let's see if this one will work," he retrieved the ring from her palm and briskly turned her left hand over. He slid the ring onto her third finger. "See, it fits. I knew it would."

"But Logan, why am I wearing a ring if we're not married? You said we were getting married. You promised me we were getting married." It was hard not to whine. If he already had a ring, why not find a preacher? The whole thing could have been settled before they left town. Her parents would have had to let her go, and she and Logan wouldn't have had to be secretive if she were a married woman.

"Don't you think I know that? I know what I told you, and I meant it. But, baby, you know how crazy it's been. This pretty little ring will have to be good enough for now, all right? You know I love you, don't you?" He leaned over. His lips were soft against her forehead. He could be so gentle. Nestling her head against his chest, she listened to the soft thumping of his heart and stared at the shiny, gold band on her finger.

"I believe you, Logan. I'll be proud to wear your ring."

He wrapped his arms around her and gave her a gentle hug. "Thanks, sweetheart. I need to do some business now, and see who's on this train who can help us out. Can you keep yourself busy until supper?"

She sat up. "I guess so. Where's my luggage?"

Logan stood. "Safe and sound, don't you worry, and I have a surprise for you later." He reached out pinched her chin once more.

She watched his back as he sauntered away, and she twisted the fine band around her finger. What could the surprise be? Maybe he'd already found a pastor aboard who could perform the service. He'd keep his promise; he always did.

Her eyes drooped with the gentle rhythm of the train; she slid over and leaned her head against the window. The noisy chatter in the compartment faded away as she fell asleep.

CHAPTER 5

THE RINGING OF A BRASS bell roused Vivian from her deep sleep. Aunt Margaret was calling the family to supper. Sitting up, she looked at the bandage around her ankle. No, it wasn't all a dream. She reached for the cane. Putting both hands on its smooth curve, she pulled herself upright. The cane wobbled, and she sat back down, gritting her teeth as the pain coursed through her ankle. Jeremy and Sarah scampered into the parlor and over to where she was sitting.

"Can I help you, Viv? You can lean on me if you want," Jeremy said.

"Sure, Jeremy. That sounds very helpful."

They hobbled their way to the dining room table where the rest of the family, except Ginny, was seated. Aunt Margaret had laid out a wonderful spread of roast beef with baby carrots and onions. A china bowl piled high with mashed potatoes sat next to a dish of Yorkshire pudding. Dark gravy in a crested silver boat also sat on the damask tablecloth.

Jeremy pulled out a chair for Vivian, and she sat down to her father's left.

Her father dabbed at the moisture on his brow with a handkerchief. His once-thick, black hair, now grey and thin, fell in an unruly lock on his forehead. It was difficult to look at his narrow face and gaunt figure. If only the old Father, the one full of life and health, would come back to the family.

"Sarah and Jeremy, would you two see if you can find Ginny and ask her to come for dinner?" Father asked.

With the blue ribbon in her hair bobbing up and down, Sarah scurried off upstairs to do as her father requested. Jeremy declared he would look in the yard.

"Vivian," Father said, dropping his napkin in his lap, "your mother tells me you had quite the adventurous afternoon."

What did it matter what had happened to her? They needed to talk about him, how sick he was, and why they had kept it a secret. Why did he always pretend he was so strong?

"I fell in front of the bakery on my way to Dr. Mason's office and hurt my ankle."

Her father wiped his brow once more with his handkerchief. "Dr. Mason's office?"

Vivian's chin dropped as the words wedged in her throat. "Wh-why did you both keep it a secret, how bad it really was? All this time we were expecting you to recover; we assumed it was just a matter of time until you would be better."

"I don't know, Vivian," her mother replied, tears streaking down her cheeks. "Perhaps I wasn't ready to accept it myself. I kept thinking, surely God would restore your father, one of His own, someone who has loved and served Him his whole life." She reached for her husband's hand on the table and clutched it. "I prayed earnestly that he would be spared, that our family could stay together." Reaching inside the cuff of her dress, her mother pulled out a hankie and dabbed at her tears for several moments. "Sometimes, it feels like God isn't listening; it feels like He doesn't care."

"Of course He cares, Tabitha," Father said. He turned to Vivian. "I'm sorry, dear, we should have been more forthright with the family. Unfortunately, it has caused a difficult situation to become even more difficult by not being completely honest." He patted her mother's hand. "I guess we thought we were protecting you. But I want you both to know I have never felt abandoned by God. For He who created the whole universe and feeds the smallest sparrow knows of our suffering, and nothing is a surprise to Him."

"But Father, what will we do without you?"

"Vivian, a long time ago I abandoned myself to His will, without question, whatever the cost. If He is glorified by taking me to Himself, I accept it. My hope is that it will not be too difficult for those of you who are left behind."

He opened his mouth as though to say more but closed it as Jeremy returned to the dining room to announce that Ginny was nowhere to be found outside. Jeremy's pronouncement was soon followed by the plunk of Sarah's little black shoes on the hardwood floor.

"I couldn't find Ginny; she's not in her room."

"I wonder where she could have gone. Did anyone see her return this afternoon after she went to visit Lady Annabelle?" Mother asked.

The adults looked at each other, shaking their heads in turn.

"Sarah, what do you have in your hand?" Vivian asked.

"I found this piece of paper with writing on it on the bed. Your room is a big mess."

"Oh?"

"There are clothes all over the floor, the bed—everywhere."

"Sarah, could I see the piece of paper, please?" Father asked.

Sarah handed the piece of writing paper to her father. He read the letter to himself, his face becoming paler as he read down the page. His hand trembled, and the letter fell to the table as he lifted a hand to his chest. Mother jumped up, and her chair tipped over onto the floor. She stepped to his side and placed her arm around his shoulder to keep Father from falling over.

"Harold, what is it?" Her voice rose. "Harold, is it your heart?"

"Tabitha," he said, his breath laboured, "I need to go and lie down; I find I am not feeling well. Would you help me, please?"

Aunt Margaret came to his other shoulder, and they supported him as he rose from the chair. Slowly they helped him down the hall toward the library where his bed was set up.

Reaching over to take the letter, Vivian slipped it into the pocket of her dress.

"Is Father going to be all right?" Sarah asked. "Maybe I shouldn't have given him the piece of paper."

Vivian tried to explain, "You both should know father is very sick; however, it's nothing either of you have done."

She wasn't sure the same could be said about Ginny; the letter burned in her pocket. "Let's eat, you two, before our supper is completely cold." She dished out a serving for each of them. The food was tasteless, and her stomach churned with every bite. Jeremy and Sarah were quiet and pushed the food around on their plates. It was a relief when they asked to be excused and went to the backyard to play in their fort.

Aunt Margaret returned to the dining room and excused Vivian from helping with the dishes. As Vivian ascended the stairs to her room, she leaned heavily on the banister and hopped from step to step. Upon reaching the second floor, she stumbled across the hall to the room she shared with Virginia. Dresses lay in mounds on the bed and on the floor. Several stockings were strewn across the top of the dresser, and a petticoat looked as though someone had stepped out of it and left it in a heap. Several of her favorite hats were scattered throughout the room. Ginny wouldn't, would she? Not only leave, but take things that didn't belong to her? The door to the closet gaped; it was empty. Where was her favorite green dress? Anger surged up through Vivian's chest. That selfish little brat! Removing several chemises from the rocking chair, Vivian plunked down in it and put her foot up on the bed. Taking Virginia's letter out of her pocket, she read:

> *Dear Family,*
>
> *By the time you read my letter, I will be on a train going west and hopefully be a happily married woman. I am so excited to become Mrs. Logan Harris. Do not worry about us as Logan knows a lot about travelling. I am sure we will be fine. We plan to ride the train as far as we can and then hire someone to take us up North to the goldfields. Logan speculates we should be rich within the year!*
>
> *If all goes well, we will return home at Christmas time. If you would like to contact me, please forward your letter care of the Dawson City Post Office, Canada.*
>
> *I do hope you will all understand and be happy for us. I am in love with Logan and he with me.*
>
> *Your loving daughter,*
>
> *Virginia*
>
> *P. S. Vivian, I'm sorry I took your two best dresses. I hope you understand the time constraints I was under. I will repay them with much better ones at Christmas when we have made our fortune.*

Vivian rubbed her forehead and tucked a stray strand of hair behind her ear. Ginny's done it; she's finally done it. She's fallen for a man and left her family. But how could she leave them? They needed each other now more than ever. All Ginny's threats and her plans to leave had never seemed real—just a foolish girl's fantasies. Vivian should have seen it coming. She should have listened, and she should have cared more. Logan must have given Ginny the money for her ticket this morning when they saw them by the summer kitchen. Vivian had not said a word to her parents when she'd returned with the children earlier. She could have stopped Ginny; Vivian was sure of it. Guilt formed a cold knot in the pit of her stomach.

Ginny, what have you done to yourself? "Hopefully a married woman?" What if he didn't marry her? What if Logan never meant to marry her at all? How could you be so foolish? Why did you trust a sluggard like Logan?

The letter slipped through her fingers and fell to the floor. Someone would have to go and bring Ginny back. If Logan didn't marry her, anything could happen; Ginny wouldn't be safe. Dr. Mason had said it could be a few weeks until she was fully healed. It didn't matter; she must go and find her sister. It was her fault Ginny had run away.

She would tell Father not to worry and to get lots of rest; she'd be bringing her sister home. They would be a family again before—better not to think about it. Her foot throbbed as she tried to stand.

"Ow," she grabbed the headboard for support. She scooped the letter from the floor, put it into her pocket, and once more hopped across the room to make her way to the library to speak with her father and mother.

The lights were off, and heavy brocade curtains covered the library windows as Vivian shuffled in. Her mother sat in the shadows, her eyes closed, a Bible in her lap. Her father lay in bed with the white cotton sheets pulled up and tucked under his chin, his face blending in with their color. His breath rattled in his chest as she neared the bed.

"Vivian, your father is sleeping. Please don't disturb him. I fear he has taken a turn for the worse."

Vivian twisted around on her good foot. Why did her mother sound so calm?

"Do you have the letter Ginny left behind?" her mother asked.

Vivian nodded.

"Could I see it, please?" Mother crossed the room to take the letter. She retrieved it from Vivian's pocket and returned to her chair where she turned on the small reading lamp that sat on the table.

Vivian watched her father's slow, shallow breaths move in and out as he slept. Mother read the letter for several seconds then gasped. Vivian turned to see her mother slump in her chair. Limping over, she spoke softly and rubbed Mother's arm.

"It will be all right." *No it won't.* "Everything is going to be fine, shh." *Nothing will ever be fine again.* "I'll find Ginny, I promise." *At least I hope I will.*

Mother's chin lifted, and her eyes flickered. She pulled her head back and gazed around the room.

"You've fainted, Mother. How do you feel?"

Without responding, Mother wrinkled the letter up into a tight ball and let it drop to the floor. "Vivian, what are we going to do with your father so sick and Ginny gone? Gone! My poor baby, we need her here; we need to be together as a family. She was always such a romantic, but I had no idea she would run off. I think I've been too harsh with her these past weeks, it's all my fault."

"Mother, you know that's not true. Ginny is thinking only of herself, as she always does."

"Oh, you sound petty and jealous, Vivian, and it doesn't become you. Is it because Virginia has more gentleman callers than you?"

"What?"

Mother turned her head away and flicked her fingers in the air. "She was always such a social butterfly, going here and there, but perhaps naïve. If I had taken more time with her, explained more about men, I'm sure this never would have happened."

Vivian had been dismissed again. Mother never listened; she only saw what she wanted to see. Vivian would stand for this no longer. "Mother, look at me." She didn't move. "Mother, look at me, please." Instead, Mother turned and stared straight ahead. She refused to meet Vivian's eyes.

Vivian stood her ground. "You think I'm jealous of a spoiled, self-centered girl who has been lying to her family?"

Mother inhaled sharply, her fists clenched in her lap.

"I don't think trying to wrap every man you meet around your little finger constitutes having bunches of gentleman callers. I may be a lot of things, as you constantly remind me, but one thing I am not is jealous of Ginny."

Father coughed, the moisture rattling in his lungs. Vivian's raised voice must have woken him. She shuffled over to the bed as Mother scurried to the other side. "Sorry, Father, I was talking too loud."

Mother glared as she plumped some pillows and placed them behind Father's back. She then continued to fuss around her husband, tucking the blankets in and around his bony frame.

"Was I dreaming, or did I hear you two arguing over this foolish situation Ginny's gotten herself into?" he asked, his voice grating like sandpaper.

"Harold—"

"It's true she has no one to blame but herself and her crazy romantic notions. I am very disappointed with the choice she's made," his speech was labored.

"But Harold, I don't think she meant—"

"Of course she did, Tabitha. If Ginny knows one thing, it's how to get what Ginny wants. But I do feel sorry for her this time; I fear she's gotten more than she's bargained for."

"I'm going to bring her home." The words spilled out of Vivian's mouth, and both parents turned to stare at her.

"What do you mean, Vivian?" her father asked.

"I am going to follow her and bring her home. She should be here with her family, especially since you are so sick."

Mother's eyes strayed to Father's; they looked hopeful.

"Vivian, I can't allow it. It's not safe. We could end up losing two daughters instead of one."

"Please, Harold, let Vivian go. I simply could not bear it if Virginia did not return."

"But Vivian's ankle is sprained." He coughed into his hand and wiped the spittle from his mouth. "She can't travel. And it's most likely Ginny won't return even if Vivian does find her."

"I am quite sure by the time Vivian catches up with Ginny she will have realized the error of her ways and be willing to return home."

"You don't need to worry about my ankle, Father. It doesn't feel like it is getting any worse; it's probably a slight sprain. I should be able to leave in a few days. Please, I need to do this."

Father didn't reply and appeared to be pondering the suggestion. How silly it must sound—the proposal that she travel across the country alone when the only travelling she had ever done was to move to Brentwood.

"I can't give you an answer right now. I will need to pray about it. It doesn't seem right, sending you off after the prodigal. I should be the one going, and if I were in any condition to go I would. We all know Ginny won't appreciate anyone trying to bring her home. The girl has been itching to leave for most of her life."

"Harold, how can you say that about your own daughter? I couldn't live with myself if we let Ginny leave without doing anything to stop her."

"Tabitha," he patted her hand weakly, "You know the girl is ornery and stubborn as a mule when it comes to listening to sense."

"It's not true. My poor baby." Mother began sobbing and ran out of the room.

Father stretched out his bony hand to clasp his daughter's. "Vivian, please keep me company for a while. I would pull over a chair myself but—" His deep chuckle caused a coughing spasm which shook the bed.

Useless against the spells that brought sweat to her father's brow and turned his face a dark crimson, Vivian fidgeted with the blanket between her fingers, waiting for the spasms to subside. How could she have not seen how poorly he was when the evidence was right in front of her? Time was so precious; perhaps it shouldn't be wasted chasing after Ginny.

"Are you sure you are not too tired? I could come back later when you've had a good rest."

"I'll be all right," he patted her hand.

It didn't reassure her, but she would stay and help him pass some time. She hobbled several feet to a ladder-backed chair in the corner of the room. It worked as a support to help her return to the side of her father's bed where she sat down.

Their quiet conversation was interrupted before it could even start by a sharp rap on the door.

"Come in," Father said.

Dr. Mason entered the room, a black satchel in his hand, and his nephew Alistair close behind him. Alistair glanced over briefly and then dropped his eyes.

"Greetings. How fortunate to find our two patients together." Dr. Mason placed his satchel on the bed and removed a stethoscope. "Margaret informs me you've taken a turn for the worse, Harold. I would like to listen to your heart. Alistair, why don't you take Vivian to the parlor and check her ankle? I'll be a few minutes."

Alistair stepped over, gave a slight bow, and offered his bent elbow. "Miss Connor, may I assist you?" He looked uncomfortable and formal. Vivian looped her arm through his and rested her weight on him as they left the library.

Vivian sat once again on the settee in the parlor and turned sideways to elevate her foot. Alistair placed a low footstool with a padded brocade top in front of the settee and sat down.

"Miss Connor . . . I, uh . . . "

"Yes, Dr. Williams?"

Alistair looked away and fidgeted with the corners of his black suit coat. What was he so nervous about?

"I feel I must apologize for my behavior this afternoon. I was so flustered by your similarity to your sister. I don't know what came over me. I hope you didn't find me rude or negligent. I certainly didn't mean to be."

Similarity to Ginny? She could only hope not in the present circumstances. It was baffling, though, how familiar he seemed to be with her sister.

"I was not offended at all; the news about my father upset me. I'm sorry I was so emotional."

"I understand, and I wish we could do more."

"But you can't, and we must all learn to accept it." Composure almost escaped her as a sense of dread knotted in the pit of her stomach. It was time to change the subject. "Dr. Williams, how do you know my sister?"

"Um, well," he worried the corners of his coat with the shiny black material beneath his fingers. "We have spent many hours together, your sister and I." His eyes filled with a sparkle she hadn't noticed until now. "She has a strong curiosity for medicine—so many questions."

"Ginny?"

He appeared concerned by her look as he replied, "I want to assure you we maintained the strictest of propriety. Lady Annabelle was present for all of our conversations. We had even talked briefly of marriage."

The room closed in as she looked at the poor soul standing in front of her. How cruel could Ginny be? How many broken hearts did she leave in her wake and why? With her palate dry as cotton, she swallowed. "Marriage, Dr. Williams?"

"Please don't misunderstand me, Miss Connor; I merely broached the subject on one of our evening walks. Ginny is so concerned about her father's health that she wishes to postpone my approaching your father. I do not consider it a formal proposal, and now I fear . . . "

"Dr. Williams, I am so sorry." Sorry he'd ever met Ginny. Sorry he was one of the casualties in her quest to fulfill her own desires. Sorry he couldn't see through the deception.

"Sorry? I was merely hoping to get your opinion on whether your father's health would permit me to—"

"She's not here, Dr. Williams."

"I understand, and as I stated before, I'm wondering if your—"

"She's not here, Dr. Williams, because she's run away."

He jumped up, bending his tall frame toward hers. "Run away? What do you mean she's run away?" His brows scrunched to a narrow "V" as he lifted his palms up. "Where? Do you know where she's run to? I'll go and find her; I'll bring her back. Why would she leave?"

"She wasn't alone."

"What do you mean she wasn't alone?"

"She's run away to be married, she hopes. His name is Logan Harris. Again, I'm so sorry."

His face drained of all color as his shoulders slumped. He brought a hand toward his brow and rubbed across it with his thumb and index finger.

The grandfather clock in the corner of the room ticked several seconds. Vivian leaned forward to hear him when he finally replied, "What do you mean, hopes?"

"She left a note. He hasn't married her yet."

Alistair looked as if someone had punched him in the stomach as he flopped down on the wooden chair next to the settee. "She's to be married . . . to someone else."

Was it a question or a statement? Maybe it would help him to talk about it. "How did you two meet? Was it at Lady Annabelle's?"

"Yes, originally, and then she came to the office asking questions and buying supplies for this ailment or that. We would visit in the evenings at Lady Annabelle's. At first the visits were brief while I checked on my patient. But over the last few weeks, I stayed longer each evening. She was such pleasant company."

No doubt she was, if there was something to be gained. But what was it? To use Alistair so callously appeared more heartless of Ginny than usual, and to entertain the thought of marriage with him was downright cruel. "When did you speak to her of marriage?"

"We spoke of it a few days ago. She didn't say yes, and she didn't say no. She merely expressed concern for your father's well-being and how broaching the subject at this time might cause him some distress. How could I have been such a fool?"

Maybe Ginny had been having second thoughts about running off with Logan after all. Maybe she was beginning to see his true nature and wanted someone to fall back on. Had Vivian given the final push during their conversation this morning? No, it couldn't be; Ginny had misled them all. "Ginny is very convincing; she's been lying to all of us for weeks. Again, I am sorry she used you."

"No one's sorrier than I am. I don't understand how I couldn't have known. She must have felt something toward me; I assure you, it was too real." His eyes looked glazed as he stared out the window.

"Dr. Williams, I'm not sure it's wise to—"

"I'm sorry, Miss Connor, if you will excuse me. I will quickly check your ankle and be on my way." Alistair sat on the stool and removed the pin at her ankle. With his left hand holding her lower calf, he gently unwound the bandage with his right hand.

She bit her bottom lip—a sharp distraction—as he prodded the ankle joint.

"It doesn't look much more swollen than it was this afternoon. I don't think you will have to be off it for more than a couple days." He rewrapped the bandage tighter; the slight tremor in his fingers was the only sign of his distress. Concentrating on his task, he once again pinned the bandage and positioned Vivian's foot on the settee.

"If you would let my uncle know, Miss Connor," his voice was tired and defeated, "I've decided to walk home, and I will meet him there. Take care, Miss Connor."

Her heart ached for him. He looked so stricken.

The parlor door opened, and Jeremy burst through yelling with Sarah racing behind him. "We've come to say good night, Vivian!" He stopped short when he saw the stranger. "Who are you?"

"Jeremy, your manners. Children, this is Dr. Williams; he's Dr. Mason's nephew. He was checking my ankle."

Alistair stood and faced the children, his tall, lanky form towering over them.

"Dr. Williams, my brother Jeremy and my sister Sarah."

"How very nice to meet you," Alistair said bending to shake each child's hand in turn. "I must be going; I think—well, I must be going."

"Perhaps you should stay for tea?" Vivian offered.

A moment passed as he hesitated. "No, I'm quite sure I must be going. Perhaps I will stop by in a couple of days and see how you are getting on."

"I don't intend to be here. I'm going after her just as soon as my father allows me." He has to allow it.

"Going after who, Vivvy?" Jeremy asked.

"Going after her yourself?" Alistair asked. "So you know where she is?"

"She's going up North to the Klondike; they're taking the train. She hopes to be rich by Christmas."

His eyes widened as his Adam's apple bobbed in his throat. "And you're going to find her? Are you sure that's wise?"

"I don't think anything about this situation is wise, but I must go for my family's sake—for Ginny's sake." For her own sake.

"Well then, I hope you know what you are doing, and I wish you the best. I wouldn't want your family to lose two daughters."

"Vivvy, what are you talking about? Who's gone?" Jeremy piped in.

"Jeremy, shh now. I thank you for your concern, Dr. Williams. I will be careful."

"Vivvy?" Jeremy said as he stepped between them raising his arms in the air and waving them back and forth.

"Jeremy, you are being rude." She reached out and tugged his shirt pulling him down in front of her on the settee and wrapped her arms around his wriggling torso. "As I said, Dr. Williams, I appreciate your concern, and I understand your disappointment. However, I feel I must give Ginny the opportunity to explain herself and come to the realization that she's made a mistake."

"I see. Very well, good-bye." Alistair nodded his head in their direction and turned to nod at Sarah. He then picked up his satchel and walked across the parlor. The clomp of his large feet echoed on the hardwood floor.

As the screen door closed, Vivian released Jeremy, and Sarah scooted over to wrap her small arms around Vivian's neck and nestle her head on her shoulder.

"He's kinda funny," Sarah said, and Jeremy strutted around the room mocking Alistair's mannerisms.

"It's not nice to make fun of people, you two." The corners of Vivian's mouth remained fixed as she held their eyes.

"Why was he acting so funny, like he was angry, and who's gone?" Jeremy asked.

She pulled Jeremy over to her and squeezed both siblings in her arms. "I think, maybe he has a broken heart and—"

"Is it Ginny who's gone, Vivian?" Jeremy finally asked.

"Yes, Jeremy, Ginny has gone on a trip without telling anyone first, but I don't want you two to worry. I'm going to follow her and bring her home."

"Will you be scared, Vivvy?" Sarah asked.

"No, Sarah, the Lord will take care of me. Now, aren't you two supposed to be in bed?"

"We're here to say good night. Could you read us some more of our story?"

"I can surely do that without too much trouble. Jeremy, would you go and get the Bible? I think I left it on the table next to my bed."

Jeremy raced off to retrieve it.

"Where did we end up last night, Sarah?"

"Joseph's brothers sold him to some traders. Do you think he'll be rescued?"

"You will have to wait and find out."

"Do you think you will rescue Ginny? I want her home."

"Me too, sweetie. Me, too."

* * *

Later that evening, Aunt Margaret summoned Vivian to her father's bedside. Her father patted a spot on the bed, and Vivian smoothed her skirt as she sat down.

"I have spent some time praying about the situation, and I still don't feel good about it. Ginny has made a grave error in leaving with this young man."

"Yes, she has."

"I fear she might not return, even if I do allow you to chase her, and the risk to you will not have been worth it."

"I know, Father. I really feel I must go, though."

"Why?"

"I was unkind. I told her maybe she should go." Vivian pushed her hair back over her ear. "I was just so tired of her behavior. I feel like it's my fault."

"You mustn't blame yourself. Ginny didn't like to listen to anyone. You realize if you go the trip won't be easy?"

"I think so."

"You've never travelled alone before."

"I'll be all right. The Lord will keep me safe, and I won't take any unnecessary chances."

"Then the Lord has given you more assurance than He's given me."

"Did you suspect she was planning to leave?"

"She's always had fanciful dreams, but I never expected her to do something this foolhardy. Apparently I haven't been paying enough attention lately to notice any one fellow in particular. I don't even remember meeting this Logan Harris more than once."

The guilt stabbed again and she twisted the cuff of her sleeve, the material worn and frayed beneath her fingers. Why hadn't she told them Logan was different from the others? He was older and suave. His advances hadn't been child's play; that much had been obvious. Ginny was a likely target—she was more spark than brains—and her thoughts could easily be turned by the promise of a pretty dress or a fancy bauble.

"I'm sorry, Father. I knew . . . kind of. Ginny has been regaling me with plans for the last two weeks about being in love and following her heart."

"Sounds like our Ginny."

"She was so sure she was going to be rich. Logan has a plan for importing supplies and selling them at exorbitant prices to desperate miners. There's one thing I don't understand, though."

"What would that be?"

"If it's as real as Ginny thinks it is, and he plans to marry her, why didn't they marry before they left?"

Father didn't reply immediately. "Perhaps Logan's supplies include Virginia?"

What was he saying? Ginny was part of the supplies? What would Logan use her for? He can't possibly mean . . . as a prostitute. Her hand flew up to cover her mouth. *No, Ginny! Please, no!*

"I can't be sure, Vivian, and I hope with all my heart it's not true. But something in this story doesn't make sense."

Her stomach lurched. *Please, Lord, don't let it be true. I know I haven't always shown it, but I love her, Lord; I want her to be safe.*

Concern filled her father's eyes. "Remember, it's not your fault, Vivian. Ginny made her own decision." He reached for her hand and held it in his own. "I appreciate your offer, and I will allow you to go and find her. If I'm correct, she will desperately need your help."

"Thank you. I will do my best to bring her home."

* * *

The blankets wrapped around her body as she twisted and turned in bed that night, and the throbbing of her ankle was a constant reminder of the day's unfolding events. Was Ginny all right, and was she truly happy? What was Alistair feeling? Could he forgive Ginny and find someone else? And then there was Ben, the handsome stranger who had come to her rescue. How easily had he swept her up into his arms. His broad chest felt so strong and safe. Maybe, when she returned with Ginny—no, it would never happen. Not with someone like him.

CHAPTER 6

A VOICE CALLING GINNY'S NAME pulled her from a deep slumber. Moving her head from side to side, she attempted to soften the sharp pain at the back of her neck and raised a hand to squeeze its source. It must have been from the odd angle of sleeping against the window. Her eyes fluttered open, and Logan stood before her.

"Ginny, have you been asleep this whole time? I'm ready to show you your surprise."

Apparently she hadn't been missed. Outside the window, stars twinkled in the blue-black night.

"What time is it?"

"Eight forty-five. Come on." Logan reached for her hand and pulled her upright, smiling as he tucked a strand of hair behind her ear. He pulled her close and whispered, "Dinner is served at nine."

Her skin warmed beneath his breath. Stepping back, her fingers trembled as she bent to retrieve her hat. Why did he have such an effect on her?

Logan led her through several passenger cars until they arrived at an elegantly carved door with no window. He turned the knob and nudged her across the threshold.

She looked from side to side. How could this be? It was as though they'd stepped into an elegant hotel room. "Logan, it's beautiful!"

Stepping forward, she ran her hand along the back of one of four short couches sitting in pairs. The rich, grey damask felt nubby under her fingers. On the other side of the car, two double beds sat facing one another with dark blue velvet curtains hanging at the corners of each for privacy. Her feet crossed the exquisitely figured carpet.

Logan put his hands on his hips and puffed his chest. "I know, nothing's too good for my little wifey."

The reference made her cringe, but it would be true soon enough. "You mean I get to stay here?" She reached out. The velvet curtains were soft and luxurious, and she brought the material to her cheek. Closing her eyes, she inhaled.

"We are staying here, darlin'."

We? Easy enough—there were two beds, and they would both be occupied until Logan made an honest woman of her, ring or no ring.

"The best part is we get it all to ourselves. No one else on the train was willing to pay the added cost. But, I happened to have already made a sweet little bundle," he patted his pants pocket. "You'll be living like a queen."

"What do you mean already made a bundle? How? Were you gambling, Logan?"

"Are you trying to tell your man how to make his money?" Logan asked. The grit in his tone was unmistakable.

Was it worth it to challenge him? He'd lost money before and told her he wouldn't be taking any more chances. But Ginny looked at their beautiful accommodations; it had been worth the risk. "I guess not."

"And I sure hope not. Let's enjoy ourselves, shall we?" His arms pulled her into a tight embrace.

Her heart thumped as he dropped his lips to her neck and slowly made his way toward her lips with soft kisses. A firm double knock sounded on the door.

Ginny sprang back and lifted a fingernail to her teeth, nibbling its edge. Had they been discovered already? Impossible. Mother and Father wouldn't have started looking until supper. By then they had been well on their way.

Logan chuckled and tweaked the side of her cheek. "Relax, darlin', it's just supper. Come in."

The porter opened the door halfway and poked his head around it. "Supper is served, sir."

"Yes, thank you. We've been working up quite an appetite."

The shame burned its way up Ginny's chest and onto her neck in a hot blush. She dropped her head and turned away as the porter entered the car carrying a large silver tray.

He placed the tray on one of the couches as he pulled down a store away table from the wall. After removing three silver domes, he placed two bowls of tomato consommé and some buttered rolls on the table. Two larger plates were set to the side with their domes left untouched. Beside each bowl he set silverware and a crystal wine glass and then lifted a bottle for Logan's inspection.

"A fine year. Proceed."

"Sir," Ginny said, "I won't be having—"

The porter hesitated.

"I'd love for you to join me, sweetheart, in our celebration," Logan motioned for the other glass to be filled.

"Enjoy," the porter said as he collected the tray and left the room.

"I've never had a meal this fancy." Ginny looked at the plates on the table.

"After you, my sweet," Logan said, gesturing for her to take a seat.

When they finished the first course, the domed plates revealed roast duck topped with currant jelly and a side of wild rice along with a small salad. Logan was the perfect gentleman during the meal. He rattled on about the trip up North, the money they would have, the dresses she would wear, and he kept her glass full.

The wine was a new experience and was bitter on the tongue. Ginny's head was growing heavy. They finished the meal with a scoop of Neapolitan ice cream from a bowl set on ice.

Arching her back, she took a deep breath. "Thank you, Logan; I don't know the last time I was stuffed with such a lovely meal. This was my surprise, wasn't it?"

"Of course, and what more could you want?"

"I was hoping—"

A knock echoed on the door. Logan granted entrance to the porter who had returned to collect the dishes, store the table, and leave.

"Now, where were we?" Logan said as he pulled Ginny over and onto his lap, wrapping his arms about her waist.

"I said I was hoping—"

"Not now, Ginny, I meant before we were interrupted," his hands roamed across her bodice.

She wriggled, pushing his hands away. "Logan, stop."

"What do you mean, 'stop'? After spending all this money, I don't intend to sleep alone, if you know what I mean."

"But you promised—you promised me we would marry first."

"You've got the ring on don't you? Isn't that enough to make you happy?" his voice held a sneering tone. "Little Miss Innocent."

"But it doesn't mean anything; it's so other people won't ask questions."

"Look," his voice softened, "I know it's not what you want, but you're going to have to trust me on this. Haven't I said I'll always take care of you?"

"Yes, you've always said that."

"And haven't I always shown it to be true?"

What about at the train station when he was nowhere to be found, or even on the train when he left her alone to sleep the afternoon away?

Logan turned her sideways in his lap. With one arm around her back, he cupped her cheek with the other hand and planted several light kisses on her forehead. His whisper reached her ear. "You know I love you, Ginny. You are so good for me."

He fingered the gold locket hanging from her neck, and a quiver ran up and back down her spine. A rush of heat followed, warming her from the inside out.

Who would ever know? They would be married soon enough. She nestled into his strong embrace, and any intentions to remain pure before they married flickered out.

* * *

The next morning when Ginny awoke, the sun shining in the window revealed the wrinkled sheets beside her in the bed. The memory of the night before swooped in like a dark shadow. What had she done? She closed her eyes as the guilt filled her heart and soul. No, no—this wasn't supposed to happen. She curled into a tight ball and pulled the covers up over her head. What would Mother and Father think? Hadn't Vivian said she was a selfish girl who would do anything to get her own way? Maybe Vivian was right.

And what if Logan didn't . . . It's all right, it's all right. He is going to marry me. He loves me. No one will ever know.

She curled further under the blankets and tightened her grip. Maybe it was a bad dream, and if she went back to sleep it would all go away. She squeezed her eyes.

Much later, Ginny prepared for the day in the private bath and left the Pullman car to go and find Logan. Pasting a tight smile on her face, she tried to meet the eyes of her fellow travellers as she walked through the cars. One after another they stared at her. Was that a smirk on that young woman's face? They knew her secret; they all knew how she'd disappointed her family and disappointed herself. The car was stifling, too full of bodies; she needed some air.

"Ma'am?"

She looked up. The porter who had delivered last night's supper held out a gloved hand "If you would come with me, Mr. Harris requested I inform you he is in the dining car."

Grateful for his rescue, she looped her arm through his.

The dining car was full and boisterous with the sound of people laughing and visiting over their breakfasts. The porter ushered her to a table where Logan and his bedraggled companions, Star and Buttercup, sat sipping their morning coffee.

What were they doing here? She dragged another smile to her lips.

"Good morning, sweetheart," Logan stood and planted a brief kiss on her cheek.

Ginny dropped her eyes to her clasped hands. She resisted the urge to reach up and wipe the kiss off.

"Thank you, Hughie, for finding my blushing bride." Logan retrieved a silver dollar from his pocket and placed it in the porter's hand.

"Thank you, sir." The porter bowed and left.

Hughie? Does he know everyone on the train by name already?

Logan motioned for her to take the empty seat next to his. "I hope you enjoyed your sleep in, honey. You didn't even stir when I got up and left this morning. Mind you, those were first rate accommodations." He patted her hand where it sat on the table.

Ginny tried to act normal and play along with the charade that they were married. She couldn't help it; the cherry red still made its way up her cheeks.

"Well now, Logan, it seems you've embarrassed the wife. Did you keep her up real late, Romeo? Is that why she slept so long?" Star winked at him and the three started laughing.

Of all the nerve! Married or not, how could Logan sit here and let these harlots be so rude? A thought pushed its way into her head. Was she a harlot now, too? Had she sold herself for a beautiful train car and a lovely meal? No, it was different. Logan loved her, and she loved him. He'd promised to marry her; it wasn't the same at all. She didn't need to keep company with women of such low moral character, and for that matter, neither did Logan. "I find I'm not very hungry. Logan, would you please escort me back to our car?" Why did he have such a firm set to his jaw like he was angry? His companions were only cheap women he'd just met.

"You go ahead; I don't intend to waste this good cup of coffee."

He was choosing a good cup of coffee over her? Star and Buttercup over her? Her hand rose.

Logan grabbed her wrist and dug his thumb into the underside of soft flesh. As the pressure increased, Ginny stopped resisting, and Logan let her arm fall into her lap. Bunching her skirt up in her fists, she stood and twisted in the narrow space between the tables. "I'll see you in our car when you have no other pressing engagements."

CHAPTER 7

THE NEXT AFTERNOON, PENCIL IN hand, Vivian poured over her travel list in the parlor. Her ankle, elevated on a chair next to the settee, was considerably better than the day before. She would be ready for travel in a couple of days.

A sharp rap struck the front door, and then a muffled voice spoke with Auntie, most likely someone with whom she had business. Vivian's eyes dropped back to scan her list. A few moments later with a considerable rustle of skirts, Mary Beth Hastings entered the parlor carrying a woven basket tied with a bright pink bow.

"And how's the invalid today?" Mary Beth leaned forward and patted Vivian's cheek. "You do look on the pale side, but I have just the thing for that." Mary Beth sat down and set the basket on the floor. She removed two shiny red apples and a quaint spray of deep purple hyacinths and set them on the table.

What a surprise—Mary Beth had followed through on her promise to visit. "Thank you, Mary Beth. How lovely." Vivian reached for the spray and raised it to her nose. She took a deep sniff and the heavy, sweet scent filled her head. Returning the spray to her lap, her fingers traced the delicate petals. "So kind of you to drop by."

"It's no bother at all; the shop is closed today as Mrs. Tredwurt is down with the flu. I popped in to ask Alistair how you were doing, and he encouraged me to stop by and cheer you up."

"How very kind of him." *Thank you, Alistair. Mary Beth would help pass the time.*

"He said you were looking quite peaked and could use the company. I think maybe he has taken a shine to you. Do we have ourselves a budding romance, Vivian?"

How does a man with a broken heart look like someone who is in love? "I don't think so, Mary Beth; the doctor has no interest in me."

"Oh, Vivian, Vivian," Mary Beth shook her head from side to side. "You're so inexperienced." She sighed as though Vivian were a simpleton. "Not like that sister of yours. It's all over town how she ran off with that big-talking Logan Harris. Have you heard anything from her?"

Vivian lifted her chin and added a note of irritation to her voice. "No, we have not, and I prefer not to talk about my sister's choices. It's a very painful topic for my family right now." Who did Mary Beth think she was anyway, barging in and talking about Ginny like that? Never mind that it was true—how did everyone in town know she had left with Logan? "She would be best served by your prayers, Mary Beth."

"No doubt about that, Vivian."

Mary Beth didn't seem fazed at all by Vivian's tone and continued to chat away about the town's people and their comings and goings. As the conversation continued, Vivian gave the occasional nod or, "My, my," which seemed to keep Mary Beth convinced of her interest.

Eventually, she ran out of new things to say and repeated herself. Perhaps there might be another motive to Mary Beth's visit.

"Have you seen Ben since your," Mary Beth wiggled her fingers in her lap, "little accident, shall we say?"

Finally—the real reason for the visit. Mary Beth wanted to see if pathetic Vivian was any competition for the gorgeous, brawny, Ben McCormack, who—in her eyes—was already Mary Beth's property. *Yes, we're riding off into the sunset together. In fact, he's picking me up this evening to do so.* If only it were true. Vivian smoothed her skirt and straightened her shoulders. "No, I haven't. Why?"

"Well, I have seen neither hide nor hair of him, either. The postmaster said he'd been in town again today, and I thought maybe . . ." she pulled at the short curls on the nape of her neck.

"Yes?" Vivian was not going to just hand Mary Beth what she wanted. Perhaps Mary Beth had sensed Ben had taken interest in Vivian—what a lovely thought.

"Never mind if you haven't seen him. But, are you sure about that, though? He hasn't stopped by to see how you're doing?"

"No, Mary Beth, I haven't seen him since he dropped me off yesterday." He was difficult to miss—the charming, farmer-type who filled an entire room.

Mary Beth searched Vivian's eyes and appeared satisfied she was telling the truth. Gathering her voluminous skirt with one hand, she bent to retrieve the basket as she said, "I'll be going now. Perhaps I shall come back and visit some other time."

"I will be home for only two more days."

Mary Beth straightened and turned to face Vivian, "Really?"

"My ankle is healing well, so I intend to go and find my sister."

"You do? How very honorable of you to go and bring the wild one home." A smile stretched across Mary Beth's face. "And in that case, I would like to do all I can to help you on your way."

Vivian clenched her teeth to keep from replying improperly.

"But do you think it will be safe? I mean a woman travelling alone—"

"I intend to be very careful and hire a reputable guide when it becomes necessary."

"Like I said, if there's anything at all I can do for you, please let me know."

"I'm sure I will be quite fine; thank you for the offer, Miss Hastings."

"Honestly, Miss Connor, I don't mean to point out the obvious, but you can barely walk. How is it you're going to prepare for the trip and be on your way as soon as possible without my help?"

When put that way, it only made sense to ask for Mary Beth's assistance, annoying as she was. Vivian picked the supply list up from the settee and handed it over to Mary Beth. "There are a couple of things on my list I could use your help with."

The two girls spent over an hour going over the items on the list and discussing the best places to purchase travelling supplies. Mary Beth offered to go downtown and buy the supplies that very afternoon.

Vivian was grateful when Mary Beth, intent on her mission, picked up her basket and left. How much prying disguised in the form of caring could one endure? By nightfall the entire town would have a fully embellished update on Vivian's plan to follow Ginny and convince her to come home, but it couldn't be helped.

* * *

Ben couldn't believe how the weather was holding. They had been able to clear a whole extra quarter, and Ben expected their biggest crop ever. It was a good thing too, what with Amos and Julie having a baby, and he getting married. He was still amazed at the fact that he would be a married man within the month. Why Audrey had suddenly become so anxious about tying the knot he didn't know. But who was he to argue; he could hardly wait himself.

Amos and Julie's mouths both dropped open last night when he told them he was heading out West and then up North to pick up his new wife. He probably should have told them about the relationship sooner. However, they promised to keep the reason for his trip to themselves so he didn't have the whole town asking him questions. It was none of their business.

The time of year wasn't the best, but at least the crops were in the ground. If Audrey would have waited until after harvest, like they'd planned, it would have been a whole lot easier to get away. It was also a good thing he had enough money set by to hire Jesse, the neighbour boy. He'd worked the farm with them for years and could be depended on to keep up Ben's end of the work. The kid was thrilled as he hoped to buy himself a team of horses and a wagon with the extra cash.

The tiny seedlings in neat rows looked green and healthy as Ben walked the perimeter of the field checking the fences for breaks. They couldn't have the neighbour's cattle crossing the lines and making a mess of the crops. As he walked, he thought about Audrey, rereading her latest letter in his mind. The girl seemed to have such a way with words. It was like poetry to his ears.

My Dearest Ben,

Greetings, my love. I surely cannot wait until we are joined in wedded matrimony. My very thoughts are all but consumed with you and your lovely farm. I do wish you would write me more about your land and the beautiful house we will share together when we are married. You must know we are very crowded here in our tent surrounded by so many others like ourselves. We hear every squabble and fight in the whole tent town. In fact, we can hear the very snores of our neighbours while trying to sleep!

However, you've promised it is but a very short time and we will be married. I know we will be so happy together. Thank you so much for the locket you sent with your picture in it. I wear it always and think of you tenderly, as it lies close to my heart.

I look forward to meeting you in the very flesh soon. We are doing our best to raise the funds for the trip. I hope it doesn't cause you undo trouble for us to come to you in the spring instead of after harvest. You must understand my anxiousness to become your beloved wife.

Good-bye for what will be only a short time.

Your Betrothed,

Audrey

Ben had ridden into town to buy his ticket for the train to Seattle that morning. Wouldn't Audrey's family be surprised to see him as they expected to be travelling down South instead of him traveling up North? It was certainly much easier this way. It would have been nice to buy gifts for the family in town, but if he did that, the tongues would begin to wag. He figured he might as well wait until he reached Seattle. And wouldn't Audrey be surprised when she saw the progress on the house? The recent letters hadn't said much about what he'd been working on. With her arrival coming sooner than he originally planned, he'd found the incentive to start working more diligently. All of the interior rooms were now finished, and the planed maple boards for the cupboards lay drying in the kitchen. It would probably take some considerable time to make them, but he didn't want to rush the work. He had to admit, it was much more satisfying when he knew he was building for someone special. He hoped Audrey would like the wood he had chosen for the cupboards and the wainscoting.

Amos asked the other day if he wasn't going overboard, but Ben wanted it to be the prettiest farmhouse ever. With everything Audrey had been through in the last couple of years, she deserved the best he could give her.

He leaned over, dug his fingers into the warm, black soil, and plucked out the roots of a ragweed. Tossing it back onto the ground, he dusted his hand against his thigh and turned for the farmhouse. There would be lots of time to work on the house again that evening after a quick sandwich for supper. Now that the plan for the trip had come together, giddiness had settled into his demeanor.

Approaching Amos and Julie's place, he noticed the doctor's wagon out front. What would Doc Mason be doing here? He ran across the yard and let himself in the front door. The house was quiet—too quiet—and Julie wasn't busy in the kitchen like usual.

"Amos? Julie?" His voice rose a notch. "Anyone here?"

Dr. Mason rounded the corner from the hallway, wiping his hands on a cotton towel.

"What's going on, Doc?"

"She'll be fine, Ben. She's putting her feet up for a bit. Amos is with her in the back room."

Ben stepped forward; he needed to see for himself. Dr. Mason reached out and put a hand to his arm; Ben stopped and rotated to face him.

"Julie had a bit of a fall this afternoon. Amos thought I should come by and check in on her. It could have been worse, but she'll be fine."

"What happened?"

"She fell off the back step trying to hang up the laundry and gave herself a good scare. The baby's fine, though; I could feel movement. Give them a few minutes, and then you can see for yourself."

Ben removed his hat and wiped the sweat from his forehead with the back of his hand. He and Amos would have to put a railing up out back. Why hadn't they done that before?

"How are you doing, Ben? I hear you're taking a bit of a journey," Dr. Mason broke his train of thought.

"You did?" They had promised they wouldn't tell.

"Amos mentioned you were going out West for a bit. Are you following the gold?"

Guess they didn't spill the whole can of beans. But why did people insist on knowing everything everybody was doing? "Uh, nope; I'm taking the train. I want to see some country I've never seen before." Smart, really smart. Farmer takes a holiday for no reason at all. Ben didn't think it was likely to put him off the scent.

"Are you thinking of moving out that way and getting your own place?"

"Doc, you know I could never leave this place. It's been in our family for three generations."

Dr. Mason looked over, one bushy eyebrow raised. Ben met Dr. Mason's eyes with clamped his lips. The doctor needed to realize there were no more answers coming for his questions. The whole town would know soon enough when he returned with his pretty little bride on his arm.

An awkward silence followed. There was no way Ben was breaking it.

Dr. Mason cleared his throat. "Have you been by to visit Vivian Connor?"

"Um." The picture of Vivian as he'd lifted her from the sidewalk and sheltered her in his arms flashed in his memory. He swallowed, "Nope."

"It was nice of you to help her out the other day when she hurt her ankle. Her father's holding his own, but I'm not sure how much longer he will last. His heart is plum worn out for someone so young."

"Maybe it's from being a pastor and carrying so many other people's burdens?"

"Maybe so," Dr. Mason moved his head from side to side. "Maybe so. Well, it would be nice if you stopped by before you left town. The family could use the distraction."

"How's Vivian's ankle doing? Will it heal well?"

"Alistair looked in on her the other night. He didn't think it was much of a sprain. I expect she will be up and at it before you know it."

The thought of Alistair spending time with Vivian made his stomach do tiny, nervous flips. It shouldn't. He loved Audrey; they were going to get married. Alistair and Vivian being together was no concern of his. But it would be the neighbourly thing to do to drop by—especially since Dr. Mason was asking. And it wouldn't be much of a problem to stop in tomorrow when he went to town again. "I might do that, Doc, if you think it would do the family some good. I feel badly about their situation."

Dr. Mason pushed his wire rim glasses up on his nose and grinned. "Yes, Ben, I think it would do the family good."

* * *

A dull throb pulsed through Vivian's foot as she took a few small steps without her cane down the front walk at Aunt Margaret's. By tomorrow walking should be easier if she didn't overdo it today.

Most of the preparations for the trip were complete, and the trunk stood ready with her clothes packed. With Mary Beth's help she'd either borrowed or purchased enough travelling clothes for six weeks. Some of the other supplies would be picked up along the way after talking to other travellers heading out into the gold fields. Father had given her enough money to supply her needs for the trip. What a waste, spending family money they really couldn't spare. Would Ginny even appreciate the sacrifice they were all making? Probably not.

Where was Ginny by now, and was she all right? *Lord, please keep her safe. Help her to remember You and Your ways. Amen.* If only Ginny would stop this fool notion, turn around, and come home; they would welcome her with open arms. It had been three days, and still not a word had been heard. The long hours of waiting gave Vivian's mind time to dwell on the worst. Dread filled her stomach when anyone knocked on the door. What if they were here to tell the family Ginny had been hurt, or even killed? There was no reason to dwell on such morbid thoughts. Ginny was wily; she could make a way for herself. But would Logan have married her by now? Was she, in fact, Mrs. Logan Harris? Vivian's heart said no, all was not well with her sister.

The horses that pulled up to the front of the house looked familiar before she even glanced up at the driver. Ben gave a quick nod of the head as he drew the horses to a stop with a low, "Whoa." The muscles in his forearms bulged against his worn, plaid shirt as he jumped down from the wagon, a bouquet of flowers in his hand.

Vivian's stomach leaped as she took in his rugged good looks, which were just as fine as they had been a few days ago. She held up a hand to shade her eyes, hoping it would make the perusal not so obvious. It was a pleasant surprise, his coming by; he'd meant what he'd said after all.

Ben's long strides brought him up the walk in moments. He held out the bouquet of mixed cut flowers tied with a delicate pink ribbon. "These are for you, Miss Connor."

"They are beautiful, Mr. McCormack," she said. "Thank you." As she reached out for the bouquet, her fingers closed around Ben's.

He looked into her eyes, and his head tilted to one side. The world tipped, and a tingle flowed from his hand to hers. Warmth flowed up from her toes through her entire body. If only she could look into his eyes forever. Was he as lost as she was?

He cleared his throat. She pulled the bouquet toward herself, and his fingers dropped.

Ben lifted his hat, wiped his forehead, and placed it back on his head. "I thought you might need some encouragement, but it looks to me like you're not doing too poorly. I expected you wouldn't be able to walk for quite some time."

"I am so sorry, to have bothered you the other day. My ankle hurts, but it's bearable."

"It was no problem, Miss Connor. I remembered Jeremy gave me permission to give you some flowers. I hope you don't mind if I didn't pick them from your aunt's yard."

Vivian laughed as she lowered her face to take a deep whiff of the bouquet. She needed to collect herself and slow the wild racing of her heart. "Thank you, Mr. McCormack, these are lovely. But you really shouldn't have just because Jeremy—"

"Actually, it's my pleasure," Ben replied.

His smile was dazzling; light sparkled from his eyes. "Umm . . . " *Think Vivian, think.* She looked down at the flowers "I should really put your lovely gift in some water. Would you like to come in?" Please, please come in.

"Sure, I have a few moments. I was wondering how your father was doing."

Oh thank you. "He hasn't changed much. He gets up for a few hours a day to visit or read, but that's about all he can manage. I think the rest of us are more frustrated than he is because we see how weak he is. He seems to have an incredible peace about the whole thing. I wish I could say the same." Vivian dropped her head, and the flowers blurred through the moisture in her eyes.

Ben reached out and gave her elbow a soft squeeze. Her breath caught.

"I'm so sorry Vivian. I wish you didn't have to go through this."

Alone? Does he mean go through this alone? He released her elbow. "Thank you, Mr. McCormack, I appreciate your kindness."

They turned together, Ben providing support, as they strolled up the sidewalk and stepped through the door.

"Hello, young man," her father called from around the corner, his voice weak.

Ben removed his hat, hung it on the umbrella stand, and then swept out his arm, indicating she should precede him into the parlour.

Father sat in the stuffed chair by the window, his legs wrapped in one of Aunt Margaret's homemade quilts. "I saw your wagon arrive; I was hoping you would come in for a visit. I don't believe we've met. I am Vivian's father, Harold Connor."

He saw the wagon arrive? That means he saw the exchange on the front lawn. But then again, what was there to see? The tingles were invisible; the heat was invisible. She must collect herself. "Father, this is Mr. McCormack. He's the fellow who gave us a ride home the other day when I hurt my ankle."

"Ah, so you're the knight in shining armor the youngsters have told me about. They were quite impressed with you. Jeremy says he's going to buy a fine pair of horses like yours when he's saved enough money. Mind you, I think his last count was six cents."

The three of them chuckled together; Vivian took the opportunity to excuse herself and go check on the children and prepare some refreshments. Her mother and Aunt Margaret were taking a garden tea tour for the afternoon—a much needed break for them—and thus left her in charge of the household.

* * *

Mr. Connor motioned to the opposite chair, and Ben sat down. Ben found it difficult not to stare at the thin, pale figure; a puff of wind could blow the man over.

"So, tell me about yourself, Ben. As you can see, I don't get out much, and it does me good to meet new people. It helps me forget about my own situation for a bit."

"Well, I farm several sections about three miles west of here with my brother. It was the family homestead, and my parents left it to the both of us when they passed on."

"I am sorry to hear of your loss."

"Thank you, sir. I was born and raised in the area, and I suppose everyone knows me or knows my family. It's a pretty close community; we like to look out for each other." It almost sounded noble when he said it that way.

"That's one of the reasons I moved my family here. My sister wrote for years about what a fine town they lived in. We never had the chance to visit until now. We lived two states away, and our church kept us mighty busy."

"Your daughter mentioned you were a pastor."

"Don't let that scare you, son. I won't bite."

"I'm not worried, sir, I know the Lord. I've gone to church my whole life."

"So, you're a believer, are you? Wonderful, wonderful. You can understand, then, how I was thankful for the Lord's provision. My sister Margaret has been so generous in giving my family a place to live. It will make things so much easier when I'm gone."

"Sir, are you sure you should be talking so finally? What if the Lord chooses to heal you?"

"He may, Ben, He may. I just feel it's my time to go. I wish I could stay, but it appears the Lord's calling me home."

What could he say to the man's pronouncement? Mr. Connor was a pastor. But what about the family he'd leave behind? It was difficult to pick up the pieces and carry on when someone left before his time.

There were still so many days when the loss of his own mom and dad sat heavy on his heart.

"I hope the Lord gives me time to talk to my daughter one last time."

Ben raised his eyebrow. "Vivian, sir?" Surely he couldn't be thinking there wouldn't be time to talk to Vivian.

"No, her younger sister, Ginny. You must not have met her. She ran off the day you brought Vivian home from the doctor."

How much could one family take?

"She headed out with some opportunist who floated into town. He said he was going to strike it rich selling supplies to the men heading out with the gold rush. I guess Ginny's head was turned by all the talk of glitter and gold."

"There are a lot of folks whose heads have been turned that way lately."

"Yes, and our Ginny never was one to listen to reason. She always thought she could do things her own way, and they would work out. I'm not quite sure why, though. That girl has been in so many predicaments, but I fear this time she's in way over her head."

Ben nodded. It could very well be true. They young girl probably had no idea what could be lurking in the minds of some men.

They continued to chat until Vivian limped into the parlor carrying a tray with iced tea and a plate of squares.

Ben jumped up and hurried over, lifting the tray from Vivian's grip.

"Thank you, Ben. If you would put it on the table. Aunt Margaret made the date squares this morning."

He put the tray on a small wooden table and took his seat again. Vivian handed him a glass of tea and a small plate with a generous portion of the squares.

"Thank you," he said. Her hands were so delicate and white that he could practically fit both of them in one of his.

Vivian sat quietly as he continued to visit with her father. She nodded her head every once in a while as if to show she was listening. But several times when he looked over, he caught her staring out the window.

"Well, Mr. McCormack," Vivian's father's voice sounded even weaker than when he'd first arrived. "I've enjoyed your visit, but I find I've tired myself out. If you will excuse me, I think I'll take a nap."

"Most certainly, Mr. Connor. I mean, I'm sure you must be exhausted. It was nice meeting you."

"Vivian, if you wouldn't mind giving me some support to the library first, I'm sure our guest would love to continue chatting with you."

Standing up, Ben helped Mr. Connor out of his chair.

Vivian took her father's arm, and they slowly moved across the parlour and through the double doors on the far end of the room.

He figured he should take this opportunity to excuse himself and go about his business; daylight was wasting. But it was so comfortable visiting with this family. Vivian loved her father; Ben could tell by the way she treated him. He knew that his parents would have liked her, too, if only they were still alive. It wasn't every family that loved the Lord either, but was his visit still Christian charity? He couldn't deny he'd wanted to bend over and kiss Vivian's sweet pink lips and to cup her face between his hands when he had looked into her eyes. No, this definitely was not Christian charity any longer. In fact, it was downright unfaithful to Audrey to think these thoughts. So why weren't his feet taking him to the door?

"Mr. McCormack? Mr. McCormack?"

Vivian's voice came to his ear. "I'm sorry, Miss Connor, I was lost in my thoughts." The skin at the collar of his shirt warmed. That look she was giving him—could she read his thoughts?

She sat in the opposite chair and smoothed the lap of her dress. "I'd like to thank you for visiting with my father; we know so few people here."

"No problem at all; it was my pleasure."

"Did he mention the difficulty our family is having over my sister?"

"He did, and I'm very sorry to hear it. It must be hard for you, waiting for word."

"I don't intend to wait much longer. I've decided to follow her and see if I can talk some sense into her."

"How do you propose to do that?"

"We're not quite sure how she intended to get there, but we do know she's headed for Dawson City. I'm leaving Wednesday morning."

"Wednesday morning? This Wednesday morning?"

"Yes, on the train. If I don't catch up with her on the way, I'll have to find her in Dawson City."

Wednesday morning on the train, the very same train he intended to leave town on. It was probably not a good idea if Vivian were along. Maybe he could convince her not to go and promise to look out for her sister himself. He didn't want Vivian getting hurt, either. "But, Vivian—I mean, Miss Connor, it simply isn't safe for you to go chasing after your sister. Perhaps I could—"

"I'm going. Ginny needs me, and I told the family I would go find her." She had her chin lifted and kept a firm tone to her voice; it was a Vivian he hadn't seen until now.

"Your father's in agreement with you running across the country alone?"

She appeared confused by the question. "I won't be alone. My aunt has secured a traveling companion for me. I am going to help a woman travel with her two young sons."

"But still, Miss Connor, I mean, how effective can you be? Your father mentioned your sister had left town with an opportunist, but what if he's dangerous as well?"

"I'll have to trust the Lord to keep me safe, I guess."

She looked at him like she was trying to figure him out, and no wonder. He raked his hand through his hair in exasperation. It wasn't his place to care about Vivian or what she did. So why couldn't he help it? And how would he explain his own travels on the train? It was time to own up to the situation. But what if things didn't work out with Audrey? Was there a chance he and Vivian—he stopped himself. It wasn't right to think this way. "Miss Connor, I implore you. Please reconsider this fool's journey."

Vivian straightened her back, "Fool's journey, Mr. McCormack? I am not sure you are in any position to give on opinion on my undertaking."

He let out his breath slowly and unclenched his fists. "You're right, I am in no position." *Oh Lord, I am so confused. Why do I care about this woman I met a week ago when I have loved Audrey for months?* It would be best to leave. Ben looked down at his feet; her stare was making his stomach clench. "I wish you well, and I hope Ginny realizes what a great family she has. I really must be going."

"Perhaps we can continue to get to know each other when I return?"

"I have no idea," Ben replied. "I can't answer that question right now. I'll let myself out; good day." He pulled himself from the chair, gave a small nod, and left.

CHAPTER 8

VIVIAN STEPPED DOWN GINGERLY FROM the carriage, straightened her grey wool traveling skirt, and adjusted her new straw hat. Mary Beth had convinced her of the need to travel in style. It had been her idea to attach the blue ribbon flowers along one side of Vivian's hat and curl the brim up to meet them.

Glancing down the platform, Vivian could see Ben walking away from Alistair and into the station. What was he doing here? Was it a final attempt to convince her not to go? It simply wasn't any of his business. She hadn't heard a word from him since the day he'd left in such a hurry. So much for thinking there might have been something between them.

Was Alistair traveling too, or were the two men conspiring together? Looking back over her shoulder, Vivian saw Jeremy helping Father out of the carriage, which would allow her a few moments to speak with the doctor alone. Her foot cramped as she proceeded down the planks.

"Good morning, Dr. Williams. What a surprise to see you here today."

"I hope I'm not a bother, but I had to speak to you before you left. You might think it a ridiculous notion, but I love your sister deeply. I've hardly slept a wink since you gave me the news she left town, and I've decided it doesn't matter."

"What doesn't matter?" What was the poor man talking about? He sounded delirious.

"It doesn't matter that she's run off with someone else. I still love her with all my heart, and I believe she loves me, too."

"Oh, Doctor, I don't think you understand." Ginny couldn't love him. She ran off with another man; that wasn't love.

"No, please listen," he pulled a ring from his pocket. It was a fine gold band with a glittering diamond and a small sapphire on either side.

"It's beautiful, Dr. Williams. Has she ever seen it?"

"No, I was saving it until it could be official. It was my grandmother's. I want you to take it, and when you find Ginny, give it to her. Let her know I still love her, and my offer still stands."

"Do you think it's wise? You don't know what or where—"

"It doesn't matter to me. I love her, I will always love her, and I want her to be my wife. Please take the ring."

She reached out and took the delicate ring. It was so pretty; Ginny would have liked it. She opened her drawstring purse and removed her sewing kit. It would be safe in there. Ginny didn't deserve such an honorable man; it would be better if he simply forgot about her. "You know I can't make any promises, Dr. Williams, but when and if I find Ginny, I will pass along your message."

"I can't ask anything more. I will be going now; I wish you safe travels." He turned away, his steps echoing on the wooden platform as he left the station.

Vivian turned in time to see Ben exit the station door and walk toward her. Her heart betrayed her with a small flutter. Perhaps he had come to say good-bye, or maybe apologize for being rude the other day? His anger during their conversation hadn't made any sense. It was so annoying that he hadn't come by Aunt Margaret's house again so they could talk about it.

"It looks as though we might be traveling on the same train, Miss Connor."

Travelling on the same train? "I didn't know you were planning to travel, Mr. McCormack. You certainly never mentioned it." And he definitely had had an opportunity to mention it.

Ben's eyes scanned the open field across from the station, and then he coughed into his hand twice. "Uhm."

"Yes?"

"You're right, I never mentioned it."

"Didn't you think our conversation the other day would have been an appropriate time to divulge your plans?"

"Probably."

Probably? It most definitely would have been the right time to tell her. Why was he being so secretive? "Why are you travelling?"

He hesitated before replying, "Business—farm business."

"Well, can you tell me how far you're going?"

"Dyea, Alaska."

Farm business in Dyea, Alaska? Why wouldn't he admit he was coming along to keep an eye on her and get to know her? "I'm hoping to catch up with Ginny long before she gets to Dawson City. I have no desire to travel that far up North." *What do you have to say to that, Mr. Ben McCormack?*

He peered over her shoulder. She turned to follow his gaze; Aunt Margaret was helping Jeremy lift her trunk to the ground.

"I'll let you say good-bye to your family." Ben stepped over to the wall of the station and bent over to retrieve the two pieces of luggage he must have left there earlier.

Why wouldn't he just come out and say he would like to get to know her? It was rather obvious to go way out of his way to travel on the same train. Although, the trip would be much safer and much more pleasant knowing that he was along.

A smile slipped to her lips as she walked toward the family carriage. Aunt Margaret and her mother were supporting either arm of her father. He looked so weak and frail. Perhaps knowing Ben would be travelling the same train would help lessen the burden of her trip? He appeared quite taken with the man. "Father, I've spoken to Mr. McCormack, and he is heading out West today as well."

Father looked at her, his weary eyes pleased with the news. He was too tired. He shouldn't have come to see her off.

"He didn't mention it the other day, Vivian, but it pleases me to know there will be someone to look out for you. I didn't feel completely secure even knowing you were travelling with Mrs. Brown."

"But, Father—"

He lifted his hand to stop her from continuing. "I know you think you are capable, Vivian, and I'm glad you feel confident. But you have never travelled without your family, and you have no idea of the danger you might encounter."

"It's not like I'm going to take—"

"Vivian, listen to your father." Mother's words stopped the protest.

"I am very proud of you for going to find your sister. This is something that should never be asked of any sibling," his voice cracked and faded.

Mother moved her arm around her father's back. "Harold, do you think you should be getting so worked up?"

"It needs to be said, Tabitha. Vivian, I love you. We all love you, and we can never express enough how much it means to us to have you go after your sister."

The words brought encouragement as they sunk in. She leaned forward and hugged her father. He wrapped his arms around her. *Lord, I pray this isn't the last time he holds me in his arms.* Mother, Aunt Margaret, and Jeremy snuggled into the embrace for a Connor family hug.

"Hey, let me in," a small voice said as Sarah squeezed her way in between her father and mother. The group laughed, and Vivian picked up her little sister.

"I am going to miss you all so much."

"I am going to miss you too, Vivvy. Do you think you could bring me and Jeremy back a present?" Sarah sniffled.

Vivian tousled her hair. "You know, I think I can probably do something about that."

The family walked down the platform with Jeremy dragging Vivian's trunk behind him. The ground shook as the train neared the station, and a loud whistle pierced the air. Jeremy and Sarah begged their aunt to take them to the other side of the building so they could get a closer look at the steam engine spewing black smoke into the air.

"Yes, let's go, children. I will see if I can find Mrs. Brown so I can make introductions before the train leaves." Aunt Margaret and the two scurried away.

Ben stepped through the main door and walked over to where Vivian and her parents stood. "Good day, Mr. and Mrs. Connor. What a coincidence, your daughter and I travelling at the same time." His voice sounded flat, as though not at all pleased with the prospect. *So why had he taken the opportunity to make such an arrangement in the first place?*

"I would appreciate it, young man, if you would keep an eye out for Vivian. She tends to think she can handle more than she is able."

"Father, I don't think Ben wants to babysit—"

Ben rubbed his neck as though uncomfortable. "I'll do my best, sir. Now if you will excuse me, Miss Connor, I'd like to take your trunk to the loading platform."

"Thank you, Mr. McCormack, I appreciate it."

Ben lifted her trunk as though it were a sack of cotton and disappeared around the end of the building. He was being so abrupt that it was almost rude. What had happened to the kind and generous man who had wormed his way into many of her daydreams?

As Vivian's gaze returned to her mother and father, she stepped back, squaring her shoulders. *Lord, please give me the strength to actually leave.* The whole idea of going to find Ginny suddenly seemed preposterous. Drawing in a deep breath, she willed her voice to sound brave. "You don't need to worry about me; everything is going to be fine. It will be a great adventure for me to be out on my own. I think it would be best if we say good-bye here. I don't want to tire you out, Father. You two go on back to the carriage, and the others can wave as I leave."

She gave her mother and father one more quick hug. She had to leave now, or she wouldn't leave at all.

Heavenly Father, please don't let this be the last time I see my earthly father. Preserve him until I return with Ginny. Lord, I love my family so much. She reached out and squeezed her father's hand and turned to walk toward the door. Opening the door, she gave one more backward glance. The corners of father's mouth scarcely turned up. Her mother stood at his side with no expression. *Walk through the door; don't look back.*

She crossed the polished station floor and exited through the open double doors on the backside of the building. Porters loaded trunks into the baggage car at the far end of the platform. Jeremy, Sarah, and Aunt Margaret stood amongst the cluster of people milling beside the shiny, black engine.

Sarah noticed her presence and ran over, throwing herself into Vivian's arms. It was hard not to wince as she stepped back to keep her balance, and the pain throbbed in her ankle.

"Hey you, be careful now. We don't want your sister hurtin' herself again before she leaves," Ben said after rounding the open doors. He reached out to steady her.

Tingles coursed down her arm at the touch of his fingers. So, he was a hero again. She wriggled her elbow out of his grasp and bent over her sister. "Sarah, you know I love you very much. I will see you in a few months. And don't you go getting taller—I want to recognize you when I get back. Be good for Mother, Father, and Auntie."

Jeremy joined the group, and Vivian wagged her finger at him. "If you are good, I will bring you each a gift when I return. But best of all I will bring you Ginny." Vivian pried her sister's arms from around her waist and stepped forward to give her aunt a warm hug.

A diminutive woman—probably in her thirties—with well-rounded curves looked on as they said their farewells. Her gown was a lovely deep blue silk with a high collar and tiny pleats running down the bodice. She stepped forward as Vivian released her aunt.

"Vivian, I'd like you to meet Mrs. Amelia Brown, a dear friend of your late uncle's family. It is so very fortunate you are able to travel together." Aunt Margaret spoke as Amelia tipped her head and reached out to shake Vivian's hand.

"Nice to meet you, Vivian. I am sure we will have a grand time together. Your aunt has kindly informed me you are wonderful with children."

"Nice to meet you too, Mrs. Brown. I look forward to our travels together."

"Amelia, may I also introduce Ben McCormack. He is a friend of Vivian's who has come to wish her farewell."

Ben removed his hat and reached out to clasp Amelia's extended hand.

"Nice to meet you, ma'am. I believe you might be seeing more of me as I have not come to wish Vivian farewell, but I intend to travel to Seattle as well."

Aunt Margaret's head snapped up, her eyes searching Vivian's. Vivian shrugged, and a look of confusion crossed her aunt's face. "But I thought—"

The train whistle blew, cutting off Auntie's comments and informing the passengers it was time to board. Mrs. Brown spun on the platform and bustled toward the train door. Vivian clasped her aunt in a swift hug and followed Mrs. Brown. Ben returned his hat to his head and followed Vivian. Each passenger stepped up the stairs and inside the train car. Holding back tears, Vivian waved out the window of the car as her brother and sister waved furiously back.

"Ma'am," said a voice, and a porter reached out his arm to indicate a bench to the right.

"She'll be seated with us," Mrs. Brown said as she motioned toward the far end of the compartment.

Glancing over her shoulder, Vivian could see Ben taking a seat in the next car. It would've been nice if he had come and sat with the rest of them. How would he get to know her if he sat so far away? He was a difficult man to figure out. Vivian proceeded to the two shiny wooden benches facing each other where Amelia was seated and arranging her voluminous skirt. Across from her sat two boys of about eight and ten with smart herringbone jackets and matching shorts.

Amelia patted the bench indicating the spot next to her. "These are my precious sons, Edward and Paul. Say hello to the nice lady, you two."

"How do you know she's nice, Mother?" the smallest one asked. "You've only just met her."

"Paul, I've asked you to say hello. Now be a good boy."

Edward shoved his finger into his brother's side, and Paul grabbed the lapels of his brother's jacket. The two tussled on the wooden bench.

"I'm certain you boys are going to be the death of me," Amelia reached over and pulled at their clothing in an attempt to part the two quarrelling boys. "What was your father thinking when he asked us to make this trip?"

Vivian squeezed herself onto the seat between the two struggling boys and spoke with a firm voice. "Hello, Edward, Paul, my name is Miss Connor." Taking each boy's hand in turn, she gave them a good shaking. They looked up as though to check if they were being chastened, so much like Jeremy. Her mouth stayed firm. The two boys straightened and placed their hands in their laps.

"Hello, miss." They chimed together. These two would prove to be a handful.

The train lurched, and the final whistle blew announcing its intention to leave the station. Vivian looked out the window; Jeremy and Sarah stood holding one of Aunt Margaret's hands. Eyes wide and faces pale, they looked as though they'd just realized she was really leaving. The scene tugged at her heart. She blew them each a kiss and touched her fingertips to the window as the train pulled out of the station and rumbled down the track. They didn't run alongside as she imagined they would, but instead stood still and listless following her departure with their gaze. Vivian brought her hand to her mouth to stifle a sob, and Amelia reached over to touch her shoulder.

"Who's that? Are they your children?" Paul asked, his small nose pressed to the train window.

"Paul, you shouldn't pry into other people's business," Edward said, tugging at the corners of his jacket in an attempt to straighten it.

"They're my younger brother and sister. I have to leave them behind, and I guess they are going to miss me more than I thought they would."

"It's very difficult to leave sometimes, isn't it? I would've never made this trip if it wasn't to meet up with my husband. He left about five months ago to seek his wealth in gold, although he had a fine job in my father's shipping business back home, mind you."

Vivian pulled her eyes from the window to face Amelia. "It's odd how the gold fever seems to take over, isn't it?"

"Yes, and of course he's discovered good claims are harder to come by than was promised. He's built a hotel in Dawson City instead. Living there will seem like the end of the world."

The end of the world—that's where Ginny was headed. It was not quite the paradise she'd made it out to be.

"Did you know people even pay for their drinks and meals with gold nuggets?" Amelia gave a soft chuckle. "I guess there's more than one way to get your share of the riches."

"My sister feels the same way. I don't know if my Aunt explained it to you or not?"

"She mentioned something about family troubles and having to find your sister. Is she all right? Do you know where she is?"

"My sister Ginny and her intended plan to take advantage of over inflated prices and make a quick dollar."

"There are many stories like that one, aren't there?"

"Yes, our whole family is worried about her; I'm hoping I can talk her into coming home before something dreadful happens."

Amelia reached over and patted Vivian's hand. "I'm sorry for the circumstances, but I'm so glad you could accompany the boys and me on our trip. I delayed it several times as I was afraid to travel alone. It came as quite a relief when your Aunt telephoned me."

The two women chatted amiably over the next several hours as the boys took turns looking out the window or walking up and down the aisle on imaginary errands. Ben didn't make an appearance. Perhaps he was planning to keep his distance for the entire trip. But then why would he go at all?

At noon, Amelia and the boys filed down to the dining car. As Vivian pulled the lunch Mother had prepared out of her valise, she noticed Ben making his way down the car. So he did intend to visit. He must have been waiting until her companions left.

"Do you mind if I sit with you for lunch, Vivian? I've brought my own for the first day, too."

He seemed so uneasy and unsure of himself; this was not at all like the visit at Aunt Margaret's. Why would she mind? "It would be my pleasure, Mr. McCormack." She brought her best smile to her face and gestured to the seat Amelia had vacated. The morning had been impossibly long without his company. There were so many things she wanted to know about him.

"Thank you." He folded himself onto the bench and pulled a wax paper wrapped sandwich from a satchel.

Munching quietly, he sat without speaking through both of his sandwiches, his apple, and a square of delicious looking corn bread. Occasionally, he lifted his gaze to look out the window.

Was she supposed to begin the conversation? Why was he at such a loss for words? As though reading her thoughts, Ben finally spoke, "Vivian, I feel I should explain something."

"Yes?" It would be wonderful if he would explain what was going on. She leaned forward hoping it would encourage him to continue.

"Well—"

"Hey, you're sittin' in our seat!" Paul said. "Mama, this man's sittin' our spot; tell him to give it back."

"Paul, you're being rude. This man is Miss Connor's friend. Now say hello."

"But he's in our seat, Mama."

"You're right about that, young man," Ben said as he stood and moved into the aisle. "I'll let you have your seat back. Perhaps, Miss Connor, we can chat later?"

Vivian looked into his eyes. Perhaps? It was not like she was going anywhere. Ben McCormack could be a frustrating man.

Ben tipped his head and turned. She watched his broad back as he retreated down the car and back to his seat.

CHAPTER 9

THE NEXT TWO DAYS ON the train were a repeat of Ginny's first: a delicious dinner, mild protests, and crushing guilt the following morning. Logan was always up and gone before she awoke and spent the rest of his day wheeling and dealing, gambling, or with his new friends. It was hard to know for sure what he was up to. She hadn't left the car since the first morning.

During the day, when Logan remembered, he brought her a bit of food from the dining car. It was difficult to eat anything; it sat in her stomach like lead. All day long thoughts assaulted her mind, one after the other. Was her family worried, and were they looking for her? Was Father worse? Was he even still alive? Would they simply write her off and forget her? She'd caused them so much grief. Would they ever let her return home again?

Logan returned to the Pullman car for a few minutes in the afternoon to announce they were scheduled to arrive in Seattle at eight o'clock that evening. He warned her to make sure she was ready to disembark by then.

She pulled the blankets up over her head and went back to sleep.

* * *

Pulling her arm away from the insistent nudging, Ginny rolled over.

"Ginny, wake up."

"Ugh," she rolled further.

"Ginny, I told you to be ready. We're almost to Seattle; get up."

She opened her eyes. Logan stood over the bed, his eyes narrow slits.

"Get ready and gather your things. You might as well say good-bye while you're at it."

She sat up, pulling the blankets under her chin. "What do you mean say good-bye, Logan?"

"That got your attention," he smirked. "Say good-bye to the beautiful surroundings. I hope you've been thankful, because from here on in the accommodations will be a lot more crowded and a lot less comfortable."

Thankful? That was definitely not one of the emotions she'd been feeling. What should have been a lovely honeymoon in such sumptuous surroundings had turned into an ordeal of daily loneliness, shame, and regret.

Ignoring her silence, Logan continued, "I was talking to some fellow who said they oversold tickets on the steamships by as much as four times what they normally do. We'll be packed in tight." He ran his finger along the edge of her jaw. "Such a pity."

Ginny turned away. It wouldn't be too horrible. With a room full of people, there was no way they could spend the nights together as they had been.

"I'll meet you in front of the station after we arrive; you can manage to get yourself there, can't you?" He put a hand on either hip. "I've got to make arrangements to transport the supplies down to the wharf."

She nodded her head.

"And Ginny?"

"Yes?"

"Maybe you could try a little harder."

"Try a little harder, Logan?"

"Maybe you could look like you're having fun, enjoying being a newlywed who's having the adventure of a lifetime, remember?"

She remembered. She remembered what it was supposed to be, what Logan had said it would be: he and his new wife, travelling up North, getting to know one another. Ginny mumbled her discontent, but Logan didn't even bother to reply as he left the car.

Upon disembarking in Seattle, Ginny found Logan on the front boardwalk of the station arguing with a small, unshaven man under a gaslight. The streets were dark except for the light from street lights dotting here and there. By their light she could see groups of men in eager discussions. The sounds and smells of livestock filled the air.

"Look, I won't do it for any less than eight dollars a load."

"Why, that's highway robbery!" Logan said, shaking his finger at the man.

Ginny stepped up and put her hand on Logan's arm to calm him. He shrugged her hand off, and she stepped back into the shadows.

"I don't know where you've come from, but this is Seattle. You interested or not?"

"Do I have any choice?"

Ginny's eyes followed as the fellow looked around the crowded station; all the other available wagons were already being loaded. "Well, now that you mention it, no. But I want ya to know my prices are the same as everyone else's. So don't you be thinkin' I'm cheatin' you."

Logan wiped his brow. "Fine, then. Get her loaded, and I'll be back."

"Sir, that doesn't include loadin'; that'll cost you extra."

"You've got to be kidding!" Logan paused for a moment as though trying to work something out in his head. "Get it done."

The fellow whistled, and two husky youths appeared out of the dark and loaded the wagon from the huge stack of supply bales.

Logan stomped off the boardwalk and onto the dusty street.

"Logan, where are you going?"

"Stay with the wagon, would you? I need a drink," he barked at her.

* * *

Several hours and three trips to the wharf later, Ginny's back ached as she scrunched into a narrow bunk fully clothed and head-to-toe with her "husband." The snores of the seven other adults and three children in the cabin echoed off the walls, and her head pounded. Only four days—if the weather held—and they would be back on land. Four days would be an eternity in these conditions. She tugged the skirt of her dress from under Logan's leg and rolled over on her side.

He grunted and fell back to snoring. The thin mattress didn't hide the joints between the planks of the hastily built bunks. Her shoulder throbbed. If only she could be curled up next to Vivian in their feather bed at Aunt Margaret's. Her eyes drooped as the rocking motion of the huge steamship lulled her to sleep.

The next morning was a frenzy of activity in the cabin as the cabin mates competed for use of the wash basin and small mirror hanging above it. Ginny waited her turn and washed her face and tidied her hair before leaving to meet Logan for breakfast. The brisk, salty air of the ocean stung her cheeks as she walked along the open deck on her way to the dining salon.

Perhaps she and Logan could start again. He was right; she hadn't been trying very hard, and neither had he, really. He spent most of his time visiting with everyone but her. And Captains could perform wedding ceremonies, couldn't they? Wouldn't that be an exciting story to tell their children one day.

"Pardon me, ma'am," Ginny apologized after her shoe caught the hem of the woman's dress in front of her.

"Not to worry—this old thing," The woman turned to address her.

"Star?" Her companion turned around. "And Buttercup? What are you doing here? I assumed you were both staying in Seattle."

"Now, darlin', why would we do that? There's as much money to be made up North for a woman as there is for a man."

The woman's drawl slithered up Ginny's spine. "So you're going to Dawson City, too?"

"Yes, didn't that honey of a husband tell you? Where is he, by the way?" Star glanced over Ginny's shoulder as if Logan would suddenly appear.

"We're meeting for breakfast."

"Well, in that case, let's not keep the poor man waiting."

Star and Buttercup linked arms with Ginny and proceeded to guide her to the windowed dining salon at the front of the ship. So much for the new start.

The room bustled with activity as waiters rushed from one table to another serving the many patrons. The room was so crowded the chairs and tables were pulled into tight circles almost on top of one another. Logan smiled at the trio as they neared his table.

"Good morning, ladies. I'm glad you've found each other; my wife is in need of some female company."

Star and Buttercup tittered as they sat at two empty chairs at the table.

A strange man sat by Logan's side. He leered as Logan stood to pull out a chair for Ginny.

She gathered her dress and sat down next to Logan as she glanced at the fellow. He had been deep in conversation with Logan as they had approached. He had a narrow mouth and pale blue eyes. His black hair was slicked back from his face, and he wore a navy suit in the latest cut.

"Virginia, this is Mr. West, my new business partner. Evan, my wife, Ginny Harris."

"Very nice to meet you, Mrs. Harris."

His obvious stare made Ginny's fingers tremor as she tidied her hair over one ear. Resisting the urge to squirm in her seat and shake off the prickling at the base of her spine, she forced a small smile to her lips. Why was he making her skin crawl? *She* was Logan's business partner. If Logan was starting another business, he sure hadn't mentioned it. They needed to talk—alone.

"And the rest of you all met each other last night." Logan scratched the corner of his eyebrow and chuckled.

Star giggled as she replied, "We sure did, didn't we Miss Buttercup?"

How on earth did Logan know they all met each other last night? He was in the bunk until the wee hours of the morning. Her stomach roiled with the ships motion, and the smell of the food in the room didn't help. "Logan, if you wouldn't mind asking for a cup of tea at the counter? I find I'm not very hungry this morning."

Logan gave her a warning glance before excusing himself to step up to the busy counter. Star and Buttercup went with him to hasten the ordering of their breakfasts as well.

"So, you're Logan's woman?" Mr. West spoke with a hint of mockery in his voice.

"I beg your pardon, sir?"

He laughed as though remembering a private joke and took a sip of his coffee before fixing his gaze on her once more.

"Tell me, how do you know my husband?"

"I don't, really; we met for the first time on the ship last night."

. "Then how is it he says you're already his business partner?"

"I guess you could say we share similar interests. We're men of the same mind when it comes to opportunity," he paused, and his cold eyes met hers, "and perhaps even other interests as well." He took another sip of his coffee as his eyes swept over her entire body. She rubbed her arms to warm the chill that settled into them.

"Your husband has a lot of good ideas when it comes to making money."

"I'm sure he does." Ginny looked up. Logan, Buttercup, and Star laughed together at the counter while waiting for their breakfasts. *Please come back.*

"He mentioned the medical supplies he's packing—very resourceful young man. I don't imagine many are prepared for disaster."

"Pardon, sir? Logan mentioned medical supplies?"

Evan placed his elbows on the table and formed a teepee with his fingers. "I haven't quite decided the best way to secure a profit on those items."

Anger surged its way through Ginny's chest, and she took a deep breath. "Perhaps Logan didn't explain. The medical supplies are mine." She met his narrow eyes with her own.

"But you're married; what's yours is his, right?" His mocking chuckle silenced her reply.

Ginny seethed as she waited for Logan to return. She sipped her tea as the others finished their breakfasts and were served hot coffee by a frazzled young waiter. Their silly banter droned on, and she ignored Logan when he tried to engage her in their conversation several times. As they finished up, he asked if she would like to take a stroll around the deck together. Finally they could talk, and she could find out what was going on and why he had told Evan about the medical supplies.

As they stepped out of the dining salon, Logan pinched her elbow and with a swift motion pulled her arm through his.

"Ouch, Logan, you hurt my arm. Why are you being so rough?"

"Keep walking," he growled into her ear and then nodded pleasantly to the many people they passed milling about the deck. Directing her further down the ship's deck, he stopped at a secluded spot along the rail. She grasped the handrail to help steady herself against the rocking motion. The wind had picked up, and the ocean breezes whipped their hair back from their faces.

"Ginny, I'm almost out of patience."

He was almost out of patience? She was the one who'd been waiting for the wedding he promised. "What are you talking about?" she snapped back.

"I asked you to try harder, and all I've seen is more of the same pouty, selfish girl from the train."

"What do you expect, Logan? You promised to marry me. I left my home and family for you. I may never see my father again." She grasped the railing tighter.

"Don't blame that on me. You and I both know I was the fastest ticket out of town, and you took it."

"Logan, how could you say such a thing?" What was getting into him? Obviously he needed to sleep instead of carousing in the middle of the night.

"I wasn't born stupid, sweetheart. It takes a bunch of the wrong kind of gumption to do some of the stuff you've done."

A twinge of remorse twisted in her stomach. Why was he bringing this up? He'd convinced her to travel with him. They'd laughed together at the naiveté of her family and Alistair. Maybe he was having second thoughts about bringing her along. "When are we getting married, Logan? Ship captains can perform ceremonies, you know."

"Ginny! We will get married when we get married, all right?" He smacked the railing with his open palm. "Stop harping at me and start making yourself more agreeable. I expect you to be nice to Mr. West and the girls, too."

"Why?" If he thought she was going to make nice with his new found friends, he was mistaken. "And why did you tell Evan about the medical supplies? You said they were mine to do whatever I pleased with."

"Like I said, he's my new business partner. We're not going to just unload the gallons of whisky when we reach Dawson anymore. Evan says if we open a saloon and water the stuff down, we'll make a killing. He has the money to either buy a saloon or build one, and I don't. The stuff you packed isn't that important; I'll tell Evan it's yours."

"You said this was a short trip. We show up, unload the supplies at a profit, and go back East to earn a respectable living. We weren't going to live in Dawson City."

"That was the plan, but the plans have changed."

She turned and grasped his suit lapels, scrunching the grey wool between her fingers. "Logan, please, I don't want to stay up North. I already miss my family—"

"Stop that whining; I've had about all I can take." He pushed her hands away and smoothed his lapels. Several passengers nearby stared at the couple at the sound of his raised voice.

Ginny bit back a reply as Logan stalked away. As she turned to the ocean, the wind whipped strands of hair from her bun, and the spray disguised the tears coursing down her cheeks. If she didn't start making Logan happy, he might not love her anymore. He might even leave her, and then what would she do? She was so far from home. The ocean waves rose and fell, their white caps breaking against the side of the ship. Like Logan said, she would have to try harder.

She was still at the rail, staring out over the ocean as Evan West stepped up beside her. He stood close enough for their hips to almost touch. He was the last person she wanted to talk to right now. *Go away.* He placed a hand over hers, and then drew it away slowly, as though his touch were a welcomed gesture.

How presumptuous. Did he not know he made her skin crawl? She drew in a long, slow breath. *Don't march away.* She faced Mr. West and smiled pleasantly. His dark eyes held no warmth. Why was he beside her?

"I see your loving husband has left you alone once again."

Why did he always sound like he was mocking her? *Keep the smile plastered to your face; it's what Logan would want.* "He felt he needed a brisk walk, and I find I'm not up to one this morning."

"Ah, but how can he stand to be away from the side of his blushing bride?"

Very easily, she thought. Not that it was any of his business.

Evan leaned over, his cloying breath warm against her ear. She pulled away before he said anything she didn't want to hear. "If you will excuse me, Mr. Evans, as I said, I'm not feeling all that well. I think I will find a quiet place to read, if possible. Good day."

"And good day to you, Mrs. Harris." He caught her hand once more and placed his moist lips on her palm.

He'd gone too far. She would have to speak to Logan about his business partner's forwardness regardless of the warning to be nice. She turned from Mr. West and raised the hem of her dress to bustle down the ship's deck, ignoring the rude snicker at her back. Out of his sight, she wiped her hand several times on the smooth calico of her dress. Who did he think he was, taking such liberties with her?

The next day she lounged in the crowded social hall on the upper deck and enjoyed some lemonade. With her eyes closed and the sun's warmth shining through the window like a soft blanket, Ginny struggled to stay awake. A shadow fell across her face, and she opened her eyes to see Logan standing next to the chair. They had hardly spoken to one another since the exchange on the deck the day before; she hadn't bothered to mention Evan's behavior. Logan was irritable enough without any more of her complaining. She'd determined to handle Evan herself and put him in his place if he continued to be so brazen.

As Logan had wanted, she'd smiled when they took meals together and laughed politely at everyone's jokes. He appeared convinced that she actually enjoyed the company. It was too bad he'd found her hiding spot.

"Ginny, I've been looking all over for you."

"And now you've found me. What do you want, Logan? I know it's not my company."

"I need you to do something." His voice lowered to a gruff whisper.

He needed her to do something? It was asking enough to put up with his new friends. "What? What do you want Logan?"

"It's part of the business deal, and I promise I'll never ask you again—only this once."

A business deal? Her math skills weren't of any note. Maybe he needed something witnessed, but surely one of the two darlings could do that. "What could you possibly want from me regarding the business deal?"

Logan scuffed the floor with the toe of his shoe, his left hand drumming against his pant leg. "Evan West has asked me if you would keep him company."

Keep him company? She sat up and placed her glass of lemonade on the table beside the rattan chair. He was the last person on the ship she was going to keep company with. "What do you mean keep him company?"

"Ginny, lower your voice."

"Logan, what are you talking about?"

"In our cabin—he's asked if you would keep him company in our cabin."

"In our cabin?" Raising a hand to her mouth, she laughed. "Why on earth would he want that? Surely our cabin must be just as crowded as his." She couldn't keep another giggle from escaping.

Logan didn't join the laughter. He didn't even look amused; his eyes were dark, unyielding.

Why does he look so serious? She swallowed. "Surely, Logan, you can't mean for me to—"

"I've arranged for a private get together at ten o'clock. You won't be disturbed."

He wanted her to keep company with Evan West, the oily man who made her sick to her stomach. Logan had no right to ask it of her. They were to be married. Why would a man offer the woman he loved in a business deal? The lemonade rose in her throat as the room spun.

"Logan, how could you? I won't do it."

"The way I see it, darling," he leaned down to eye level and put her chin between his fingers. "You chose to come with me. I need you to do this for us—for our future. Evan won't invest if you don't."

She pulled away, and he reached over, pinching even tighter and turning her face back toward him. "Don't what, sell myself? The thought makes me ill."

"Like I said, Ginny, just this once, and after we've hit Dawson, we'll have it made."

Logan leaned in as she whispered, "Please, don't ask me to do this."

"I don't have any choice. Our good luck on the train has left me. Now I owe Mr. West a considerable sum, and he owns our cargo."

Ginny gasped. He owned the cargo they'd worked so hard to get. "And my supplies? Logan, how could you gamble away my supplies?" They wouldn't be able to survive.

"He'll forgive the debt and set us up in business if you do this one thing."

Tears trickled down her cheeks, and he wiped them away with a smooth thumb.

"Logan, do you really love me?"

He pressed his lips to the top of her head and murmured, "Of course I love you. Haven't I always taken good care of you?"

Her chin dropped to her chest as she closed her eyes.

"Think of it as an investment in our future. This is something you can contribute." Logan reached out and grasped her elbow, lifting her limbs to a standing position.

The surroundings grew foggy as he led her across the deck and down several levels to the door of the cabin. Logan opened the door and she stepped inside, crossing the empty room toward their bunk. The door closed behind her with an ominous click, like a jail cell closing in the deepest dungeon. She sat down on the bunk, and several moments later a tap sounded on the door. Evan West stepped in.

CHAPTER 10

TWO DAYS LATER, THE AFTERNOON sun fell through the train window and onto their backs as Vivian read a Bible story to the boys. She wriggled her shoulders and looked up to find Ben staring at her from his seat at the end of the train car.

He smiled, and she smiled back in return. Perhaps it would encourage him to come and sit with her. Apparently understanding the invitation, he stood and walked down the aisle to where they were seated.

"Hello, Miss Connor."

"Mr. McCormack."

"Mrs. Brown," he nodded to Amelia, and she dipped her head in return. "Miss Connor, could I talk to you for a moment?"

"Please do," Vivian said, her stomach doing an uneasy flip-flop. Something in the tone of his voice didn't sound right.

"Come along, you two; let these folks have some privacy. Paul, Edward, follow me." Amelia beckoned to her sons.

"But Ma, we were right at the good part where Goliath gets a big rock right to the middle of his forehead. I like this part."

"Paul, let Miss Connor and Mr. McCormack talk, and we'll go for a stroll through the train to stretch our legs."

"Can we buy a root beer, Ma? I'm awfully thirsty."

Amelia smoothed the boys' jackets after they stood to join her. "Perhaps. Come along now. Vivian, Mr. McCormack, if you'll excuse us." The three sauntered away as Ben sat down across from Vivian.

"Miss Connor, there's something I've been meaning to tell you."

Was this it? Was he going to say he's admired her from the first moment they met? Well, maybe not the first moment, with her boot stuck in the hole in the sidewalk, but perhaps shortly thereafter. The day he gave her the flowers must have been when it happened. He couldn't deny what he'd felt when she'd touched his hand. Vivian clasped her hands in her lap, leaned forward, and then closed and opened her eyes slowly.

His Adam's apple twitched as he swallowed. His eyes dropped to the floor, and he was silent. The silence stretched on, and she waited. It must be difficult for him to express his feelings. Perhaps she could encourage him; she reached out and touched the rough cotton of his sleeve.

He startled as though burned and then brought his hand up to run it through his hair.

"Mr. McCormack, you were going to tell me something."

He exhaled loudly as his neck turned crimson. "What I was going to tell you was . . ."

"Yes?" *Please, please tell me.*

"I'm engaged."

"You're engaged? You're engaged to be married?" What? He had never mentioned a fiancée—not even once!

"Yes, I'm getting married. It's why I'm on this trip. I'm going to meet my fiancée Audrey in Dyea, Alaska, and we're to be married. It's all been planned for some time now."

Vivian sat back, letting her shoulders slump, and stared out the window. She couldn't look at him; he might see the dashed hopes and dreams. A sickening hole formed in the pit of her stomach.

"Ben, I mean, Mr. McCormack, you have never once indicated an attachment to anyone. Why didn't you tell me the first day we met? Surely you knew, even then, you were to be married. I'm at a complete . . . I thought—"

"Vivian, I honestly don't know. I should have told you and your family. I know I've had many chances, but I couldn't bring myself to do it."

Through the corner of her eye she could see him clench and unclench his fists in his lap. Yes, he should feel miserable, too.

"I hope you won't be upset with me. I don't want it to spoil the rest of our trip. I do think of you as a good friend, Miss Connor—a great friend, actually."

"A great friend you haven't been honest with. I should have known you were engaged from the first day I met you. But as for the rest of the trip, don't worry—we will be parting ways very shortly."

"Miss Connor, I'm so sorry. I didn't mean to deceive you. I know I should have told you immediately. I feel like a fool." He leaned forward and touched the sleeve of her dress.

She snatched her arm away and turned to face him.

"Please," his voice sounded desperate. "Let me do what your father asked and help you get to Dawson City safely."

She looked up at the ceiling clenching her teeth to keep the tears from springing to her eyes. How could he ask her to continue on under his protection, as though everything were the same, as though her heart weren't breaking? Why didn't he know of her affection for him? It had been made quite obvious. Perhaps Ginny was right; she was awful at this "romance stuff." However, it made one decision easier to make. "Amelia has asked me to accompany her by steamship all the way up the coast to Dawson and continue to help with the boys; I'm going to say yes. I couldn't afford it on my own, but she has graciously offered to pay my way. I know it will take a few weeks longer, but under the circumstances, I think it will be best."

"But what about Dawson City? It's not safe, and I'd like to know you're all right."

She wasn't all right, and she didn't know if she would be all right ever again. It was most definitely no longer any of his concern. "Mr. McCormack, sir, were you intending to make the trip up to Dawson City your honeymoon and also take me along to make sure I was all right? What could you possibly have been thinking?"

"I hadn't gotten that far, but I'm sure we can work something out." He paused for a moment and took a deep breath. "Perhaps you and Audrey will be the best of friends."

Was the man truly insane, or was he just a simpleton? If she never met the girl, Audrey, or whatever her name was, it would be too soon. "I'm not quite sure what world you're living in, sir, but I would venture a guess it is not the real one. No woman wants competition for her new husband."

"I don't look at it that way at all, Miss Connor—"

At her sharp intake of breath, he stopped. Her fingers itched to slap his face, and she clutched them together. *One must never make a scene.*

"Miss Connor, I'm sorry. I didn't mean it that way, honest. You're a beautiful girl with an amazing ability to take care of people," Ben leaned over and placed one large palm over her trembling hands.

"Don't touch me."

He pulled his hand away and leaned back. "Why are you so upset? I don't understand. I know I should have mentioned it right away, but I'm telling you now. Doesn't that count for something?"

He didn't understand how much she thought of him, how much she admired his kindness and strength, and how much she had hoped for a future. "Mr. McCormack, I consider our conversation finished. If you would kindly go back to your seat, I would like to be alone, thank you."

"Miss Connor, could you please explain—"

Her voice raised several decibels, "I believe I asked you to leave me alone, and I trust I'm communicating quite clearly, unlike yourself, sir."

Several heads turned their way at the sound of her raised voice.

Ben rose, his splayed hands out in front of him as he backed away. "Fine, fine, I'll go, but please let me help you in Seattle, at the very least." He ran a sinewy hand through his thick hair. "Miss Connor, I'd like us to part as friends."

His deep brown eyes begged a response she couldn't give him. She turned her head to the window in dismissal, releasing a slow breath as he walked down the car and returned to his seat.

As she continued to gaze out the window, a familiar verse ran through her mind. "Lo, I am with you always, even unto the end of the world." *Lord, I need You with me; thank You.*

How could she have misunderstood? If the posy of flowers and the warm conversations didn't mean anything to him, then why, when they'd touched, did it seem like her fingers were on fire? And if he had a fiancée, why were there any flowers or conversations in the first place? He should have dropped her off at Dr. Mason's, gone about his business, and not returned.

Mile after mile of newly sprouted fields passed outside the window until Amelia and her two boys returned. As she continued to stare out the window, the boys moved into their seats and sat quietly.

A half hour passed before Amelia asked, "Would you like to talk about it, Vivian?"

"I don't think so; I don't even understand it myself."

"Are you quite sure? Has Mr. McCormack said something offensive?"

"No, not offensive."

"Would you like me to pray with you?"

"Yes, thank you." Amelia took Edward's seat and put her arm around Vivian asking the Lord to comfort her and give her a sense of His everlasting peace.

Vivian prayed silently that the Lord would help her endure through the remainder of the trip while Ben was still with them.

CHAPTER 11

THE NEXT DAY SHORTLY BEFORE lunch, the porter walked the length of the train informing the passengers of their imminent arrival in Seattle. The boys jabbered to one another and then tussled each other for the window seat. The rest of the passengers located and collected their belongings and prepared to disembark.

Vivian accounted for all her effects and firmly secured the clasp on her brown leather valise. Then, with the aid of her reflection in the window, she tucked stray hairs into the bun at the nape of her neck. The change in scenery as they neared the Seattle station drew her attention outside the window. Pack animals and stacks of supplies lined every street resulting in narrow passageways and crowds of people attempting to navigate the tight corridors. Some of the men shoved their way through. The train's piercing whistle blew as it slowed and then chugged to a stop.

"End of the line folks," the porter repeated as he walked through the car. "Those of you who need a hand collecting your luggage, let me know."

Vivian stepped up to ask for the porter's help when she glanced over and noticed the anxious look in Ben's eyes. He wasn't going to make their parting easy. Several times since yesterday he had walked down the car and attempted to draw her into conversation. It hurt too much to know he was getting married to someone else, so she had rebuffed his attempts. He could wish all he wanted; they were not going to be friends. She could probably let him carry her luggage, though. She nodded her head his way, and he returned a wide smile. Grabbing one of each of the boy's hands in her own, she spoke to Amelia. "Amelia, why don't the boys and I go and wait outside the main doors to the station while you deal with your luggage?"

"That would be fine. Boys, mind Vivian, and I will meet you in a few minutes."

The swarm of people as the three stepped off the train was un-expected. People pushed and prodded from all directions. Vivian lost her hold on Paul's hand for a brief moment and gripped the neck of his jacket to keep him from being pulled away from her. She clasped both boys' hands tighter as they pushed their way across the plat-form and up to the double doors of the station. Upon reaching them, they put their backs to the wall and watched the frenzy of people disembarking, greeting travellers, or collecting freight. Amelia and Ben would find it difficult to navigate the throng.

After twenty minutes the crowd dissipated a little, and Ben joined them hauling both Vivian's trunk and his own luggage. He placed them both on the platform, and the boys scrambled on top of the trunk to see over the crowd.

"Isn't it something," Ben said, wiping his brow with the back of his sleeve. "I never expected all these people. It seems like half the world is heading up North, and the other half can't wait to go home."

"How will we ever find a hotel?"

"I asked the porter about a decent one. He gave me a name but said he wasn't sure it was still open; everybody has been losing their staff to the Klondike. It's a couple of blocks up, so it's even closer to the harbor. He also said the owners were pretty honest and wouldn't raise the room rates on you overnight. Can you imagine?"

"No, I can't." He must have taken her refusal to answer him about his helping in Seattle as an affirmative. Could he not leave well enough alone and go on about his own travels? Amelia and she were capable of finding a hotel on their own.

She was about to say so when Amelia appeared through the crowd, her hat askew, pulling a small wooden cart loaded with their belongings. A look of exasperation was etched on her face.

"Well, I never in all my life have seen so many people. I hardly had room to breathe, let alone collect our things. Apparently you can rent wagons out front to take you to your hotel, although I don't know how they get through all the hubbub. I didn't think to ask my husband about a place to stay in Seattle; I had no idea it would be so busy."

"If you don't mind, ma'am, I've already inquired into a decent hotel."

Amelia's eyes darted form Ben's to Vivian's and back as though wondering how she should respond.

Please tell him to go; we will be fine on our own.

"Thank you, Mr. McCormack. We will take you up on your offer. Come on, boys, hold Vivian's hands; let's see if we can make it through the crowd."

"Can we ride on the cart, Ma?" Edward asked.

Amelia opened her mouth to reply when Ben interrupted, "Sure you can. I'll throw our luggage on, too, and you boys can climb up on top. Mind you, be careful you don't fall off."

"Thanks, Mr. McCormack," they said together.

The group forged their way to the street side of the station. Ben opened a path with the cart for Vivian and Amelia through the crowd.

Several wagons sat parked along the boardwalk with drivers perched on their seats. On the closest wagon a grizzled, wiry fellow of indeterminate age poked a broom straw between his teeth. "You folks lookin' for a ride? I'd be happy to escort you. I can even load your luggage for an extra charge."

"And what would you be charging for your service, mister?" Ben asked.

"Ten bucks will get you over to any hotel providin' it ain't too far out, and it's an extra dollar to load you up."

"Ten dollars? Well, I never," Amelia said, and she fanned her face with her hand.

"If I were you, I wouldn't complain none. I'm one of the cheapest." He pointed his thumb toward the row of wagons behind him. "These boys are chargin' twelve dollars a ride. He twirled the straw with his fingers. "You know, it's a wonder I'm still drivin', what with everybody else taking off to make it rich. Are you folks interested or not?"

"We'll take it, and it's my treat, ladies. But I'll load up myself, mister. The name's Ben McCormack. Pleased to meet you."

"And my name's Pete, but everybody calls me Bender."

"Why do they call you Bender, mister?" Paul piped up from his perch atop the trunks.

"Uh—" Amelia said.

"It's a long story, son, and probably not fit for your young ears. Would you two like to sit up front with me? We'll let the love birds and your mama sit in the back."

"Sir, we're not love—" Vivian said.

"Sounds fine to me," Ben interrupted. "Can I give you ladies a hand up before I load the luggage? Mr. Bender, we're staying at the Diller Hotel on First Avenue."

Vivian glared at Ben, and he smiled, reaching out his hand to help her up into the wagon. She squeezed his fingers hard, and his smile broadened.

With everyone loaded and the trunks in the back, the wagon moved in jolts down the dusty street.

Bender looked over his shoulder at Vivian several times before finally speaking. "If you don't mind me saying so, ma'am, you look awfully familiar."

Familiar? Had Bender seen Ginny? Alistair had noticed a resemblance, but in these crowds would it even be possible? "Sir, if I may question you further, what do you mean I look familiar?"

"I coulda swore I gave you a ride a few days ago. It's hard to forget a pretty face like yours. Although, I must say, you are travelling a whole lot lighter. I made three trips down to the wharf last time."

It must be Ginny. She had made it to Seattle. *Please, let her still be here.* Her voice wobbled as she replied. "You must have met my sister—my younger sister."

"Well, now that you mention it— "

"I've been trying to find her. Was she all right? I mean, did she look happy?"

"Happy? Can't say as I rightly know if she was happy or not."

"She must have been with someone—her husband, perhaps?"

Bender looked back, one eyebrow raised as he answered, "She was with someone; it wasn't clear if it was her husband or not. A bit of a temper, that fella. You'da thought the world was out to get him."

So it hadn't taken long for Logan to show his true colors. *Ginny, what have you done to yourself?* Perhaps Logan's poor behavior would make it easier for Ginny to listen to reason; she would be ready to return home. Vivian had to find her.

"Did you drop them off at a hotel? Can you take me there now, sir? I need to know if she's safe."

"She isn't staying anywhere in Seattle. Like I told you, I took them directly to the wharf. They were shipping out that evening."

Vivian clenched her fist in her lap. She was so close. If she hadn't injured her foot and had left as soon as they'd discovered Ginny was missing, she would have caught up with her. *Lord, give me patience.* She would find her. She would find Ginny and bring her home. More than likely Logan hadn't married her, and she would be free to leave. Vivian would have to continue on up North with Amelia and the boys. *Oh, Ginny, please be all right.*

Ben reached over and covered her fist; she batted his hand away.

Bender continued to prattle away from the front seat. "Looks like we're in for a long ride. The town's been crazy for months now, what with some of the miner's actually retuning with gold. It seems like people are in fever. Do you know The Portland returned last week with a ton of gold on her? I was down at the dock when she pulled in and seen it with my own eyes when those fellows held up their bags of gold. Why, some of them could barely lift them."

The sights and sounds of the chaotic city distracted Vivian as the wagon rumbled up the street, and Mr. Bender regaled the group with stories. The streets were lined with groups of men dressed in heavy plaid coats and wide brimmed hats and their pants tucked into high top leather boots. Many were engaged in eager conversations, while others sat together on the sidewalks playing cards. Precarious, ten-foot high stacks of supplies filled the sidewalks and stuck out onto the roads leaving narrow passageways that lead up to the stores. Hand printed paper signs were tacked randomly on the stacks inviting buyers to Klondike specials of heavy blankets and wool clothing.

Hopefully the wool garments she and Mary Beth had packed would prove to be sufficient for the cool northern mornings. Poor Mary Beth—if she thought Vivian had been competition for Ben's attention, she would surely be crushed when she learned of his marriage. How did the man keep such a secret in a small town like Brentwood? It didn't matter; Mr. Ben McCormack and his comings and goings were no longer any concern of hers.

She gathered the edges of her skirt touching Ben's thigh and tucked them under her legs until there was a distinct gap between them. Ignoring his inquisitive glance, she turned away.

A tall fellow leaning against one of the stacks caught her eye. "You folks be needing any supplies for your outfit?" he asked. "There's a real good sale across at Seattle General. I've been in there myself and couldn't believe the prices."

Vivian shook her head and focused on a short, burly prospector attempting to load a sway back mule with more than it would ever be able to carry.

"If you change your mind, it's Seattle General. A real nice place to find—" the man's words were lost in the clamor as they continued down the street.

The only occupant of the wagon apparently not captivated with the unusual sights of the gold rush town was Mr. Bender. He continued to distract them with the laments of the ever increasing costs of living in Seattle.

As they neared the harbor, the crowds became thicker and more agitated. Amelia commented on the sign for the Seattle Transport Company and then asked, "Mr. Bender, could we stop here for a moment? I need to pick up the tickets for our trip to Dawson City."

"I don't think you'll be getting any tickets, ma'am. From what I've heard, they've been booked solid for months now, and the prices have pretty near tripled."

"I guess it's a good thing, then, that my husband purchased our passage before he left Seattle. He said they would be held here at the office until I arrived, and I could book the departure time when I picked them up. If you would kindly stop the wagon, I would like to do so now."

"Sure thing, ma'am." With a slight movement of the reins, he directed the horses to the right as far as they could go in the crowded street and brought the wagon to a stop.

"I'll go with you, Amelia, if you'd like," offered Vivian. Sitting so close to Ben was unsettling even if she didn't care for him anymore.

"Please do, Vivian. I fear the crowds are a bit much for me. Mr. McCormack, would you mind keeping an eye on the boys?"

"We'll be fine, won't we boys?" Mr. Bender answered. "Would you two like to feed the horses some oats while we're waiting?"

"Sure," they said in unison. Mr. Bender bent over and pulled a small burlap sack from under his seat and then handed it to Paul.

"You two go ahead; Mr. Bender and I have it covered." Ben shooed the two women away with his hand.

Amelia and Vivian lifted their skirts and stepped carefully while crossing the street to avoid the droppings of the many pack animals tied or hobbled wherever there was a few spare feet. The prospectors standing around watched their progress, and several stepped forward to lend their arms. However, the ladies murmured a polite, "No, thank you," and continued toward the office.

"My, my, Vivian, have you ever seen a city like this? It appears to have gone crazy. It's no wonder Arthur was so excited when he wrote home. But if what Mr. Bender says is true, I'm sure glad he had the foresight to purchase our tickets before he left. I hope it won't be too difficult to purchase one more for you. I so want you to be able to come with us."

And what if they couldn't get another ticket? There was no way she could turn around now; Ginny needed her. But, to be a third wheel to Ben and his new bride would be awful. They would simply have to purchase another ticket. "I appreciate you wanting to purchase a ticket for me. But what if they are three times the price? I don't want you to feel beholden on my account." Vivian held her breath and tried to keep her voice even; it wouldn't do to sound desperate.

Amelia looped her arm through Vivian's. "We will have to wait and see."

They stepped through the doors of the office; the room was filled with men in their odd prospector's outfits. They raised their voices in an attempt to talk over one another, and the room reverberated with outrageous remarks.

Along the front wall behind a full length wooden counter, three harried clerks waited on those who had reached the front of the lines. After a few minutes of politely waiting, Vivian realized the only people moving were the ones pushing and shoving their way through the throng. She wedged her elbow between two men and reached back to grasp Amelia's hand. Pulling her along, she pushed and wriggled her way to the front counter.

They stood before a young man with a curl of blond hair on his brow and a pair of gold wire rim spectacles. With his pointer finger he pushed the glasses up the bridge of his nose and then spoke. "Can I help you?" he asked.

"I sure hope so, young man; I've never seen such a crowd in all my life," Amelia said as she raised her hankie and dabbed at the sweat droplets beading on her forehead. "My name is Amelia Brown, and my husband purchased tickets about four months ago for me and my sons to take a steamship up the coast. He said they would be held here at the office until I came to claim them."

"Umm," the clerk cleared his throat and pulled at the collar of his shirt. He then shuffled some papers on the counter, his eyes darting left and then right.

"Son, did you hear me?"

"Yes, ma'am, it's just that I started working here yesterday. I'm not trained yet, you see, and my boss said if I ask any more questions he won't keep me on, regardless of whether everyone keeps quitting to join the rush or not."

"I'm sure he'll overlook it this time—it's an unusual circumstance—and I will tell him how very helpful you were."

The young man hesitated for a moment, pushed his spectacles up once more, and then crossed over to a large desk covered with untidy stacks of papers. Behind it sat a grey haired fellow, his suit jacket buttons straining across his large girth. When the young man spoke, the older man wiped his brow with the back of his sleeve and threw his pen down on the desk.

As the young man continued speaking, the older man nodded and then retrieved an envelope from the top left drawer. Glancing up at Amelia and Vivian, he smiled and rose slowly from behind the desk. The young man scurried out of his way as the older man took heavy, deliberate steps over to the counter. Sweat poured down from his mutton chops in rivulets.

"Mrs. Brown, you do indeed have three pre-purchased tickets for the Sally Girl, one of our finest steamships. We should be able to put you on board in about three days' time if everything goes according to schedule. However, there has been one significant change since your husband purchased the tickets."

"And what would that be, sir?" Amelia asked.

"We no longer have private rooms."

"But I thought my husband paid a premium to make sure the boys and I had a room to ourselves?"

"At the time he did, but the passage rate has more than doubled since he purchased the tickets, and with the high demand we find ourselves booking as many passengers as we possibly can."

"And how many roommates can we expect?"

"I promise you, ma'am, no more than seven."

"Seven for a three-bed stateroom? Oh dear."

"I assure you, at Seattle Transport Company we do our best to maintain a clean and comfortable excursion even with the added passengers."

Amelia pulled at the hankie in her fingers and looked over at Vivian.

Vivian spoke up, "Would it be possible to secure passage as one of the ten in the same stateroom?"

"And who would you be?"

"The children's governess."

He tapped the envelope on the counter twice. "I see. Well," looking at Amelia he continued, "I suppose, but I hope you realize how great a favor I am granting you. These men are desperate to go up North, and they would riot if they discovered I was selling another passage on that ship. It has been sold out for weeks. However, you will have to accommodate eleven persons in your room."

"Thank you, we're very grateful," Vivian said.

"The cost will be one hundred twenty dollars."

Vivian gasped as the man opened a drawer under the counter and pulled out another ticket. "Amelia, I don't expect you to pay such an amount. I can find another way. Mr. McCormack—"

"We'll pay anything, sir. Would you kindly just give me the tickets so I can go out and get some fresh air?"

"Certainly, ma'am."

After completing the transaction, Amelia and Vivian pushed their way to the back of the office and stepped out onto the sidewalk where they met Ben.

"I was about to come and find you two. I thought maybe you were having some trouble."

Amelia swiped at her forehead with her hankie and then stumbled forward. Ben reached out to steady her elbow.

"It's a madhouse in there, but we did manage to secure passage for Thursday morning. It's a good thing Amelia's husband bought the tickets ahead of time, or we would have been stuck here for weeks," Vivian said avoiding Ben's gaze.

Ben continued to steady Amelia's arm as the three ambled over to the wagon.

"What's wrong, Ma? Are you sick?" Edward asked.

"I'm fine son—worn out, that's all. Sorry to keep you all waiting."

"No problem, ma'am. Ain't nothing gets done quickly around here anymore," Mr. Bender quipped as he urged the horses forward into the melee.

"Mamma says we ain't supposed to use the word ain't," Paul noted.

"Paul, let Mr. Bender do his job," Ben said. "Keep a lookout for the Diller Hotel, would ya?"

The wagon crawled toward the docks as the streets were now even more crowded than before. The narrow passageways between the stacks of supplies were packed with men. The crowd would part to let the wagon pass and close back in behind it just as quickly. There was no break in the conversations; each man was engrossed in his dealings either to secure passage to the Klondike, to find provisions to live on, or to hire some help.

At least passage had been secured to travel with Amelia and the boys. Vivian wouldn't have to rely on Ben and his new bride. And, as he would probably head out in the morning, avoiding him for one evening would be easy enough. Her cheeks grew warm as she thought about his disclosure on the train. Why had she been so sure he had taken an interest in her? Looking back over his visits, he had never actually led her to believe there was anything more than friendship between them.

Sitting beside Ben on the wagon, Vivian drifted to imagining a future without him. It would be difficult to watch him back home with his new wife and eventually a family. She would miss

Ben McCormack, but that was something he would never know. She hugged her shawl tight around her shoulders even though the sun shone against their backs.

"You doing all right, Vivian? Are you cold?" Ben asked.

She turned her head away from him and adjusted the hem of her dress before speaking. "I'm fine, Mr. McCormack, you don't need to worry about me. I'll manage."

His fingers curled around her hand, and she pulled it from his grasp as though touched by a hot kettle. "Mr. McCormack, please."

"Vivian, don't be angry. I don't want us to part like this."

"It looks to me like neither of us has any choice in the matter, Mr. McCormack. I would appreciate it if you would leave me to my thoughts, thank you."

"Vivian, I—"

"Thank you for your consideration."

The muscle in Ben's jaw tensed as he looked away and over toward the steamboats lined one beside the other in the harbour. At least he hadn't persisted.

Mr. Bender turned the wagon to the right and down a side street as the boys chattered and stood up to point out various sights to the group. Amelia would put a hand to their shoulder, and they would sit for a moment before popping up again to point out something else. Ben remained silent by Vivian's side.

Mr. Bender pulled to a stop in front of a four-story structure with "Diller Hotel" printed in large green letters on the sandstone archway over the front door. Patrons bustled in and out and up the wooden stairs.

"Well, the place appears to still be open," Ben said as he jumped from the wagon and started unloading the mound of luggage piled in the back.

"Boys, could you give me a hand back here so Mr. Bender can be on his way?" The two scrambled from the front seat and tussled their way to Ben's side.

"Hold up now," he said, "there's plenty for both of you to carry. No need to fight about it."

"Boys, I have half a mind to banish you to our room if you don't start behaving."

"Ah, Ma, we're anxious to help, that's all," Edward said.

At his quick reply, soft laughter spilled from Vivian's chest and both Edward and Paul smiled up at her.

"Alright, you heard your mother," she wagged her finger at the boys. "You two better behave, or you won't be able to go exploring with me tomorrow."

Ben looked at her from under his dark lashes, and Vivian glared back. *I dare you to comment, Mr. Ben McCormack.*

"You mean we get to go along, Miss Connor, when you and Mr. McCormack go exploring? That would be real fine."

"I'm sorry, Edward, but Mr. McCormack is otherwise disposed. I'm afraid you'll have to settle for me."

Edward glanced over at Ben and then back to Vivian and put his hand on his younger brother's shoulder.

"That's all right; we'll still have fun, won't we, Paul?" he said. Paul nodded his head as Ben let one of the trunks thump to the ground.

"Boys, let's get a move on," he said as one after the other, their belongings dropped to the dusty planks. When he finished, he secured his cowboy hat on his brow and circled to the front of the wagon, extending a ten dollar bill to Mr. Bender.

"I'll be seeing you folks; safe travels as you seek your fortune," Mr. Bender said as he pocketed the money.

No one bothered to correct him as they retrieved their baggage and transported it up the wooden stairs into the hotel.

* * *

After checking in, Vivian had taken the boys to a fenced garden area behind the hotel so they could run around and get some exercise. Amelia had retired to her room after saying she could feel one of her headaches coming on.

Ben told the women he was going to wander amongst the crowds down at the dock and ask about prices for passage to Dyea. He hoped to secure a spot on a ship by offering to shovel coal for the boilers. The steamers had been losing their workers to the rush, and judging the majority of characters they'd seen eager to leave town, they were ill prepared to pound a nail—let alone scoop shovelfuls of coal for hours on end. How would they survive up North in the harsh conditions with all the hard work?

With a fair bit of luck, he'd secured working passage on a small steamship departing midmorning Wednesday. That left only two days of Vivian ignoring him; he couldn't wait to get out of town.

After a good night's sleep in the comfortable hotel bed, he felt more refreshed than he had in a week and decided to breakfast with the others in the hotel dining room. They all sat at a large table which sat perpendicular to a tall, narrow window. The location provided a street level view of the busy city. The boys talked over one another asking questions about Seattle and its strange mix of folks.

Vivian marvelled to Amelia over the beautiful chandeliers hanging from the tall ceilings and the creamy gold-edged china used for the breakfast service.

"Ma, these flapjacks are so good. Do you think I could have some more?" Edward said as he shovelled another mouthful in.

"My, you are one hungry boy today."

Vivian pushed her plate across the table. "Here, Edward, you can have mine if you like. I find I'm not very hungry this morning."

"Thanks, Miss Connor, I still feel like one of my legs is empty."

Ben laughed along with Vivian and Amelia at Edward's response. Vivian seemed more relaxed today; maybe she would listen to some sense and not take the boys traipsing around Seattle all alone. Who knew what trouble the girl could get into with the crowds of men acting so crazy over gold? It couldn't hurt to try and talk reason with her. He cleared his throat. "Miss Connor?"

"Yes, Mr. McCormack?"

"I'm not busy today like I thought I would be. I secured passage down on the docks to continue my journey up the coast last night, and I leave Wednesday morning. So if you don't mind, I'd love to go with you and the boys to sightsee around Seattle. I've never been to a coastal city before, either."

Vivian stared at her coffee cup on the table for a few moments. "I appreciate your offer, Mr. McCormack."

Ben found this unlikely. He knew there was bound to be a "but" involved.

"But that won't be necessary. The boys and I will be fine; we wouldn't want to hold you back."

There it was. "Vivian—Miss Connor, the city is not safe."

"Please don't exaggerate, Mr. McCormack. If I am at all unsure about our safety, we will come back and play croquet in the garden. It is a lovely spot to relax if you find you have too much time on your hands."

"I really must insist. I walked down by the waterfront yesterday, and the crowds are senseless. You could easily become separated, and then what?"

"Very well. However, I find I do not wish to endure your company. So, if you do insist, you may follow us from a distance."

Endure his company? He was beginning to think she might be the most stubborn, irrational woman he'd ever met.

"As you know, Mr. McCormack, we wouldn't want anyone getting the wrong ideas about our relationship."

He deserved the jab, but couldn't the woman forgive and forget? It was still no reason to put the boys at risk. "Don't you think you are being a bit unreasonable?"

Vivian pushed the chair back from the table and stood. Her small fists clenched along her sides. "Edward, if you're finally finished eating, I think we should get a start on our adventure. I am going upstairs to retrieve my gloves. Come along."

As she turned, both boys followed her through the crowded dining room and up the wide staircase to their rooms on the next floor.

"Mr. McCormack, do you honestly think Vivian and the boys might not be safe? Should I require them to stay at the hotel?" Amelia asked.

"As Vivian allowed, I will follow from a distance. It's not likely they will run into trouble. The woman is so feisty; who would want to tangle with her?"

Amelia chuckled and reached over to pat his hand with her pudgy, ring laden fingers. "I don't know what it is about you, Mr. McCormack, but you do not bring out the best in that girl. I suppose it is just as well since you're planning to be married shortly. Perhaps it is wise that you keep your distance; it will give her heart time to heal."

Ben lifted his chin and folded his arms across his chest.

"Pardon? I think you've got things a little mixed up, Mrs. Brown. I am getting married, but as for Vivian . . . Her feelings for me are purely . . . " He paused, searching for the best word, "venomous."

"My, my, Mr. McCormack, aren't we in a mood today? I think maybe you're looking at Vivian's behavior from a skewed angle. But if you'll excuse me, I am going to sit out in the back garden and read while the boys are being kept busy. Would you care to dine with the rest of us for supper this evening?"

"Yes, ma'am, I will see you then."

Amelia left the dining room while Ben continued to sit and drink his coffee.

What could Amelia mean by a skewed angle? Vivian had been nothing short of rude and miserable to him. If that was how a woman showed she cared, who needed it? But he still wanted to make sure she and the boys were safe while he could. He'd do his best to keep an eye on them today—from a distance, of course.

CHAPTER 12

VIVIAN CLUTCHED PAUL AND EDWARD'S hands in her own as they stepped out into the busy street and pushed their way through the crowds of people.

"Ow, Miss Connor, you're holdin' my hand awfully tight. Do you think we could walk beside you? We're not going to run away or nothin'."

"I'm sorry boys, but there are too many people here. I don't want to lose track of you." She continued to clutched the boys' hands tightly in her own. "I think our first stop should be a candy store. What do you think? Is your leg starting to empty out yet, Edward?"

"Do you think we can even find a candy store around here? Looks to me like everybody's buying dried food, judging by all these signs," Edward said.

"I can see a general store down the way a bit. Surely they'll have some candy. I know my little brother and sister love the peppermint sticks. What do you boys like?"

She didn't hear their reply as she stumbled forward and then regained her step. She felt the pressure from a crowd forming to watch a couple of men who were facing one another with their fists raised in the air and a sorry looking, sway back mule tied to the side of a wagon nearby.

"I'm telling you, I saw her first!" the short, red headed fellow making jabs at the air with his fists yelled at his tall, shaggy haired opposition.

"I believe you're mistaken, Will, I offered to buy her two hours ago. I had to go rustle up the money. But I'm willing to fight you for her, fair and square." The two circled one another, and the crowd pressed in yelling out insults and encouraging the men to fight.

Vivian pulled the boys in front of her and pushed shoulders out of the way to make room for them to pass. Escaping the crowd, the three once more took each other's hands and walked toward the general store.

Out of the corner of her eye she noticed a familiar stance and turned to see Ben leaning against the wall of a saloon two doors down. His fists were clenching and unclenching, and his eyes were stony. He must have been unhappy about the crowds and the fighting. She tucked her chin down to hide her smile as they stepped up onto the boardwalk.

The Seattle General Store was teeming with male customers all shouting out what they wished to buy, as though somehow it would make their order appear faster. Four harried clerks hustled back and forth behind the lengthwise counters and added to growing piles stacked in a roped off area at the end of the store. Vivian turned with the boys to leave. There was no point in waiting; it would take all morning to buy the candy.

"Lookee here, boys, we got ourselves a lady on the premises." The voice was loud and authoritative. It came from a tall, slim fellow by the window as he pressed a lit cigarette to the bottom of his cowboy boot and tossed it on the floor.

Several customers looked over at the speaker and, as if taking their cue from him, nudged the others back to leave room for Vivian and the boys to move forward through the crowd and up to a counter.

Vivian looked over at the dark haired man and nodded her head in a thank you; he had well-chiselled features and two or three day's growth of beard. His direct stare made her want to squirm. She turned toward the counter and tightened her grip on the boys' hands. Was Ben still lurking about outside? Maybe it hadn't been such a good idea to take the boys out by herself in such crowds. Perhaps she should go and find him and ask him to come with them; the boys would be disappointed if they went back to the hotel now.

"What can we help you with, ma'am?" one of the clerks asked Vivian.

"We are here for some candy, if you have any."

"Candy, huh. Now ain't that something."

"Momma says we're not sup—" Paul piped up and then bent over as Edward elbowed him in the ribs.

Vivian stepped between the two boys.

"Everybody else here is frantic for supplies to go up North, and you folks want candy." The clerk bent down under the counter. "Now, let me see. I think we do have some over here." He pulled out three jars: the first containing peppermint sticks, the next containing black liquorice, and the last containing salt water taffy.

Paul stared at the jars with his tongue sliding across his lips.

"Well, boys, what'll it be?"

They didn't say a word as their eyes darted from jar to jar.

"If you don't mind, sir, we'll take a few of each. It appears the boys can't make up their minds," Vivian said. They needed to get out of the store. The hair on the back of her neck tingled, and she wriggled her shoulders. Perhaps the man by the window was still staring.

The boys nodded to the clerk, and he placed several pieces of each candy in brown paper wrapping and tied them with a string.

"Gee thanks, Vivian—I mean, Miss Connor. This is real nice of you," Edward said as he reached for the package.

Vivian gave the clerk some change, and the throng opened once again to let them through. Some of the men doffed their woollen caps and gave Vivian a slight bow.

The man who spoke earlier still stood in front of the window. His eyes raked up from her hem before meeting her eyes. The smile on his face mocked her as he removed his hat and tipped his head. "Ma'am, you and your sons have yourself a nice day now."

"She's not our mother, mister, she's—"

Vivian tugged Paul's hand and dropped her chin as they passed the man.

"Don't bother thanking me; it was nothin', miss." He spoke to Vivian's back as she hurried the boys out into the sunlight.

* * *

Ben exhaled as he watched Vivian and the boys leave the general store. He'd crossed the street, stepped into a bakery, and purchased a lemon tart while he was waiting. The tang still zinged on his tongue as he wiped the crumbs off his cheeks with the back of his sleeve and stepped off the boardwalk.

Following these three around was ridiculous. He would go and talk to Vivian to see if she'd come to her senses. It would be safer if they all walked together. He watched as Paul pulled a package out of Edward's hand, and Edward grabbed it back and smacked the side of

Paul's head. Vivian put her hands out and stopped the boys by giving what appeared to be a sharp reprimand. The boys hung their heads. Vivian opened the parcel and handed each boy a piece of candy and they continued down the street.

It looked like they were headed for the docks. Ben knew this wasn't a good idea; if they went down there, they were sure to be separated. The crowd was a lot heavier along the water; it pulled both directions as though no one really knew where they were going.

He followed them down the street and quickened his pace to catch up. Within moments the mass of men quadrupled. Paul and Edward craned their necks to look up at the towering steamboats as Vivian pulled them through the shoulder to shoulder crowd. Several seconds later Paul's head disappeared, and Edward and Vivian continued to be jostled through the mob.

Ben swooped down to pick the young boy up off the ground. Paul held a dust-covered peppermint stick in one hand as he wrapped his arms around Ben's neck. Ben took several more large strides, pushing men out of the way, and gripped the back of Edward's collar. The young boy fell back against Ben as he held him tight with the other arm. The crowd was relentless in its push toward the water, and his stomach gripped as he saw Vivian being pulled further and further away.

"Edward, hold on to my belt and don't let go. I'll get you boys out of here."

"But what about Miss Connor, Mr. McCormack? We can't leave her alone out here, can we?" Edward rubbed his eye with his fist.

"I'll get you two to the sidewalk. You stay there, and I'll go after Miss Connor."

He elbowed through the crowd carrying Paul while Edward kept a tight grip on his belt. They pushed their way to a bench in front of the post office; Ben leaned over and sat Paul down on the smooth boards. Edward sat beside him.

As Ben stood upright and looked over the crowd, all he could see of Vivian was her blue bonnet bobbing along in the press of people.

* * *

Vivian righted herself again. The pressure from the crowd was inescapable as it propelled her further and further away from the boys toward the docks.

Lord, please let them be all right.

A few moments later she felt a firm grip on her elbow; it was the forward stranger from the general store.

"Miss, if you don't mind, I'd like to offer my assistance." He forced an opening in the crowd with his shoulder pulling Vivian along with him. "The boys are safe over here in a restaurant; if you'll come with me."

She'd been harsh in her judgement of the man—what a relief that he knew where the boys were. "I lost them back in the crowd. I'm so glad you found them."

The stranger maintained his grip on Vivian's arm and led her away from the steamships toward a row of dilapidated buildings on a grassy ridge along the shore. "They are fine, Miss . . ."

She raised her voice over the noise of the crowd, "Connor, Miss Connor." Her bonnet slipped to the side, and she righted it. Her arm was beginning to ache from the tugging.

"Miss Connor, then. Yup, they're fine, and a spunky couple of boys they are," he laughed. It sounded forced, almost hollow.

"Where are we going? I'm not sure—"

"Don't you worry, Miss Connor, we'll go on over here to my friend Henry's restaurant, and you'll find the boys having a soda." His long finger pointed halfway down the boardwalk. "The crowd usually quiets down around noon when the men go and rustle themselves up some lunch."

As they neared the buildings, he pulled her forward and wrapped his arm around her shoulders. Pulling her in tightly, he moved them through the crowd.

Vivian almost tripped over the hem of her dress as she allowed herself to be led along the mud-encrusted boardwalk. Several yards down they turned in through a weathered door hanging at a crooked angle on its hinges. It scraped the floor with a screech as they entered; the man still held her to his side.

The breeze from the ocean wafted in through the missing windows as several men sitting around two plank tables and drinking alcoholic beverages gawked at them.

"Well lookee here, boys. It appears Jacob finally had someone take him up on his offer. Mighty pretty one, too." The speaker was a grimy, squat fellow with a bulbous red nose and several teeth missing from his smile.

"Offer? What offer? What is going on, and where are the boys? Sir, you said—" The words were cut short as Jacob pushed her ahead of himself. She stumbled to the floor, and her bonnet was crushed under Jacob's foot as he stepped forward to put his hand under her arm.

"The boys are in the back," he said as he lifted her to her feet and propelled her toward the far end of the room.

As he passed the fellow who'd spoken, Jacob hit the man on the back of the head, and the man's forehead smacked on the table. The others all looked nervous as the fellow rubbed the red welt beginning to form.

"What did you go and do that for? I was only trying to make conversation."

Jacob turned back and stepped toward the man, his chest puffed out, dragging Vivian with him. All of the men, including the one with the welt, got up from their chairs and filed through the outside door.

Panic filled her stomach. "You said we were going to a restaurant. Where are the boys?" She struggled against Jacob as he dragged her several steps and kicked a large crate away from the back wall.

The boys aren't here. How could I have been so foolish? She kicked Jacob's shin and clawed at his arms around her waist. "Let me go! I insist you put me down!" She thrashed and flailed in his grip.

He pulled a ratty burlap sack nailed to the wall aside; it revealed a three foot hole where the back wall had been cut away. There was no way she was going through that hole. She screamed, twisted in his grip, and scratched at his cheek. Her scream was cut short as he grabbed a handful of her hair and tugged it, wrenching her neck and dropping her to the floor. Giving her a shove, her head and shoulders poked through the hole, and her skirt caught on a nail. It ripped from her thigh down as he pushed her the rest of the way through.

Jacob crawled over her. His stench was sharp in her nostrils as he grabbed a rag that lay on the floor and stuffed it into her mouth. She gagged and clutched at the dirty cloth. He pinned her arms to her sides and threw her over his shoulder.

It was so hard to breathe; she squirmed against his back as he carried her through the dusty store room. His shoulder rammed into her stomach on every step of the narrow stairs leading down into a low-ceilinged, earthen cellar. The cool air smelled musty.

Jacob carried her to the far end of the narrow room and reached out to grab a length of rope hanging on a rusty nail. While he tied Vivian's ankles together, she pulled the rag from her mouth and screamed, her fists beating against his back. He wrapped her torso a couple of times with the end of the rope and plunked her down on a crude bench along the mildew-covered wall.

"What are you doing? Let me go!" No one would hear her down in this hole.

He laughed as he continued to truss her up with the rope. The frayed jute bit into the flesh of her ankles and wrists.

Taking her chin in his large palm, he spoke in a husky whisper, "I don't mean to hurt you none, Miss Connor, I just sometimes can't resist a pretty face."

"Let me go! Please, let me go!" Tears trickled down her cheeks as she pleaded.

He patted the top of her head smoothing her hair. "You'll be fine here for a while. I've got some business to attend to, but I'll be back, don't you worry." He picked the rag up from the floor and stuffed it back into her mouth. Then he removed the handkerchief from around his neck and tied it across the rag.

At the scent of his sweat and grime the bile rose in the back of her throat and she doubled over. His boots turned to leave, and she lifted her head. She was still screaming through the rag, and he kept walking. She hurled herself off the bench and landed with a crunch on the floor.

He glanced back over his shoulder and shrugged as she wriggled on the damp ground.

"Well, have it your way. I thought the bench would be more comfortable." He laughed and tramped up the stairs. As he closed the door behind him at the top, Jacob plunged Vivian into complete and utter darkness.

* * *

Ben turned toward the two boys. Paul had dusted the end of his peppermint stick, and it now protruded from his mouth. Ben put his hand on Edward's shoulder. "Edward, you two stay put and don't move for any reason. I'll go and get Miss Connor and be right back. Don't worry, I'm sure she'll be fine."

Tears pooled in the bottom of Edward's eyes; he swiped at them with the back of his hand. "I think she's the one who's going to worry about us," he said.

"You're right; she will be worried and will try and come back and find you as fast as she possibly can." He averted Edward's stare as he thought of the danger Vivian could be in. The boy didn't need to be burdened any further. "But you two need to stay here." The two boys nodded, and Edward put his arm around Paul, who burrowed into his brother's side.

Ben turned and jumped off the sidewalk running back out into the dusty street, hoping to catch a glimpse of Vivian in the fevered crowd. How would he ever find her? He forced his way in the direction he'd last seen the bobbing bonnet. A burly headed man jabbed him in the ribs as he pushed past.

"You going to put out a fire?" he snarled at Ben's back.

Several minutes later he heard a familiar voice as Bender, the wagon driver, pulled up in front of a dilapidated shack along the water's edge. Two young men jumped over the side of the wagon and unloaded their belongings from the back.

"Now don't forget you boys owe me twelve bucks; that'll be six from each of you."

The two pulled the money from their pockets and paid Bender as Ben approached the wagon. "Mr. Bender."

"Oh hello, young man. How's our fine city treating you? Do you need a ride somewhere else? I'd be happy to go and pick up—"

"Mr. Bender, it's Vivian, the young woman riding with us yesterday."

"I remember that pretty, young thing for sure—your sweetheart. She didn't look none too happy, if you don't mind me sayin'."

"She's missing, Mr. Bender."

"Missin'? Whadya mean, missin'? You guys have a fight?"

"No, we didn't have a fight, and she's not my sweetheart. But that's not the point. She brought the boys down to the docks, and they became separated. I've been trying to find her, but it's like she's disappeared."

"Oh? I'm sure I don't have to tell you what happens to some of them women who get kidnapped and stowed away on the steamships going up North."

Kidnapped? Not likely. She's probably lost in the crowd, the stubborn woman.

Bender snugged up the reins and shook his head from side to side. "This is not good at all. I'll tell you what: I've got a few buddies who work the wharves, so-to-speak. I'll go and see if anyone has seen her." He gazed out over the crowd. "It's mighty packed down here today; let's hope for your sake she's makin' her way back up to the Diller. I'll leave word at the front desk if I hear anything, and you can do the same."

"Thanks, Mr. Bender, I appreciate your help."

Mr. Bender's tongue clicked against the top of his mouth, and the wagon pulled away from the shack to go and find some of his cohorts.

Ben went to find the boys. He had to get them safe before he found Vivian.

* * *

Oh, God, please help me.

Vivian whimpered as she lay on the cold, damp floor; her tears formed a puddle on the hard-packed earth. Both hands and feet were numb from the rope cutting into the skin, and the back of her throat burned from screaming through the rag tied in her mouth.

I am sorry I was headstrong about taking the boys out when I knew it could be dangerous. Please forgive me, Lord I don't want to die. God, please!

I will never leave you, nor forsake you. The familiar verse came un-bidden into Vivian's thoughts.

Is that You, Lord? Are You really here? Help me, Lord, I need You. She pulled her knees toward her chest, curling into a tight ball as the sobs shook her body. *Lord, I need to know You are here.*

. . . neither death, nor life, nor angels, nor principalities, nor things pres-ent, nor things to come, nor powers, nor height, nor depth, nor any other created thing will be able to separate us from the love of God, which is in Christ Jesus our Lord.

At the familiar words from the dog-eared family Bible Father read every evening after supper, a peace came over her. It started at her toes and washed up over her torso as if a fuzzy, warm blanket were wrapping itself around her.

She relaxed, and her breathing slowed. *Thank You, Lord, for reminding me You are here.*

Vivian rolled onto her back and rocked forward and backward to work into a seated position. Not a single ray of light pierced the darkness of the dank basement. Something scurried past her leg, and she cringed.

Lord, now what?

* * *

Ben pushed his way through the thick crowd along the docks. Where was Vivian? He caught a slip of blue material in the corner of his eye and elbowed his way several yards over to the left, which earned some choice words from those around him.

"Vivian, is that you?" He asked, grasping the elbow of the woman in front of him who was wearing the blue bonnet.

A gruff voice answered his question, "Excuse me, sir, but that's my wife you're holding on to."

The woman turned, and Ben's hopes fled as he looked into the tiny brown eyes and the pinched mouth. "I'm not the woman you're looking for." She pulled her elbow from his clutch. "Move along, mister."

"I'm sorry. I didn't mean to bother you."

Ben's shoulders slumped as he wiped his brow and turned toward several ramshackle buildings posing as storefronts on a knoll overlooking the harbor. He was four hours into searching for Vivian along the docks, and there was still no sign of her. Every dockworker he spoke to claimed to have not seen any petite blonde woman dressed in blue gingham, providing they were telling the truth. Maybe Mr. Bender was having better luck with his local cronies? Ben stepped up onto the boardwalk and peered through the windows of the small, crudely built shacks. There was not a woman in sight. *Lord, where is she? I need to find her; please keep her safe until I do.*

Ben reached the end of the walk and turned around to press through the storefront crowd one more time and then hike his way back to the hotel to see if they'd had any word. Who knew, maybe Vivian had been sipping coffee in the dining lounge for a few hours already? The thought wasn't convincing. She was out here some-where. He looked to his left over the crowd in the harbor.

His shoulder collided with someone, and he turned to see a short, unkempt fellow with a nasty welt on his forehead rubbing his jaw. "Hey mister, watch where you're going," the man growled at Ben. "I should have stayed in bed this morning," he muttered to himself.

"Sorry about that, mister."

The man's eyes travelled from Ben's chest up to his face.

"I guess I'll survive. I've had worse. Is there any chance I can set you up with some provisions for going up North? Tools, maybe, or food? How about some wool blankets—I've got lots of those."

"Uh, no thanks, but I'm looking for a woman about this high," he held his hand at chest level, "with golden blonde hair and beau-tiful green—"

"Can't help you out with women, nope. That's not my area of specialty." The man touched the welt on his forehead and grimaced. "Well, I'll be letting you get on your way then." He coughed into his hand, wiped it on his dungarees, and then whipped around to walk away.

"That's not what I mean. She's missing, and I need help to find her," Ben called to the fellow's plaid back as he continued down the planks.

Not his area of specialty? Ben's stomach reeled as the realization struck him. Mr. Bender wasn't joking; someone was kidnapping women. *Lord, how could they?* The odd fellow might be his only hope of getting any information; Ben ran after him and grabbed at his arm.

The fellow turned, arms raised up over his head. "Whadya want?"

"You can relax, sir, I've changed my mind. I think I might be interested in some of those wool blankets after all."

"You are?" The fellow dropped his hands, and a wide, gap-toothed grin split his face. "I was beginning to think I'd made a poor investment." He reached out his grimy hand, and the two shook. "The name's Willy. I've been trying for years to get people to call me Bill, but Willy's the only name that stuck."

"Nice to meet you, Willy. My name's Ben."

"Well, I got me about a hundred blankets or so. How many do you need?" He looked to Ben like the kind of guy who might be bribed with alcohol.

"Not near that many, but I need a few. Would you like to talk about it over a drink? Let's see if we can come to some sort of an agreement."

"Ben, you are my kind of customer. There's a saloon right around the corner; follow me." Willy took off with a peppy spring, all injuries apparently forgotten.

Ben knew it was not the best idea to take advantage of the poor guy's problem, but how would he get any information about Vivian if he didn't? And who knew what could be happening to her by now;

it'd been hours since she'd first disappeared. Willy had to know some-thing—anything that could give him a clue to where she might be. Ben would have to be careful he didn't spook the guy.

"There she is," Willy said as they rounded the corner. He pointed to a large wooden sign painted in black letters which read "Oliver's." It hung at a slight angle over a pair of brown, wooden saloon doors.

Waves of raucous laughter bellowed from the saloon doorway as Willy and Ben neared it. "I got into town yesterday—what a mad-house," Ben said.

"Yup, the men are wild and in a fever; I've never seen anything like it before. I hope I can recoup my investments before the whole thing dies down."

Just shy of the swinging door, Willy stopped and adjusted the bowler hat atop his head and straightened the collar of his shirt. Ben followed him into the saloon where the bartender stood behind a long, dark wooden bar wiping a glass with a white rag. He looked their way.

"Willy, stop right there. I told you your tab needs to be paid up before you plan on drinking here again."

"Don't you worry, Oliver, we're paying customers today. Me and this here fellow are doing business."

The bartender lifted an eyebrow as his eyes moved to Ben's. Ben straightened his shoulders, removed his hat, and nodded toward the bartender who put the glass down on the polished bar and reached for another under the counter.

"Well then, what'll it be, boys?"

"A Coca-Cola for me, and for my friend here . . ."

"That's not a man's drink."

"What I drink is my business. You want something or not?"

"Whisky, straight up."

Grabbing their drinks, Willy led Ben toward the window, and they sat down at one of the crude wooden tables. Willy lifted his glass to his lips, and his Adam's apple dipped several times before he returned the glass to the table and wiped his hand across his mouth.

Ben realized he'd have to try and get some information while Willy could still think clearly. "So, why'd you invest in blankets, Willy, instead of heading out for the gold itself?"

"Believe me, I would have done so, but my wife said if I did, she'd chase me down and bring me back by the scruff of my neck. And she'd do it, too. No one fools with Esther." He took another swig. "She went on about how a man with seven kids has no business chasing the end of some stupid rainbow. I guess I agree with her. Besides, I ain't meant for all that privation stuff. I can't see going that long without my creature comforts."

"I know what you mean. I don't plan on getting into the gold rush myself."

Willy's chin snapped up, and his beady eyes focused on Ben. "Whadya talking about? I thought you were needin' some wool blankets to go up North?" He fidgeted with the empty glass on the table; his eyes darted toward the window.

"How about I get you another drink, Willy. You still thirsty?" Ben hoped it would be enough to settle the fellow down and keep him talking. Willy rotated the glass in his fingers and nodded. "Bartender, could I get another couple of drinks for my friend?"

The two men visited for several minutes talking about the crazy antics of the gold rush. Now that Willy had figured out he wasn't going to make a sale, he seemed happy enough to get himself some free drinks.

Ben's mind raced to find a way to bring the conversation around to Willy's earlier comment about women. His eyes strayed to the window, and he saw Bender driving down the road with an empty wagon.

"Excuse me, Willy," Ben said as he stood up and then ran to the door. "Bender!" he yelled out into the street. Bender turned and raised his hand to Ben, and then he pulled the horses to a stop and tied them to a hitching rail across the street. A moment later he stepped through the double doors. Squinting through the thick cigar smoke, he said, "Willy, are you trying to swindle my friend Ben here?"

Willy looked up at Bender and fiddled with his glass again, his hand shaking.

"You know I wouldn't do that, Bender. We were havin' a friendly conversation. Besides, he's the one who pretended to be interested in some blankets. I ain't swindling nobody."

"You best not be, or you'll be answering to me. Is Jacob up to his tricks again? You know what we told him last time. He tries that once more, and we'll run him out of town on a rail."

Willy scrambled to his feet. His glass tipped over, and a stream of amber liquid flowed across the table.

Returning his cowboy hat to his head, Ben pushed his chair back and stood. There was no way he'd give Willy the opportunity to bolt.

Bender clenched his teeth and spoke across the table. "You tell us what we want to know, or I'll make sure you never work in Seattle again. Even worse, I'll tell your dear, sweet wife how you really make your money."

"Ah, come on. You wouldn't do that." Willy raked his hand back through his hair, and it stood up on end. "Besides, I don't even know what you wanna know."

"Has Jacob been taking girls again?" Bender asked.

Willy traced a finger around the edge of the puddle. "You know I can't tell you nothing. Look at my forehead. Jacob will kill me."

Bender raised his voice several notches. "Hear that, everybody?"

The saloon fell silent as customers turned their attention to Bender. He climbed up onto a chair. As he spoke, he poked the air with his forefinger. "Willy here is going to let some fool criminal ruin everything for all of us. The whole place will be crawling with deputies if word gets out Jacob is smuggling women again."

Ben's stomach rolled as he heard the words from Bender's lips. This Jacob was smuggling women. Could Vivian have been the victim of some treacherous smuggling ring and already deep in the hold of some steamship heading up North? Maybe Willy would talk if Ben hit him.

Bender pointed his finger at Willy. "Tell us what you know, Willy, and we'll take care of Jacob. You'll have to lie low for a bit. That boy's been told we won't stand for his kind of trouble."

The other patrons nodded their heads, and one lifted his drink in salute of Bender's comments. Ben opened and closed his right fist. He watched Willy scan the room and saw beads of sweat break out across his forehead.

"Well, what do you have to say, Willy?" Bender asked from his perch atop the chair.

Willy's chin dropped to his chest as he answered. "Jacob walked into Cracker's place today with a pretty little blonde on his arm.

That's all I know." He shrugged his shoulders and lifted his palms in the air as he backed toward the door. "I tried to make conversation, and this here is what I got for my efforts," he said as he pointed to the egg-shaped bruise on his forehead.

Ben's heart pounded in his chest. He took two steps and grabbed Willy by the scruff of the neck. The table tipped over, and the glasses crashed to the floor. Willy's face turned a deep shade of red as he gasped for breath, and his feet dangled in the air. The other customers stood up from their tables and crowded around the spectacle, no doubt trying to figure whose side they'd be on if things broke out into a full-fledged scuffle.

"Where is she? Tell me right now, you no good . . . or I swear I will—"

Bender jumped off the chair and squeezed Ben's arm. "Now, Ben, settle down. This ain't no way to solve your problems. Besides, he can't tell you what he knows if he can hardly breathe."

Ben dropped his arm slowly bringing Willy to the ground and released his collar. Willy bent over, chest heaving as he gasped for breath.

"Bender, it's time to take your friends out of here. I won't have my place broken up," the bartender said above the rustle of the restless crowd.

Ben jerked Willy's arm, and the crowd parted while he dragged the sorry scoundrel to the bar. He tossed a five-dollar bill on the shiny surface.

"Thank you, sir," the bartender said as he nodded his head and tucked the money in the front pocket of his apron. "Let us know if you need any help finding her. As Bender said, we're a respectable town, and we don't like what Jacob's been doing."

Ben dipped his hat to the bartender and then hauled Willy out the saloon doors with Bender on his heels. The sound of chairs scraping on the floor followed them out.

Bender stopped an audience from forming as he spoke, "Stop right there, boys. This is private business." The men who'd made it through the doors muttered to themselves as they returned to the bar.

Ben kept his hand clamped on Willy's forearm as the three stood on the edge of the boardwalk. *Lord, what am I going to do? I have to find Vivian, I have to. And I'm sorry for losing my temper; I don't know what's gotten into me. Father, please help me.* After exhaling through his teeth, Ben spoke. "Okay, Willy, I'm going to ask you again: Where is she?"

"Do you think you could let go of my arm? You're liable to break it."

"Nope, I don't think I can do that." Ben exhaled again, and his fingers tightened. "Answer my question."

"Ouch, I told you before I was at Cracker's place when they walked in."

"Cracker's place?"

"Down by the wharf."

"Where I first met you."

"Ya."

Ben dropped Willy's arm, turned on his heel, and jumped from the boardwalk.

"But, I don't think . . . "

Anything else Willy said was lost as Ben rounded the corner and ran straight into the crowd.

CHAPTER 13

VIVIAN SHIVERED ON THE COLD, damp floor. The chill had crept into her bones; pain throbbed in every limb. She'd heard chairs scrape on the floor and the dull voices of men as they came and went upstairs, but it had been quiet for several hours now. How much longer would it be before Jacob came back?

Thoughts about Ginny filled her mind again and again. Was Logan a man like Jacob? Was he a man Ginny had put her trust in only to be deceived? Was she hurt or abandoned? *Lord, please no.*

And what was Jacob's plan? He could kill her and bury her body in this filthy cellar. It's not likely any of the men would talk; they hadn't tried to help when Jacob had hauled her across the room. Maybe he wanted her alive; that would be much worse. She squeezed her eyes shut, and the melody of her favorite hymn thrummed at the back of her throat.

* * *

Ben pushed the squeaky door open and thundered into the empty room. Rickety chairs sat around several tables; three were knocked over. He bent forward and sucked in a jagged breath of air. His chest was going to explode.

"Vivian!" He kicked at a chair; it slid across the floor and toppled several others. "Vivian!" He pushed his way through tables and they fell to the floor in his wake. Once more he roared, "Vivian!" and picked a chair up over his head. He threw it across the room, and the flimsy walls reverberated with the sound as it fell to the floor in pieces. "Where are you?" He scanned the room. "Vivian, where are you?" *Oh God, where is she? Please, don't let him have taken her away. Lord, if You'll only—*

Ben eyes fixed on an upended, wooden packing crate; it was the only one in the room. More chairs hit the floor as he crossed over to the crate. It tipped over and fell when he kicked it, exposing a burlap sack tacked to the wall. He knelt to the floor, pulled the sack aside, and peered into the room. A small, dirty window on the back wall allowed enough light to see stacks of dusty crates filling a small storeroom. After glancing back over his shoulder he crawled on his hands knees through the opening.

* * *

Vivian opened her eyes. Someone was back. She could hear yelling and furniture scraping across the floor. Was it Jacob? Was he angry?

She pulled her knees in tighter. *Lord, please, I don't want Jacob to come back. I'm so sorry for every mean thing I've done. I didn't want Ginny to go, not really; I know it's all my fault. I need to help her. Lord, please let me help her.*

* * *

Ben lifted a couple of the crates and set them back down.

"Vivian, can you hear me? Vivian, are you in here?"

As his eyes swept the room, he saw the door on the back wall. When he pulled the knob, the door stuck on the warped floorboards, and Ben gave it another yank. The cold, musty air hit his nostrils as he stepped down onto the top stair and waited for his eyes to adjust in the dim light. Anger surged through his chest when his eyes landed on the trussed up form curled up on the on the dirt floor.

"Vivian?" he said as he took the stairs three at a time, crossed the room, and lifted her into his arms.

Her eyes flashed with terror, and her body went limp. Ben tightened his grip and knelt to the floor. He laid Vivian back down, carefully removed the gag, and pulled a dirty rag from her mouth. She remained unmoving.

He untied the rope from her body and the rope binding her wrists and feet. There was a long tear in the skirt of her dress. He gritted his teeth, and his hand made a fist. He needed to stay calm for Vivian's sake. She was safe now.

He gathered her up, and as he held her in his arms he searched her ashen face for damage. With one finger he pushed the damp hair back from her forehead and traced the mud-streaked edge of her jaw.

Her eyes fluttered and opened. "Ben?" Her voice was gravelly. "Ben? Is it really you?" Her eyelids fluttered, and her eyes rolled back into her head.

"It's me," Ben murmured against her forehead. "Vivian, I'm here. You're going to be all right." His arms tightened around her body, and he rocked her back and forth.

Her eyes opened once more, and he loosened his hold. Vivian raised her fingers and pressed them to her left temple.

"Vivian, are you all right?"

"My head hurts. I'm so thirsty."

"Did a man called Jacob bring you here?"

"Yes. He must have followed me from the general store. Have you seen the boys? Are they all right?"

"I took them back to the hotel; they're fine." What about the rip in her dress? His chest clamped in a vise. "Vivian, did Jacob—did he hurt you?" He readjusted his arm and pulled her in tighter.

The quiet went on forever.

"No, not like that."

The air rushed out of his chest.

"He said he was coming back." She hiccupped. "Oh, Ben, I'm so sorry. I should have listened to you when you said it wasn't safe." She wriggled and put her arms around his neck. Weeping against his chest, she was barely audible. "I'm sorry. I'm so sorry."

His arms tightened, and he cradled the back of her head in one hand as he whispered into her ear. "It's all right, shh, you're going to be all right."

Vivian leaned back, her green eyes searching his. She looked so vulnerable, so beautiful. "Ben, I'm so glad you—"

He couldn't resist. Her words were cut off as he brought his mouth to hers.

She startled and then melted into his embrace. She was so perfect in his arms. He didn't want to let her go. He could keep her safe; he would make sure no one ever hurt her again. His heart raced in his chest as he squeezed tighter and kissed deeper. A picture popped into his head of a girl with dark eyes and dark hair—Audrey. He pulled away from Vivian. "Please forgive me. I shouldn't have done that."

She raised one finger to his lips. Her eyes sparkled. He drew in a slow breath and closed his eyes as she spoke.

"Thank you for arriving in time. Thank you for being my hero."

Ben shook his head and groaned, and then he stood up, bringing Vivian to her feet. She stumbled as her knees gave out, and he stepped forward, wrapping his arms around her again. "Vivian, please, I can't do this. You know I'm promised."

She pulled back from his arms and sat on the rough bench along the wall. Her face was pale and her eyes stricken.

Stupid, that was so stupid. Why had he kissed her? Was it love, or was it relief? One thing was for certain: it wasn't fair. It wasn't fair to Vivian, and it sure wasn't fair to Audrey.

"We need to go," Vivian said, and as she attempted to stand, her knees buckled again.

He reached out and held her arm to help lift her to her feet. She pulled it from his grip; tears made white streaks down her dirty face. He swooped down and gathered her in his arms, crossed the room, and ascended the stairs one at a time.

"Let's get you back to the hotel," he said. "Amelia's worried sick, and the boys are beside themselves. They think it's their fault."

Vivian stayed silent as Ben carried her up the stairs and through the storeroom. He put her down carefully so she could crawl through the trap door, and then he picked her up again to carry her through the debris of broken chairs and overturned tables.

As they stepped out the door of the building, Bender met them. His chin bore a nasty scrape, and one eye was puffy and blackened. His good eye widened as he took in Vivian's dirty and dishevelled state. "Ben, I see you found her."

"Yes, down in the cellar, trussed up like some sort of animal. If I get my hands on that varmint . . . "

Vivian still didn't stir.

"She all right? I mean, he didn't touch her, did he?"

"Not like you're thinking, but she's tired and cold. I need to get her back to the hotel."

Bender took the dusty hat from his head and looked down, fidgeting with the brim. "We found Jacob; we caught up with him in one of his hidey holes. Me and my buddies knocked the stuffin' out of him. That's when he told me where she was. I came straight over to see if he was tellin' the truth." He raised his eyes to Vivian's wearing a look of near reverence. "I'm awful sorry for your trouble, ma'am," he said.

Vivian nodded, pushed a few stray strands of hair behind her ear, and squirmed to release herself from Ben's grip. He snugged her up tighter against his chest.

Her voice held a year's worth of weariness as she spoke. "Mr. McCormack, if you would put me down, I'd like to walk now, thank you."

Ben bent over to put Vivian's feet on the boardwalk. As he let go, she wobbled and then gained her footing. Vivian covered her mouth with her hand and cleared her throat. She looked so vulnerable and wounded. How much of that was his fault?

"Mr. Bender, I'd like to thank you for your concern and quick thinking. I don't know what might have happened if—" her voice hitched, "if Jacob had returned."

"I don't want to think about that myself, miss, but I sure am glad you're all right. Jacob's had it coming for some time now." Bender straightened his shoulders and took a deep breath. "I got myself in a few good licks. It was quite a ruckus down the street. My buddies will make sure Jacob is run out of town on a rail, and he better not even think about steppin' foot in these parts again."

"Thanks again, Bender. I'd best be getting Miss Connor back to the hotel. She's been through a lot." Vivian's eyes fluttered, and she swayed on her feet. Ben reached for her elbow and held it. "Are you sure you can walk? I don't mind carrying you."

Vivian shook her head and raised her chin. "I'll be fine, thank you. If you could give me your arm." She turned toward Bender, "Thank you again, Mr. Bender. I can never repay you." Vivian looped her arm through Ben's, and he secured it with his other hand as they stepped off the boardwalk into the muddy street.

* * *

Every bone and every muscle screamed in agony as Vivian pulled her body out of the blankets and sat upright in bed the next morning. Amelia and the boys had near drowned her in their welcome the night before. Thank the Lord things had worked out the way they did. If Ben hadn't found her, if Bender hadn't found Jacob—a shudder wracked her shoulders. She wouldn't think about it.

Ben would leave today. His steamship traveling up the coast to Dyea departed at nine o'clock, only one hour away. If she lay back down and curled up in the blankets, perhaps sleep would overcome her once more. Nobody would blame her if she slept the day away, and it would be just as well to miss the good-bye. How could she look in Ben's eyes again and not be reminded of his kiss and how good it had felt to be held in his arms?

A timid rap sounded on the door.

"Good morning, Miss Connor. Are you coming to eat breakfast with us?" Paul asked. "I'm even hungrier than I was yesterday."

She opened her mouth to reply.

"You probably need a good breakfast after yesterday, too," Edward said.

So both young emissaries had been sent.

"I can smell the pancakes from here." Vivian's stomach growled.

"Mamma and Mr. McCormack are already down in the dining room. Mamma sent us up to ask if you would join us before Mr. McCormack leaves," Edward said.

She couldn't pretend to be asleep now. She would have to face the good-bye. "I would love to have breakfast with you. Give me a few minutes, and I will meet you in the dining room."

"I'll tell Mamma you're coming." Phillip's quick thumps retreated down the hall.

"Miss Connor?"

"Yes, Edward?"

"Do you mind if I wait here?" The boy was so sweet, but it wasn't fair that he should sound so worried.

"Of course, Edward. I'll be with you shortly."

Dressed in her best silky pink gown with a row of tiny pearl buttons down the front, Vivian stepped through the hotel room door. Edward sat hunched on the floor with his back against the wall. He leapt to his feet and offered his arm for assistance. Looping an arm through Edward's, Vivian gritted her teeth and took a tentative step. Soreness gripped her from head to toe. "We'll have to go slow; I find I'm not feeling that well."

Edward's head bobbed up. "Would you like me to go and get Mr. McCormack? He could help you better than me."

She patted his arm. "We'll be fine."

Edward led her down the hallway. "We sure are glad Mr. McCormack saved you yesterday. After we waited and waited for hours, we were mighty afraid for you."

"I am glad, too. I think he was sent by God. What do you think?"

"I think so, too." Edward smiled and the light returned to his eyes. He chattered as they walked toward the dining room.

Amelia looked up and spoke as they neared the table. "I'm so glad you could join us, Vivian, before Mr. McCormack continues on his journey."

"Good morning, everyone," Vivian said.

Edward pulled out a chair next to Paul, across from Ben, and Vivian sat down. Ben's eyes rose from his menu.

A flame lit in her stomach. The tossing and turning all night long and the chiding and correcting had all been of no use. He was still gorgeous, and he was still her hero. She swallowed as his look bore through her. He must feel something for her, or else why was her heart fluttering like a wild bird? It couldn't be just her imagination.

Ben cleared his throat and closed the menu. "I find I have no appetite, so if you folks don't mind, I'll say my good-byes here and head down to the wharf." He stood, and the chair scraped across the floor.

So it was going to be like that. He hadn't changed his mind.

"But you said—"

"Let him go, Paul. You don't want him to miss his ship, do you?" Edward said.

"Why can't Mr. McCormack go with us, Mama?"

Ben cleared his throat again, "This is good-bye then. Mrs. Brown," he bent toward Amelia. "Edward, Paul, I have enjoyed meeting you, and I wish you well in your travels to meet your father." He shook each boy's hand and stepped over to Vivian.

Vivian fiddled with the silver place setting as he spoke. "Miss Connor, I leave you in good hands. I hope you find your sister, and I hope your family appreciates your sacrifice. Take care." He touched the tips of his fingers to her fidgeting hand and then stepped back waving to everyone as he turned toward the door.

For a moment the words were stuck. "Mr. McCormack," Vivian said to his back, "could I see you out?" Her legs wobbled as she stood.

Ben slowed and replied without turning. "It's time for me to go. I've said my good-byes." He pushed his hat down on his forehead.

Vivian took two steps. Her knees buckled, and she crumpled to the floor.

"Vivian!" The table rattled as Amelia jumped up.

Ben was at Vivian's side.

"Vivian, are you hurt?" Amelia asked.

"I'm sorry; I find I'm still unsteady from being tied up in the cold for so long. If you wouldn't mind helping me up, Mr. McCormack, I would like to see you out." His eyes flickered. "Please."

Ben lifted her from the floor and wrapped his arm around her. If only this wasn't the last time he would hold her close. With Vivian's shoulder snug against his side, Ben guided her to the hotel door and out onto the veranda.

A long, wooden bench sat in the far corner. Vivian motioned toward it with a flutter of her hand. The two of them sat side by side facing the street. She could get through this. "Mr. McCormack, I had to speak to you before you left. I never thanked you for finding me. I hate to think, well, if things had turned out differently."

"You don't need to thank me, Vivian. It was my fault."

"Your fault? How was it your fault?"

"I never should have let you go with the boys. I knew it wasn't safe."

"You can't blame yourself for that. I was stubborn; I should have listened to you. And I'm sorry I kissed you. I had no right; I know you are going to be married. I hope you and God can forgive me."

Ben bent over, put his face in his hands, and groaned. "Vivian, you know full well you didn't start it. I appreciate your trying to let me off the hook. It shouldn't have happened. I was just—I don't know, just so happy you were alive. I'm sorry." He sat back up and stared up at the ceiling.

He was so happy she was alive? Was that all? *How about, I think I might be in love with you or when I kissed you I realized how much you meant to me?* The crushing weight on her chest made it difficult to respond. "I guess this is good-bye, then. I wish you well on your journey and in your new life." It was a lie. She didn't wish any of those things.

"Good-bye, and Vivian, I want you to know . . ." His hand slid over and curled around hers on the bench.

"Yes?"

"I want you to know . . . " He brought his head down and stared out at the goings-on on the street. "I'm sorry, I have to go. Good-bye." The bench shifted as he stood up, and then he walked through the hotel doors.

Five minutes later he returned, tipped the edge of his hat in her direction, and sauntered toward the wharf with his bags.

CHAPTER 14

THE BELEAGUERED TRAVELLERS ROUNDED THE corner on their barge laden with supplies. Ginny lifted a hand to shield her eyes from the sun as the buildings of Dawson City came into view. It wouldn't be much longer until they could all part company, and she could put the most grueling three weeks of her entire life behind her.

After keeping company with Evan West, there were days she didn't want to leave the cabin. How could she ever lift her head in public again? After the first time, she'd made it plain to both Evan and Logan that their little arrangement was over. Logan had been angry and had stomped around and yelled about her unwillingness to help them get ahead. Evan had appeared happy enough to shift his attention to the lovely, full-figured Buttercup. But it hadn't stopped him from mentioning Ginny's lack of cooperation to Logan. Since then, Logan spoke to her only when he had to.

Star had decided to part ways with the company in Dyea as women of her extraordinary talents were in short supply in the sprawling tent town, and she stood to make a bundle. Maybe she'd been the smart one; the hike up to and over the Chilkoot Pass had almost done Ginny in. It was a good thing Evan had the money to pay packers to cart their supplies over the pass; they would never have made it otherwise. He'd also bankrolled the boat up to the rapids as well as the barge and guide who had brought them the five hundred miles downriver to Dawson City.

The barge pulled in to shore slowing as it jockeyed for position among all the other sailing contraptions. Gazing up over the throng of people and possessions on the shore, Ginny saw the buildings of Dawson City. They were real buildings made of sawn wood and appeared to be everything Logan had promised. It would be his first fulfilled promise since they'd left home.

"Logan, where do you plan to stay tonight?" Evan asked him.

"I've heard the Triple J Hotel is the best in town, and I wouldn't mind trying it out. Nothing but the best for my baby." He attempted to put his arm around Ginny.

She shrugged him off. Baby? So she was his baby again? Most likely he wanted someone to warm his bed now that he might actually have one.

"Are you still sore at me, Ginny? Look, we made it, didn't we? I said I would get you here, and I did." He stood up and spread his arms out toward the town. He almost fell over as the barge caught up on the muddy bottom of the river. "Welcome to the Paris of the North." Logan had lost his dapperness after the steamship. His clothes were rumpled and filthy, and four days' worth of beard mottled his face.

"Sure, you got me here, Logan." He would have to pardon the lack of thank you. "Where's that hotel you were talking about?"

"You two ladies go on ahead. The Triple J is on the corner of Fifth Street. You can see it from here. We'll catch up with you when we've made arrangements for the freight." Evan casually gestured toward the city.

Ginny and Buttercup located the satchels they'd packed with a half decent change of clothes that morning and disembarked. Ginny dropped her eyes from the hungry gazes of the men along the shore as the two women pushed their way through the mass of people and belongings. Dawson City's streets were mud-packed but lined like any other she would find back home with barbershops, restaurants, saloons, dance halls, and a theatre. The duo trudged up to the Triple J, and each of them took a room for the night.

Ginny ordered a hot bath immediately. With the warm, sudsy water against her skin, she peeled away the weeks of grime and discomfort. After her bath, she slipped Vivian's daisy print dress over her head; it was the only clean one left to wear. It wasn't her favorite, but it would have to do. As she did up the last button, someone knocked on the door.

"Ginny, it's me. Let me in."

She crossed the room and opened the door. Logan bumped her shoulder as he entered the room dropping his battered leather grip on the floor. "I can't tell you the last time I've been so glad to see a real bed," he said.

Ginny swept her arm through the room. "Well then, take a good look, Logan, because this is the last glimpse of this bed you're going to get until we are man and wife."

"Ah, sweetheart, cut me some slack, would you? We just got into town." He removed his cap, wiped his forehead with his sleeve, and tossed the cap onto the bed. "What am I supposed to do? Wash up, shave, and march you right over to the closest church?"

She planted her feet on the smooth floorboards and held his eye. "Yes."

"Ah, baby, don't be like this."

"Don't be like what, Logan?" He deserved her mocking tone. "Make you keep your word?"

The vein in Logan's neck bulged as he gritted his teeth. He stomped over, snatched his cap from the bed, and turned. His face was etched in scarlet. "You know what? This isn't going to work. I can't take any more of your whining and complaining; day and night you're going on and on and on." His right fist opened and closed.

He wouldn't.

"You haven't treated me right since the day we left Brentwood," he accused. The words stung. It wasn't true. "I figured out a long time ago I should have taken one of the other girls up on their offer."

"Other girls?" The contents of her stomach rose into her throat. "What other girls, Logan?"

"Do you actually suppose you're the only one I was keeping company with?" His laugh was harsh, grating on the ear. "What did you think I was doing all that time you were sweet-talking Alistair? I could have had any girl in town I wanted. And you know what? Any one of them would have been a lot more fun than what you've turned out to be."

Ginny cringed. Alistair hadn't deserved to be used, but neither did she. "Logan, you said you loved me and that you were going to marry me."

Logan smirked. "I couldn't marry you even if I'd wanted to. I'm already married. I haven't seen my wife in two years. She's back home with our son."

Ginny sucked in her breath. The room spun, and she reached out a hand to the washstand.

Logan fished in his pocket, pulled out a small roll of bills, and threw them onto the bed. "We're through. I'll have your trunk sent up, but that's all you're getting from me. I don't want to ever see or hear from you again." He bent to pick up his bag before stomping through the door and slamming it. The walls rattled as he marched down the hall.

Already married and with a son? Ginny fell to her knees and then crumpled to the floor. He had never meant it; he had never meant a single word. He didn't love her, he wasn't going to marry her, and they were never going to build their fortune together. How could a man be so cruel?

Alistair's kind face rose in her mind. It wasn't the same. Yes, she'd used him, but she'd never made him any promises. She'd never promised him forever.

And there were the nights she'd spent with Logan. How could she have been so stupid? She'd given herself to a con man, and he'd given her to someone else. A whimper slipped through her lips. They had been right about her. Vivian was right about her. There was no way she could go back home now. There was no way she could face her family again. Why hadn't she listened? Wrapping her arms around her knees, Ginny curled up into a ball. It wasn't long before she drifted into sleep.

A bright stripe from the sun shone across the floor the next morning when she heard a soft knock on the door. Ginny sat up and rubbed her aching shoulders. "Logan, if that's you, go away."

"Ginny, it's me, Buttercup. What did you do to get Logan so hopping mad?"

"Go away. I don't want to talk about it."

"Ginny, come on, open up."

"I said go away!"

"Fine, suit yourself."

Buttercup's skirts swished as she turned and sauntered back down the hallway.

Every limb cried out in pain as Ginny pushed up off the floor and climbed onto the bed. The soft mattress was like a cloud. Her eyelids drooped, and sleep over took her once more.

Several hours later the grumbling in her stomach woke her. She reached for the roll of bills still lying where Logan had tossed it on the end of the bed. Five, fifteen, twenty-five, thirty-five, forty. Forty dollars wouldn't get her very far in Dawson if all the rumors were true.

What if Logan didn't pay the hotel bill? There was no way she would have enough for more than a few days. A sharp jab pierced her stomach. She'd have to find something to eat soon.

Ginny rolled from the bed and crossed the room to open the door. Her trunk sat in the hallway. The relief of seeing it when so much else was gone was sardonic. She bent over and tugged on the leather strap to drag it to the end of the cast iron bed. Opening the lid, she let her breath out slowly; everything was exactly as she had left it. She spent the next half hour making herself presentable. She would have to go and see who needed hired help. There must be some sort of job in this town she could do.

Ginny stepped from the main hotel door into the bright sunshine. Men milled about in groups on the muddy streets. Judging by the clamor, each one had a better prospecting tale to tell. Their matching outfits were amusing; they all wore tattered wool shirts and patched trousers. Many of them wore shabby beards and were rail thin, as well. It appeared to be hard to get a good meal in Dawson

City. The men's eyes burned on her back as she lifted her skirt to protect it from the mud and proceeded down the street.

Where to start? What was she even good at? She kind of liked to bake, but only when she absolutely had too. Maybe she could start there. Ginny stepped through the door of the bakery and inhaled the delicious, fresh bread scent. She hadn't eaten since noon the day before. The biscuits, muffins, and cookies in the glass case made her mouth water.

"May I help you?" asked a plump, middle-aged woman whose hair was wrapped in a tight bun.

"How much would two biscuits cost?"

The woman slid the back of the case open and reached in with her tongs to pinch a biscuit. "That will be three dollars," she said as she plopped the biscuit in a small paper bag and reached for another. Three dollars. Logan's money wasn't going to last long at these prices.

The woman shut the display case with a firm click and glanced at Ginny over the top of the counter. "Do you still want them or not? I've got lots of customers who do if you don't."

Saliva surged into Ginny's mouth at the same time the annoying pain in her stomach stabbed again. "Yes, I'll take them, thank you." Ginny handed over the money in exchange for her breakfast, lunch, and perhaps even supper. "Would you happen to need any help? I mean, do you have any work a person could do in your bakery?"

Ginny shifted from foot to foot as the woman scrutinized her from head to toe.

"Have you ever worked in a bakery before?"

"No, I haven't, but I like baking, and I'm very willing to learn."

The woman gave a snort. "Are you in Dawson by yourself, young lady?"

"Well, I was . . . " How could she explain? "I guess so."

"And what did you say your name was?"

She hadn't given her name yet, but why would it matter? No one here would know her from anybody else. "Ginny Connor, ma'am."

"Ginny Connor. Well, hmm, can't say as we need any help right now. My husband and I pretty much have everything looked after. Good day." The woman looked away and helped the next customer in line.

Ginny left the bakery and sat on the rickety wooden bench against the wall outside to eat her expensive biscuits. Why the curt dismissal? It seemed as though the woman had been interested until she'd given her name. She bit into the soft, cake-like texture of the biscuit as her stomach stabbed again. The warm biscuit lost its appeal, but she forced herself to eat it anyway.

The spot on the bench provided a good view of the activity on the street. Miners stood in a long line in front of a small tent several doors down. A crude sign advertised shaves for fifty cents. Several other makeshift tents also offered hot baths or baked beans and pork. Maybe a restaurant could use some help; there were at least four shingles advertising their establishments on this street alone.

"Miss, you've dropped your purse."

Her eyes focused on the tall fellow with the typical miner's outfit, reaching out with her drawstring bag.

"Thank you, sir." She said retrieving it from his grasp. How could he know it held her last thirty-seven dollars? "I'm so glad you've returned it. I don't know what I would have done if you hadn't."

He beamed at her, the smile lighting up his thin face. "I had no other choice, miss. It's the code of the North. Nobody steals from anybody, even if they can. Dawson City is one of the safest places you'll find."

"Well, thank you. I appreciate it."

He tipped the tattered brim of his hat. "You have yourself a good day now," he said as he walked away.

Ginny spent the next several hours talking to restaurant owners trying to find someone who might take her on as waitress, cook, or even a dishwasher, but had no luck. Exhaustion seeped into her legs until they weighed twice as much as they had when she'd left the hotel. She returned to her bed and climbed in under the wool blanket to rest.

Buttercup returned and insisted Ginny open the door. Why wouldn't Buttercup go away? It wasn't like they were friends, and she didn't want to talk about Logan. She didn't want to talk about anything. Ginny huffed as she crossed the room and opened the door. "Do come in," she said and indicated the round table and chairs by the window.

Both women took a seat and arranged their skirts. Ginny's hand lifted to smooth the hair around her ear.

"How are you feeling today, sweetie?" Buttercup's eyes looked worried—maybe it was pity.

"Better, thank you for asking."

"Are you sure, Ginny? You don't look so good, and you've been getting thinner and thinner. It looks like you could up and blow away."

With the severe stomach pain and horrendous headaches, she hadn't felt like eating much. "I think it's all the strain. I really didn't think the trip would turn out this way."

Buttercup reached over and patted her hand. "Life's rarely what you expect, honey. Sometimes we have to make the most of it."

Make the most of what? There was nothing left. She had no marriage, no family, no tidy sum of riches, and it would appear no one wanted to hire her, either.

"Have you decided what you're going to do? If I had any money I'd help you buy a ticket home. But I will, Ginny. I'll have money soon."

"I can't go home; I can't ever go home."

Buttercup's voice was a whisper. "I suppose not, what with your daddy being a pastor and all."

Ginny stared out the window. So Buttercup knew how far Ginny had fallen. But it was true; Father wouldn't want to see her now even if he was still alive. She picked at the hangnail on one of her fingers and several drops of blood fell onto her skirt. "I'll have to find a job; I have to learn to take care of myself."

"I don't know if Logan will forgive you, but maybe—"

"It's over between Logan and me. He said he never wants to see or hear from me again. Did you know he was married?"

Buttercup scratched at an imperfection on the table with a shiny red fingernail. "Honey, men like Logan are different. He doesn't care if he's married or not."

Ginny crossed her arms. "Well, I care."

"I know that's how you feel right now, but I thought you should know he and Evan have taken over the Yukon Hotel on Front Street. The former owner made his money and wants to go back home to his family. We're all busier than bees. I'm sure we could use some more help."

Was Buttercup suggesting Ginny go back to Logan and put herself under his power again? There was no future in that; they could never actually be man and wife. And he didn't love her; he was probably already looking for his next girl. "I can't. I just can't."

"All right, well, you can still think about it. I've got to get back to work. You take care of yourself, Ginny. Get some food into you." Buttercup stood, and the two exchanged a tight hug before she left.

Ginny rubbed her forehead and pressed her temples; another headache was on its way. She didn't have the energy to go back out looking for work. She went to the front desk and ordered another bath. The warm water, rich with the scent of lavender, eased her weary thoughts and muscles.

The next morning Ginny groaned upon waking and rolling over as she flung the blanket off. The room was stifling, and even her skin hurt. Why did she have to get out of bed at all, other than not having a job and her last dollar probably going to the hotel bill? She rolled over again, her dark hair falling across her eyes, and took in a deep breath. It would be so easy to go back to sleep. But the streets beckoned; she needed a job before the end of the day.

Trudging up and down through the mud rendered no results. Each time she enquired about a job and gave her name the proprietor would shake his head and respond by saying they didn't have any openings. Her strength couldn't carry her for more than a couple of hours at a time, and she returned to the hotel.

Wednesday morning a note had been pushed under the door of the room from the hotel staff asking her to pay the bill of eighty dollars. Eighty dollars for three nights? It was outrageous. Apparently Logan meant what he had said about not covering the hotel bill. But she didn't have eighty dollars and had no way to get it. She kicked at the trunk at the foot of her bed and the lid slammed down. A lot of good a trunk full of dresses would do if she had nowhere to sleep. She chewed the inside of her lip. Maybe someone in town might want to buy them. They were wrinkled after the trip, but they would be as good as new after a wash.

* * *

After selling several of her favorites for twenty dollars apiece to the ladies working at the saloon next door, she entered the Horseshoe Saloon, a two story, false-fronted wooden structure with the name emblazoned in large letters across the top of the building.

The bartender, a whippet thin man with a wide waxen mustache, raised one eyebrow as she approached the polished bar.

"Sir, do you have any women working here who might be looking for dresses?"

"Suppose so. You'll find them in the back room."

"Would you happen to need any help with dishes or cleaning?" The desperate sound to her voice was annoying even to her own ears. She dropped her eyes to the floor.

"What was your name, miss?"

"Connor. Virginia Connor."

"Hmm, I've heard about you."

"You have?" What was there to tell? She was young, foolish, and not that interesting.

"Ya. Word on the street is you took Logan Harris for quite a bundle. Time came for him to ante up with his partner and the money was gone. Logan said you spent it all."

"What? I didn't take any of Logan's money."

He went on as though she hadn't spoken. "This town don't take kindly to stealing. If you were a man, you would have already been run out of town. As it is, you won't find a respectable job of any sort; you are too much of a risk."

"Is that why nobody would hire me? I didn't take Logan's money; he gambled it all away. I don't even know if he had any money in the first place."

"A likely story. Take my advice and buy yourself a ticket home." If only it were that easy. She lifted the bundle of dresses in her arms a little higher and turned for the door. "Don't be coming back, miss."

Logan must have spun quite a tale. It didn't matter that it was a lie—everybody seemed to believe him.

The stomach pain was difficult to ignore when she stopped by the hotel desk and paid the bill. As she held the stair railing and ascended to her room, each step was slower than the last. She had only two dresses to her name and five dollars in her purse. One more night in the hotel and she'd be out on the street; she was too tired to fuss over it. She lay down and slept the evening away again. The next morning her head reeled, and the sheets were damp with perspiration. Maybe she could use Buttercup's help after all.

The Yukon Hotel was easy enough to find. It was a long, narrow, two-story structure built of wood. Painted white with a balcony across the front, it looked like a respectable business. She pushed the door open and stepped inside. The front of the room was full of men seated at round wooden tables who seemed to all turn in unison and stare.

"Well, would you look who's come to visit?" Evan drawled from several feet away. He put two bottles down on a table and walked over to face her. "I thought Logan told you he didn't want to see you."

"I didn't come here to see Logan. Where's Buttercup?" Ginny wiped her brow; the building was more like an oven than a hotel.

"She's not here; said she'd be back later this afternoon."

"Do you know where I'd find her?"

"Can't say."

"Did you know Logan's made it impossible for me to work in Dawson City?"

"I heard you stole from him. It's not his fault if your reputation precedes you." His lip curled up as he gave an ugly snigger.

Ginny grasped the back of an empty chair to keep her balance; her knees shook inside her skirt. "You know it's not true, Evan. What am I supposed to do?"

"Hmm, well you're not fit for the typical establishment; you're too thin. Have you looked at yourself lately?"

She looked down at the folds of her skirt bunched around her waist. The man had no mercy.

Her hands trembled, and heat crept up her neck as she tucked her blouse further into the waistband.

"I do have a suggestion." Evan's smile was slimy as he ran his hand through his slicked back hair. "There are some cabins not far from here. I find the customers and send them on back. You spend time with them, and I give you a percentage of the money." At his words, the whole room sucked in its breath.

One tear slid down Ginny's face. What did it matter anyway after all she'd done? She couldn't disappoint her family any more if she tried. And besides that, it looked like her only other option was starving to death. Her voice cracked as she asked the question, "Where?"

"Come with me."

Evan led her to a strip of crude, one-room shacks away from the ornate buildings of the main street. A few girls milled about speaking in a language she'd never heard before. She leaned on a fencepost to catch her breath. All she really wanted was sleep.

Evan seized her wrist and pulled her up to the door of one of the shacks. As the door swung in, the room revealed a broken chair, a small table with an oil lamp, and a single bed.

"Welcome to paradise," Evan snorted as he pushed her into the room. "Oh, and, Ginny . . ."

"Yes?"

"Maybe try and be a wee bit more welcoming with the men than you were with me." He laughed and turned to close the door behind him.

Ginny spent the longest day of her life waiting for a knock on the cabin door, and her stomach dropped when she finally heard one. "Come in," she said as she sat on the bed.

The door opened to the unkempt beard and dirty garb of most of the miner's filling Dawson's streets. She would think of home, her brother and sisters, and it would soon be over. Her spine shook involuntarily as the grinning fellow removed his hat and stepped through the door.

The days stretched into weeks. Ginny didn't know how many customers there'd been, and she didn't care. She also didn't know when they'd moved her to the shanty at the end of the row. The last thing she could remember clearly was Buttercup spooning sips of hot broth into her mouth.

CHAPTER 15

BEN SAT WATCHING THE WATER twist and turn from his bench on the deck of the paddle wheeler; his heart weighed a ton. Ever since coming aboard he hadn't wanted to talk to anyone. He was bored with the ridiculous conversations of the gold seekers. Sure, they were all going to be rich. Some of them hadn't worked an honest job their whole lives; they most likely wouldn't apply themselves to their claims, either. There was no way the gold was sitting on the ground; there was no such thing as nuggets as big as chicken eggs. Eventually they left him to himself and probably wondered why he was going up North in the first place. They must have found it odd that he wasn't interested in hearing how a man could become a millionaire in one afternoon.

He pulled a tattered letter from his pocket and gritted his teeth as the image of Vivian's face when they'd said good-bye rose in his memory.

Dearest Ben,

I cannot wait to be your wife. I know we will be very happy together, and I am so glad we will be able to come to you soon. I am trying not to sound over anxious, but you can't possibly know how difficult it is for my family in Dyea. We all look forward to spending time with you and your family when we get

home to the farm. We are doing our best to raise the money to
come to you.
Your Beloved,
Audrey

With any luck Audrey would be prepared to leave shortly after he
arrived and they'd found a church somewhere. In a way, he was kind
of changing the whole family's plan as they would no longer have to
travel back with her. It would be so good to be back home working
his own land where everything made sense.

The captain had announced yesterday at supper they should arrive in Dyea by the end of the week if the weather held out. Several
of the men had commented it would be a wonder if the ship were to
even hold out; it looked as though it had been resurrected from the
mud along the shore of some forsaken island, let alone the fact that
they were overloaded by five times.

Three days later, the ship pulled into the Dyea inlet, and the at-
mosphere on the deck grew restless as the boat drifted toward the
shore. Fights broke out as the men argued over who would be the first
to strike it rich and bring the spoils down South to their families. It
wouldn't be long until he would meet Audrey, and she would help
him forget Vivian.

Ben lifted his hand to shade his eyes from the bright sun. It was
hard to believe the sight that met them as they pulled into Dyea. Ships
of all description lined the shore; cattle boats, coal shuttles, steamships, and ancient paddle wheelers—several of which were listing
to one side—and would never set sail again. Bundles of goods and
wooden crates floated in the water bobbing against the side of the

boat, and huge ungainly piles of supplies lined the beach. The tide was in, so the boat pulled in to the dock without any trouble. The sailors called out to one another as they prepared the ship for unloading.

The scene was no less chaotic as Ben wandered up Main Street. Wood frame saloons lined the street, and men caroused in various states of inebriation. Several false fronted hotels boasted of their comforts, and large gambling houses offered to take gold dust or nuggets in fair trade.

He bent his head to enter a small log café and ordered a cup of coffee.

"That'll be a dollar fifty," the man behind the counter said as he poured the steaming liquid from a metal pot.

A dollar fifty? Ben wondered if the stuff had gold dust in it. He scrounged in his pocket and put the change on the counter. One long sip down his throat made it well worth it; it was the best coffee he'd tasted since setting sail. "You know where a fellow could find tent town?" he asked.

"I don't suppose you can miss it if you head on up the street a way. Look to your left when you come to the fancy Opera house."

After finishing his coffee, Ben bid the man good day and trundled up the street. It would take a while to get his land legs back. When he reached the Opera house, quite a sight greeted him. Tents of every shape and size were crammed together with piles of supplies almost as far as the eye could see. Some of the tents were well supported and appeared to hold themselves up, while others looked as though they were set up in haste. Groups of men milled about deep in discussion, and he supposed they were either bargaining for supplies or selling their excess. Packhorses and dogs wandered in and out of the groups of men. The whole scene looked unreal.

He let out a deep sigh. Locating Audrey and her family in this mess would not be an easy task. He might as well go find somewhere to stay first; he turned and retreated down the mud caked street. He should have asked Audrey for more details.

Stopping at the first hotel he came to, he took a room. He could go down and retrieve his luggage from the shore later. Then he decided to start the search; he figured someone here would have to know Audrey's family. He could ask the scruffs loitering amongst the tents.

Several hours later Ben had been offered everything from corn-meal to candles, shovels to pack mules—all real cheap—but no one could tell him where Silas Mayberry's family stayed. Hot and tired, he stepped into line to buy something to eat from a ramshackle tent with a wooden sign posted out front that read, "Beans and biscuits $2.00." It must be some pile of beans for that price.

While in line, he scanned the surrounding tents for anyone who might look like the picture he pulled out of his shirt pocket several times every day. When Ben finally reached the front of the line, a small, slim woman stepped out of the tent and brushed loose tendrils of dark hair out of her eyes.

She looked up at Ben as she spoke. "Can I get you some beans, young man? The biscuits are fresh from the oven."

Ben's throat constricted; it was dry as a cornhusk. She was an exact replica of the picture, only older. He'd found the Mayberrys.

"Sir, if you're not interested in my vittles, move yourself along so I can help the next customer." Ben was elbowed to the side as the next man stepped up with four fifty-cent pieces in his grubby, out-stretched hand.

"Mrs. Mayberry, I swear I can't get enough of your biscuits. They're selling beans all over these parts, but nobody makes a fluffy biscuit like you do."

"Thanks, Henry, and like I said, I'm not going to give you a deal even though you think you're my best customer, in case you were going to ask again."

A tow-headed young boy of about eight brought out a tin plate with two large biscuits and a heaping pile of baked beans. He passed it to the woman, who in turn passed it to Henry and pocketed the coins in her apron while the young boy returned to the tent. A few more customers were served. They ate standing up and then returned their plates and spoons to a sudsy bucket parked next to the tent. Eventually, the woman spied Ben standing off to the side.

There was no way he was leaving.

"Do you not have any money, son? Is that the problem? I can give you some beans if you like, and then you'll have to move along."

"Nope," his voice croaked as he ran his finger around the inside edge of his collar. He'd waited so long, and now here he was standing like some kind of buffoon.

The tent flap opened again, and a much younger version of the woman standing in front of him emerged. She had a slight form, pretty, with dark, wavy hair pulled into a braid down her back. She looked about the age Audrey was when they took the family photo-graph. It must be her younger sister Caroline. She stepped over to the side of the tent and picked up the bucket with the dishes. Without a glance in any direction she returned to the tent and disappeared behind the flap.

"Don't you be getting any ideas, young man. That's my daughter, and she's engaged to be married to a fine farmer out East. Now either eat or run along."

That wasn't Audrey, it was Caroline. The woman must be mixed up. It was understandable, though, working as hard as she was. "Mrs. Mayberry, it's me—Ben McCormack."

Mrs. Mayberry's face lost all its color as she spoke, "Oh my, Mr. McCormack. Um, what are you d-doing here? We were planning to meet you down South." She stepped forward and turned the plank around to show they were now closed. "Sorry, boys, we're done selling for now."

The men grumbled as they wandered away from the tent.

Mrs. Mayberry cocked her head and twisted the long hair by her ear for several moments before speaking. "As you can see, we're not at our best. We've been working hard for weeks to make enough to buy passage out of here. We were hoping—well, never you mind. You're here now, and that's all that matters. Give me a moment, would you please?" She turned with a quick swish of her skirt and entered the tent. A muffled conversation went on for several minutes—some of it high pitched—before she returned and stood in front of him.

He swallowed, raised his eyebrows, and glanced over at the tent, but she still didn't speak. "Is there a problem, Mrs. Mayberry? Could you let Audrey know I'm here?"

"No, I can't do that."

"Why not?"

"She's not here right now."

"She's not here? Where is she?"

"I don't know where she's gotten to. You have to understand, Mr. McCormack, this is all a bit of a shock. We weren't expecting you to come to Dyea. I don't know quite what to tell you."

"Florence! Florence!" A tall, red haired fellow, unshaven and un-kempt, stumbled his way toward Ben and Mrs. Mayberry with his large leather boots scuffing up the mud.

"Florence, I jus' need two more dollars. Jus' two more dollars and I swear I won't ask for any more today." He stepped closer to Ben. His foul breath was strong enough to injure a man's nostrils. Several small faces peeked out from the tent flap. Mrs. Mayberry stood fro-zen, her eyes darting from the man to Ben and then back again.

The man turned to Ben as though noticing him for the first time. He brought his right index finger up to push into Ben's chest while attempting to steady himself with his other outstretched arm.

"Look here, mister. Are you attempting to bother my woman?" He poked Ben a couple more times. "What's goin' on here? Florence, is this man bothering you?"

"Silas, I'd like you to meet Mr. Ben McCormack," Florence put her arm on Silas's and pulled him to her side. "Audrey's fiancé."

"Fiancé? Are you that farmer from back East?"

Ben lifted his chin and nodded.

"I never expected—well, this calls for a celebration, my friend." Silas stepped away from Florence and turned to put his arm around Ben. "Yes sir, this calls for a celebration. Florence, don't hold supper for us. This fella and me got to get to know one another. Gotta see if he's good enough for my daughter. Yup, gotta see if he's good enough for my little girl."

"I'm not sure that's such a good idea, Silas. It doesn't look like you're thinking too straight right now."

"Don't you worry none; we'll be fine. Come with me, uh—"

"Ben. The name's Ben."

Ben grasped the back of Silas' belt to aid in navigation as the man draped himself over Ben's shoulders. Sure, Ben could celebrate; maybe Silas could answer some questions, like where his oldest daughter might be. Florence looked worried as they turned toward Main Street. The faces from the tent had already disappeared.

"Silas, don't keep the boy out too late; he's had a long journey."

Weaving Silas through tent town proved difficult, but eventually Ben was directed to Silas' favorite watering hole. The two men took a seat in the ramshackle bar.

"Hey, Barney, I'll have a—"

"Not so fast, Mr. Mayberry," Ben stopped him before he could order. "We're here for coffee, and that's it." Ben looked over at the bartender, who gave him a nod and reached for a large blue coffeepot sitting on the sooty heating stove behind the counter.

"Coffee? I don't need any coffee."

"I think you do. We're here to talk about your daughter, remember? You want to see if I'm good enough for her."

"Yeah, all right." Silas slumped into the rickety wooden chair and gave the leg of the rough sawn table a kick. The coffee arrived, and Silas' was half gone before his eyes perked up and he spoke. "Hey, you lookin' to make a few bucks while you're here? And what are you doing here anyway? I thought we was coming to you."

"I thought it'd be a lot easier this way. Now you folks can go where you want; you don't have to escort Audrey all the way out East."

Silas looked at his mug as he swirled the coffee in the bottom. "So, you don't want the family around, huh?"

"I didn't say that. I said it would be easier for your family if you didn't all have to travel."

"Well, you probably still need some cash to start your married life off flush. You and me, we could go into business. I've got a whole bunch of ideas up here." He tapped a crooked finger to his temple.

"What were you thinking, Mr. Mayberry?"

"Call me Silas; we're probably going to be kin, after all."

The bartender refilled their mugs with steaming coffee. Silas slurped his up in one long swallow and then wiped his mouth with a tattered sleeve.

Ben pushed his own mug across the table. "You look like you've still got a thirst, Silas. Go ahead. And what do you mean, 'probably' kin? Do you think Audrey is having second thoughts about marrying me?"

Silas stilled like a rabbit sensing danger.

"You're probably wondering if I know for sure she's the one I want to marry because we've never spent any time together, other than on paper. But I know, Silas, Audrey's the one for me." Ben pushed the thoughts of Vivian out of his mind.

Silas leaned back in his seat, scratched the side of his dirt-ringed neck, and took a deep breath. "You're right there. I'm a little nervous about that girl not knowing you for real. Sometimes she gets things in her head and, well, a father doesn't know what to do." He leaned forward and rapped the knuckles of his right hand on the table. "Now, about you and me going into business. There is a whole pile of ways a man can make a buck without even digging for gold in this country. Why I've been thinking . . . "

Silas went on for two and a half hours about every hair-brained scheme known to the North. The more sober he got, the louder and faster he talked. He didn't even appear to notice when Ben gave the occasional grunt or, "You don't say?" Ben had more important stuff to figure out while Silas was talking. Why had Audrey taken off? Could the surprise have been a little too much for her to handle? Maybe he'd done it wrong and should have let her know he was coming. He had to admit, though, he admired Audrey even more after meeting her drunk of a father.

It had been a long day, and between Silas' jabber and the heat of the cook stove, Ben's head nodded. He rubbed his eyes and ran his hands down his face to try and stay awake.

"Well, son, I guess I better let you get some sleep. We can talk about all this some more later."

Silas must have finally noticed Ben's lack of participation. It took some doing for Ben to rouse himself from the table. "Good night, Silas. Tell your family I'll see them in the morning."

CHAPTER 16

THE EARLY MORNING AIR HELD a crisp bite as Ben trotted to the Mayberry's makeshift home the next day. Tent town already bustled with men and animals, and a long line of men waited for the popular biscuits and beans.

"Good morning, son," Silas said as he gave Ben a sharp slap to the back. "How'd you sleep?"

Ben had tossed and turned most of the night knowing today was the day he would finally meet the woman he loved; her father didn't need to know that. "I'm fine, Silas. Is Audrey here? I'd like to meet her now."

Silas removed his battered hat and swiped at his forehead with a grimy hankie. "See, the thing is, Ben, she's gone to visit a friend."

"She's gone to visit a friend? What are you talking about? Did you tell her I was here?" What was going on in that woman's head? After all the wonderful letters repeating her excitement in seeing each other, why would she run off to visit a friend? "Is she scared, Silas? Is she thinking of changing her mind about marrying me?"

"No, no, Ben nothing like that. I guess the pre-wedding jitters got to her. You showing up here unannounced spooked her is all. You'll have to be patient."

"What do mean, spooked her?"

"Nothing I can do, son," Silas reached out and squeezed Ben's shoulder. "You just hold out here with us, and eventually she'll show up."

Ben had no other option; everyone in the family was tight lipped about where Audrey might be. He spent the next two days helping the family run the canteen, as they liked to call it. Silas was behaving himself and hadn't been drunk again since the first day. The other kids all appeared to know their roles in keeping the business running smoothly and darted about without saying much. He'd never seen so many biscuits and beans in his entire life.

He'd approached Mrs. Mayberry several times as she scurried back and forth from the Yukon stove in the tent to the men waiting in the line for vittles. She didn't appear to want to answer any questions about when Audrey might return judging by the way she clamped her lips and avoided his gaze. She'd sent him to the general store several times to pick up some ingredient or other they were running low on. Somebody would have to start talking soon.

The next morning was the day for answers. Several clouds marred the vivid blue sky as he marched toward tent town. Stepping up and over tent strings and other paraphernalia had become second nature as he made his way to the familiar grey tent.

Not a soul was lined up at the plank table used as a counter where Florence Mayberry sat alone winding a hankie around her hand.

Ben swallowed, the uneasiness building in his chest. "Mrs. Mayberry, it's time for me to know the truth. Where is Audrey?"

Mrs. Mayberry didn't look up as she replied, "In the tent, Mr. McCormack. Take a look yourself."

Why did she sound so weary? Had something happened to Audrey?

His heart thumped like a drum. Here it was: the moment he'd been waiting for. He was about to meet the woman he'd been dreaming about for months. He hustled over to the tent flap and lifted it aside. Audrey's younger sister Caroline and her brother Jonathan were mixing batches of biscuits in large metal bowls atop a steamer trunk. Caroline looked over and then shifted, turning her back toward him.

"Mrs. Mayberry, she's not here. It's only Caroline and Jonathan." He turned around. Mrs. Mayberry's head was in her hands. "She's there, Ben."

Nope, he saw only Caroline and Jonathan. His Audrey sure had a knack for disappearing.

"Audrey come on out," Mrs. Mayberry called wearily.

Caroline removed her floury hands from the bowl and brushed them on her apron. Straightening her shoulders, she brushed past Ben to exit the tent and stand beside her mother.

Still holding her head in her hands, Mrs. Mayberry mumbled, "Ben, meet your intended, Audrey Nina Mayberry."

He couldn't breathe.

Lord, no! He shook off the grey haze threatening his vision and stumbled forward to grab the girl's upper arms. "You're not Audrey. You can't be. You're only a child."

Audrey wrenched her arm from his hold. "I just turned thirteen, and I don't care what Ma and Pa say. I am not going to marry you!" Her eyes flashed as she tossed a long black braid over one shoulder, lifted her skirt from the dust, and stalked away.

As his stomach reeled, Ben's eyes followed her narrow back between the tents until she was gone. What in blazes was going on? Where was Audrey, the girl who could melt his heart with her letters?

He thrust his bottom jaw forward, gritted his teeth, and took two long breaths. "Mrs. Mayberry, you've got some explaining to do."

"Mr. McCormack," her hands fluttered around her collar, "I can explain later. You're angry right now, and it wouldn't do for me t—" She jumped as his fist hit the table.

"I need answers, and I need them now."

Her eyes stretched open, but her mouth stayed shut.

He leaned across the table, his voice a low rumble, "I said, now."

Mrs. Mayberry reached out, her fingers skimming his sleeve. He jerked his arm away and leaned forward, both fists on the table. His eyes locked on hers.

"I'm so sorry, I never thought it would end this way. It—well, it seemed a good idea at the time, but I never should have listened."

The words were ground out slowly through his clenched teeth, "What seemed like a good idea?"

"The advertisements and the letters."

"Go on."

She twisted a hankie around her raw fingers and stared at the ground for a full minute before she whispered, "It was Silas's idea."

"What was Silas's idea?"

"Putting the ad in the paper, looking for a beau for Audrey . . ."

Lord, still my hand. I want to hit this woman.

Two streams of tears trailed down Mrs. Mayberry's cheeks. "I know she's only a little girl," her chest heaved, "but I didn't know what else to do."

"Woman, I need you to tell me the whole story. The girl I thought I was going to spend the rest of my life with—the girl I've loved for over six months—just marched off, and she's a child. Why?"

Her words came out in a rush. "I was desperate. Right after we arrived at this excuse for a town, Silas lost our entire outfit to some hack who said he could sell it for triple what we paid for it and then sell us replacement goods at below cost. How could Silas have been so stupid? And if that wasn't bad enough, he invested all our hard cash with some fellow who said he'd designed a new way to mine gold that would make us all rich. The guy's been long gone for over a year. That's when Silas started drinking, and we got desperate. Do you know how many of my relatives invested in our trip up here? We were supposed to bring them all back some profit, and now we've got nothing."

"What does that have to do with the ad and the letters? Why did you get Audrey to write the letters if she wasn't . . . "

Mrs. Mayberry's face blanched; she looked ashamed.

No, no, no. He rocked back on his boot heels. "She didn't write the letters, did she?" Mrs. Mayberry had been writing them all along. *Lord have mercy.* He'd been exchanging love letters with a married woman for six months.

"I am so sorry. The whole idea was bad from the start. But you've got to understand, I was desperate. I was desperate to get my family back home. Me and Silas, we thought maybe you would send us money to come and visit you, and we could use that to get out of here. But I know now Silas would have taken that, too. He's gone, you know. He figured you weren't going to take kindly to the lying, and he's taken all we've earned. I don't know what I'm going to do now."

The Mayberry family could disappear from the face of the Earth for all Ben cared. His heart ached for all the beautiful letters and all the time he'd spent reading and rereading them. Audrey didn't exist.

The girl he thought he was going to marry didn't exist. All the hopes, dreams, hard work for months, and this whole trip were for nothing. *Lord, why?* Vivian entered his mind, her silky blonde hair and warm green eyes beckoning him. His head was pounding. "I've got to get out of here," he said as he pressed his temples with his knuckles.

"Perhaps you should sit for a bit; you don't look well."

Ben dropped a thick roll of bills on the table. "Here's some money to help get your family home."

"But—"

"Stop. I don't ever want to hear another word from you again." He turned and staggered his way through the maze of dilapidated tents.

* * *

The next morning Ben's head still hammered as he shifted the canvas duffle bag purchased in Dyea to his other shoulder and traipsed down the wagon road leading out of town. He knew he probably wouldn't get very far today. He ached all over like he'd gone several rounds with the town rowdy. For several miles the trail had been littered with trunks and other paraphernalia that the Klondikers had decided were either unnecessary or too awkward to carry. It was a good thing he'd traded his own trunk for the duffle. He wouldn't have been able to carry it far up the trail.

The path meandered through a deep green forest of spruce and birch. It was hard to appreciate it as he couldn't stop thinking about yesterday. What an absolute fool he'd been. He should have known. Looking back, there was no way those letters were written by a teenage girl. If he hadn't been so proud and had sought the Lord regarding Audrey, he was sure it wouldn't feel like someone had stomped on his heart right now. He needed to stop figuring he knew what God's plan was and start asking Him.

Lord, I'm sorry; I should have waited on You. But I didn't, and now I'm out here in the middle of nowhere. Please show me Your direction. Please help me to know Your will. Is it Vivian, Lord? You know I'm attracted to her, but I also broke her heart. Will she ever forgive me? Should she?

He had to get to Dawson City and help her whether she forgave him or not. If he didn't pick up his pace, he'd never reach Sheep Camp. It was said a man could get a decent meal and a half decent bed there.

Shortly, the trail led into a narrow canyon about fifty feet wide. Household goods were still tossed to the side and piled up against huge boulders dotting the trail. Upturned trees with their roots exposed made it difficult to navigate. He didn't stop to gab with the other travellers complaining about the conditions. He had enough problems of his own.

Entering Pleasant Camp at the far end of the canyon, Ben dropped his duffle to the ground in front of a crude shack and rifled through his pocket for a couple of dollars. With those he purchased the customary beans and bacon and a couple mugs of tea. Those who tried to engage him in conversation quickly figured out he wasn't up for talking and instead left him to his brooding.

Shortly before the sun's descent, Ben entered Sheep Camp. It was nestled at the base of the Coast Mountains, the peaks of which towered over a deep bowl with tents pressed so tightly together that a man found it difficult to get a footing. He shook his head as he read the crude signs in front of hastily built log cabins or canvas tents. They advertised everything one could imagine from cook stoves to rubber boots, laundry services to first class hotels.

Ben slowed in front of a roughly built two-story sided with tar paper and barked slab planks. The large, white sign poking out above the door read, "Hotel Northern: meals, lunches, and beds." It would do as well as any other. He slung his duffle off his shoulder and stepped through the door. The smell of unwashed bodies and stale breath stuck in his throat. When he coughed, several pairs of eyes lifted to take him in. He crossed the dirt floor and stepped up to the rough-sawn counter off to one corner.

"I was wondering if I could get a bed for the night?" He asked the wiry man behind the counter with a grizzled beard and hollow cheeks.

"Sure can. Did you need a place to store your outfit too?"

"Nope, just a bed will be fine. I'm travelling light, thanks."

"You plan to go over the Chilkoot Pass, young man?" The fellow looked up from his ledger, and the pen in his hand stilled.

"Yes sir, I thought first thing tomorrow. Why?"

"I'm assuming you know about having to own a year's worth of supplies to take over the pass with you in order to enter Canada?"

"One year's worth? You kidding me?" Ben envisioned the roll of bills he'd thrown on the table in front of Mrs. Mayberry.

"No son, I ain't. The Canadian Mounties don't want anyone starving in Dawson like they did last year. I'm surprised you haven't heard about it until now. You came up from Dyea didn't you?" The fellow raised one bushy eyebrow as he asked the question.

Ben regretted shrugging off so much conversation along the way.

"Have you got enough money to supply yourself? It'll be about five hundred dollars or a thousand pounds in weight, depending on how you want to look at it."

Five hundred dollars? He had only fifty bucks and the hope he could find Vivian and help her find Ginny before the cash ran out. "Any chance a guy can get a job around here? One that pays real well?"

"Can't say there's much to do if you didn't bring it in with you. Although, you look like a strong fellow, and the packers are always looking for help."

"The packers?"

"The guys who carry the supplies over the Chilkoot pass. It's back breaking work, and not many of the white men last long."

"Where could I find out about doing some packing?"

"There's a big shack north of here that says Packer's Rest out front. Tell Bill I sent you."

Ben lifted his duffle and turned to leave.

"I suggest you take a bed before you go; I don't have many left. We fill up and then some every night."

Ben paid the hotel owner and left his bag sitting on his bed to claim it. After trudging through the mud for several minutes, he spied a crude shack which boasted the name Packer's Rest above the door. Loud guffaws filtered out onto the street through the cracks between the uneven planks. The laughter ceased as Ben entered the dimly lit room. "I'm looking for Bill, the fellow at Hotel Northern sent me down this way."

A brawny man about six foot five with a big, burly chest and a mop of black curls spoke up, "I'm Bill, and what can I do for you? Did you need some packers? Our rates are about the best in town."

"I'm looking for a job."

Several men in the room looked at each other and chuckled.

"Well, that's a story we hear just about every other day now, isn't it boys? What makes you think you can pack?"

"I've worked hard all my life, sir."

"Ain't no sirs around here. Call me Bill, and what is it you've been doing all your life?"

Ben cleared his throat to remove the dry cotton feel from his mouth. "Farming."

"Farming—that might do. What do you think boys? Should we give this here fellow a shot?"

Several of the men made comments on Ben's height while several others commented on his youth. It was like they were buying a new horse. He shifted his weight to his other foot and stared at the floor.

"I guess it's unanimous, we'll let you give it a try. Don't take the comments to heart; we were having us some fun. There's not much out here in the way of entertainment. So you think you can haul a hundred pounds for about six hours a day?"

"No problem." A hundred pounds on flat land would be no problem. Over a mountain—well, that might take some getting used to. But did he really have any choice?

Bill looked Ben in the eye. Ben looked right back without flinching.

"Do you know where you're packing, or are you just foolhardy, boy?"

"Probably a little of both, sir—I mean, Bill."

Bill's deep laughter poured out of his chest as he put his arm around Ben and drew him over to the table where the rest of the men sat. They emptied two chairs, and Bill and Ben sat down. Bill went on to explain how the system worked. The customer was charged fifty cents a pound, the packer made twenty-five cents, and the boss, meaning Bill, made the other twenty-five cents. If a packer carried a hundred pounds a day he could make twenty-five dollars.

Ugh. He'd be stuck here for more than a month by the time he made the money to buy his own outfit and then carry it over the pass, too.

"Welcome to the club, Ben. Arnie, pour our new employee a drink, would you?"

"No thanks, Bill. Fellas," Ben nodded his head to the men around the table, "if you don't mind, I'll be getting back to the hotel. I've had a long day, and I mean to start packing tomorrow."

"Sure thing, Ben, but I can guarantee you one thing: today will feel like a church picnic after tomorrow. We'll see you at first light."

Several comments about Bill never seeing the inside of a church, let alone a church picnic were tossed around the room as Ben walked to the door and stepped out into the crisp, cool night.

* * *

Ben wiped the sweat from his eyes and with no break in his step shifted his pack to his left shoulder. He didn't have to concentrate on packing up the Chilkoot Pass anymore. His legs kept moving through the day and long into his dreams. Why would anyone be foolish enough to spend the money it took to transport their supplies over the pass on the slim chance they might find some gold? If he heard one more story—ever—about gold sitting on the ground like goose eggs, it would be too soon.

The day had begun at four in the morning, just like it had for the last five weeks, at The Scales. He paid the toll and started up the steep pass, climbing with the steady stream of men fifteen hundred gruelling steps straight up the side of the mountain. Many of the men were so bent over they practically brushed the ground with their noses. Their loads were too heavy, and they wouldn't take advice from the seasoned packers. They'd be out of commission for several days, guaranteed. A man had to pace himself. He'd learned that the first week out. He'd been so sore that his aches had ached. During the climb, he didn't dare step out of line to rest on a flat spot, either. The men were following so close it could take hours to break back onto the trail.

It took five and half hours for a climb, and all of about two minutes to get back down using the snow chute. He was on a first name basis with the Canadian North West Mounted Police in their big buffalo coats at the summit. Once in a while on a calm day, he could manage two trips, each with a hundred pound pack. Bill told the others he never expected Ben to last more than a couple of weeks. But, within a few days, his own provisions would all be stacked at the summit, and he could legally enter Canada.

A man could do a lot of thinking as he climbed. Where was Vivian, and had she found Ginny? Maybe they were already on their way home, and all this would be for nothing. And then there was Audrey—the Audrey who didn't exist. What a fool he'd been to throw away love with someone he could see and touch for someone who was only a dream. Audrey had become nothing more than something he'd made up in his mind that was so amazing there wasn't a woman alive who could measure up. He didn't deserve Vivian. But, she was well worth trying for, and he could probably arrive in Dawson by the end of next week. He was bone weary, though. He didn't know if he could make it.

CHAPTER 17

AFTER SEVEN WEEKS ON CROWDED steamers, Vivian's heart leapt at the sight of Dawson City nestled on the south shore of the Yukon River. She would miss the boys and the distraction their business provided. They had given her less time to think of Ben. And there was no way she would ever forget the breathtaking sights of the vast mountain ranges and deep green forests she had seen along the way. But the delay in taking the northern water route meant she hadn't caught up with Ginny when she'd hoped to, and who knew what trouble that girl could be in by now. The thought of it had plagued her day and night. For relief, she read the small black Bible Father had given her when she'd first learned to read. The favorite passages were almost worn through.

"I will lift up mine eyes unto the hills, from whence cometh my help. My help cometh from the Lord, which made heaven and Earth."

Oh, Lord, I'm so glad You are here to help me and Ginny. Please protect her, and help me find her. And, Lord, be with Ben and Audrey as they start their new . . .

She couldn't do it; she couldn't pray for them. The air in her chest would almost choke off when she thought about Ben and Audrey getting married; they'd be enjoying their honeymoon by now.

But thinking about Ben and remembering how safe she'd felt in his arms when he'd rescued her that day was no problem. And there wasn't a day gone by that she couldn't escape thinking of his kiss—the one that had changed her whole world.

She was drawn out of her reverie as the crew called out orders for disembarking and organized the passengers to prevent injury or trampling in all the excitement. Vivian stepped away from the railing, her eyes searching the deck for Edward and Paul. It would be difficult to say good-bye to the boys and Amelia; they'd spent so much time together. But she'd promised she would visit them often while she was still in town.

And whether they owned the hotel or not, it wasn't right to stay on with Amelia and the boys any longer as Amelia had suggested. She'd already been more than generous by paying such an exorbitant amount for Vivian's travel on the Sally Girl, and Vivian needed the freedom to search for Ginny.

As the steamship pulled up to the shore, it appeared as though the whole town had shown up for their arrival. Thousands of people waited at the water's edge to secure some of the fresh supplies packed in the hold of the steamship.

Vivian looked over the crowd. Her gaze settled on the lanky shape of a fellow standing about halfway through the throng. From the back he seemed familiar, and she shook her head. There was no way she would know anyone up here other than Ginny or Logan.

As the ramps were lowered, the foursome joined the slow parade of passengers making their way to land amid the cheers and catcalls of the ragamuffin crowd. The luggage wasn't going to be unloaded until later in the day, so Vivian would secure her lodgings and send word back as to where it could be delivered.

Progress proved to be slow, and it was an hour later when they finally walked through the mud and up the street toward the town's main intersection. Vivian gasped when she felt a hand snake around the inside of her forearm.

It was happening again. Screaming, she pulled away and stepped toward Amelia before turning to face her attacker. Edward and Paul flanked her sides with their small fists raised in the air.

"Dr. Williams?" she gasped.

"Vivian, I'm sorry I startled you. I should have spoken first."

"Boys, it's all right; he's a friend." She patted the boys on the head. They lowered their fists but continued to glare.

It had been an eternity since she'd left home. "Alistair, I can't believe you are here." She abandoned all social propriety and stepped forward to embrace Alistair, wrapping her arms around his slim frame.

Alistair's hands remained by his sides. His ears were red to their very tips when she released him and stepped back. "I don't know when I've ever been so happy to see someone. But what are you doing here? Have you found Ginny? Is she all right?"

Alistair straightened the lapels of his rumpled jacket. "I am pleased you are happy to see me. I wasn't sure if you would consider it an intrusion or not. I've been here only a couple of days, and unfortunately I haven't found Ginny. I can answer your other questions over tea, if I may escort you?"

"That would be lovely," Vivian said and turned to face Amelia and the boys. "Mrs. Brown, Edward, Paul, this is Dr. Alistair Williams, a family friend from back home."

"How nice to meet you," Alistair bowed his tall frame as he took Amelia's hand. "It looks like you've made some fine friends, Miss Connor; these boys are ready to defend you with their life."

Maybe she could tell him someday how close she'd come to a life of abject misery or how her own stubbornness had jeopardized the safety of the two boys, but not today. Thinking about it still made her sick to her stomach. Vivian straightened her shoulders to reply, "We have grown very close."

"Vivian, I can see you are in good hands, and we are anxious to find Mr. Brown. So if you would please excuse us?" Amelia placed a hand on Vivian's shoulder.

"Oh yes, of course. And thank you so much for giving me the opportunity to travel with your family." Vivian clasped Amelia's hands briefly and then kissed each boy on the forehead.

"Vivian, do look us up in the next day or two and let us know how the search is going. Come, Edward, Paul."

Amelia reached out a hand for each boy. The boys took their mother's hands, and the three turned to proceed up the street. Both Edward and Paul looked over their shoulders as they walked away. Vivian waved and watched them until they were swallowed up by the crowd.

Alistair offered his arm, and the two sloshed through the ankle-deep mud churned up by the crowd milling in the makeshift market. Tents and tables were crowded together to sell fruit and vegetables and even ice cream. Provisions from the trail looking like they'd seen better days lay in heaps and piles so customers could pick through and purchase what they needed. Some of the sellers had a desperate look in their eye as they haggled with the newcomers from the boat.

"Alistair, what is all this?"

"People trying to go home. Most of them have lost almost everything trying to get here, and now they just want to turn around to go back where they came from."

"But what about the gold?"

"Oh, there's gold for sure, but it seems to be in the hands of very few. Almost all of the rich had made their money before the rush began. You've got to feel sorry for these other folks."

As they reached the end of a street, Alistair helped Vivian step up onto the raised sidewalk. It was still covered with dirt but allowed for easier progress. Large wooden buildings boasted first class hotel, dance hall, or theatre further down the way. It was amazing, and Ginny's stories didn't seem all that farfetched anymore. It was like the town had sprung up out of the mud.

Alistair led her into a small café which had an impressive French menu; he ordered an assortment of fruit, cheese, and small cakes to go with their tea.

"Please, Alistair, tell me how you ended up in Dawson City."

He looked down at the damask tablecloth and fiddled with a spoon for several seconds. "I came for Ginny. After you'd left, I was beside myself wondering if you would find her. My uncle said I might as well follow you as I was useless at the office. I arrived Wednesday."

"And you've looked for her?"

"I have waded through so many people asking questions that I don't know where I've been and where I haven't anymore."

Poor Alistair—he loved Ginny enough to come all this way. It must be difficult knowing she was with someone else. "How did you get here, Alistair?"

"Over the White Pass, and I can't even begin to tell you how awful it was. It was just miles and miles of men in such frenzy you would have thought them all mad. I saw men beat their horses until the sorry beasts jumped over the cliffs to be spared." He popped a cinnamon tea cake in his mouth and talked with the lump of it in his cheek. "Miss Connor, I've never seen country the likes of which we toiled through. It was only the thought of your sister that kept me going."

Ginny didn't deserve his commitment. Vivian turned away and nibbled on a piece of cheese. "It sounds like you had a terrible trip."

"You can't even imagine. We climbed over hill upon hill and then boulders ten feet high, which led us into quagmire so thick it could pull a man under. I treated so many broken limbs and torn ligaments along the way that I lost count. The trail was littered with thousands of dead horses; I finally had to shoot my own to put it out of its misery." He placed his elbows on the table and covered his eyes with his hands. "There were so many times I wanted to give up. Then I would think of Ginny and worry that maybe she'd been abandoned by that no account—well, whoever he was—and then God would give me the strength to go on." He reached across the table to grip Vivian's hand.

How could she respond? She was grateful he'd endured so much to find her sister. She gave his hand a return squeeze. But would Ginny care? It was not likely; it would be cruel to pretend otherwise.

"Thank you for persevering, Alistair."

"No one I've talked to has heard of or seen Ginny. I've spent hours every day scouring the town. I meet every ship coming in to shore in case she was delayed. There are thousands of people here; I never expected so many."

He was completely devoted to Ginny. Why couldn't someone love Vivian that way? Why couldn't Ben have loved her that way? It was of no use to constantly think of Ben and what would never be. Finding Ginny must be foremost in her thoughts, or Vivian would go mad. She straightened her spine and pulled in a long breath. "Alistair, I am so thankful you decided to follow Ginny. Between the two of us, we'll find her. I know we will."

"Miss Connor, I know you're hopeful, but we don't even know if she's in Dawson."

Vivian remembered the doctor's ring in her bag. She picked the embroidered pouch up from the table and rummaged through the other contents until her fingers lit on her sewing kit. She opened it and removed the ring. Holding it across the table she said, "Here, take this back. I am certain we will find her, and when we do, you will need it."

Alistair reached over and took the ring from Vivian's grasp looking almost hopeful as he tucked it in his inside jacket pocket.

The rest of the afternoon flew by as they talked about Vivian's family back home and both Alistair's and Vivian's travels up North. Alistair's voice rose, and his long limbs flailed about as he spoke of the hardships on the trail.

When Vivian raised a hand to stifle a yawn, Alistair apologized for his lack of consideration and offered to direct her to reputable lodgings.

On the boardwalk, he tucked her arm through his and led her to a small clapboard hotel several doors down which promised to have the cleanest rooms in Dawson City. The two bade each other farewell and promised to meet the first thing next morning at the same café to devise a plan on how to best find Ginny.

CHAPTER 18

THE NEXT MORNING THE SKY was painted azure blue as far as Vivian's eye could see. She stepped from her hotel and out onto the boardwalk refreshed after a good night's sleep. She knew her restfulness was due in part because she'd been so exhausted from the weeks on the steam ship and otherwise because Ben's smile had only invaded her dreams once last night. With any luck, soon he wouldn't appear at all.

A smile rose to her lips as she remembered the previous evening with Alistair. His company had proven delightful. It was comforting to know she wouldn't be alone in the search for Ginny.

Alistair pushed his chair out and stood at their table as Vivian stepped into the small café from the afternoon before. The table held a hearty spread of two bowls of oatmeal and a plate of toast. Mugs of steaming coffee sat beside each bowl. A growl emanated from her stomach as she walked toward the table near the window.

Alistair pulled her chair out. She sat down and adjusted the folds of her skirt.

"Good morning, Miss Connor, you look much more rested today."

"Thank you, Alistair. The hotel lodgings are very comfortable." And she didn't dream of the married Ben all night long.

"If you don't object, I've developed a plan for our search. Thousands of people have invaded Dawson City. Our best bet is to talk to as many people as we can, as fast as we can. Just about everyone goes through a restaurant, a dance hall, or a saloon. As difficult as it might be, I think we should start with those establishments. I've already talked to several of the local pastors and they've promised to send word if Ginny contacts them."

"There are several churches in town? That's a good idea. I'm sure Ginny would attend one; I mean, I think she would attend one if she could." *Oh, Ginny, where are you?* Vivian's eyes closed to fight off the nausea rising in her stomach. Alistair's hand curled around her fingers, and she opened her eyes as she jerked her hand back.

Alistair returned his hand to his lap and cocked his head to the side as though asking a question.

"I'm sorry. I don't know. Somehow being here in this chaos has made her situation all the more real to me." Why did Alistair's touch feel like a betrayal of Ben? Would she never be free from the man's shadow?

"I understand, and that's why it's important we find her as soon as possible. There's a small Methodist church two blocks up and around the corner. The pastor was particularly helpful and wanted you to know if you needed anything to be sure and ask him." Alistair's gaze left her face and roamed to the window. He chewed the edge of his lip for several seconds. "Miss Connor, it pains me to say this, but we need to remember the company she's keeping. If our hunch is right, Logan Harris is not the most upstanding fellow, and he may well have brought Ginny down with him."

"I can't even think about that. She's my sister."

"I'm sorry, but we may have to."

* * *

Late that afternoon Vivian sat on a low plank bench outside the Yukon Hotel. She removed her left boot and rubbed her instep and big toe through the heavy wool stocking ignoring the stares of the grubby men loitering on the sidewalk. It served her right for not breaking the boots in on the trip up like Mary Beth had suggested. A good hot soak in Epsom salts back at the hotel would probably help. She and Alistair must have covered miles trudging up and down the streets inquiring into every restaurant in town hoping to find Ginny before they resorted to the saloons and dancehalls. However, not a single soul recognized the pretty face in the photograph she proffered at every establishment. More often than not, the proprietor would comment on the similarities between them and then shake his head saying he hadn't seen anyone like Ginny come through the door.

It was disheartening working her way through the tight crowds of unruly men only to have someone shake his head and go back to what he was doing. Ginny must have arrived weeks ago. Why did no one seem to remember her? Alistair, on the other hand, appeared to have no end of zeal. He'd left Vivian in front of the hotel a half hour ago to chase down a couple of prospectors he'd overheard talking about some dance hall girls.

Vivian bent over to put her boot on and tugged the long row of crisscrossed laces up the front. She was to meet Alistair in fifteen minutes at the church he'd mentioned the day before.

The sun showed no hint of waning overhead as she neared the small, white clapboard church. The heavy, carved door opened with a creak as she depressed the thumb latch and stepped inside. It was empty. Her boots scraped on the rough hardwood as she walked to the front of the sanctuary and knelt in front of the altar to pray.

Dear heavenly Father, please help us find Ginny. It's so crazy here; I know she needs Your protection. And Lord, give me the strength to find her and the faith to know You are with her. Guide our path. In Jesus' name, Amen.

The front door creaked again, and quick steps made their way to her side. Alistair knelt on the floor at arm's length. His murmurings carried a comforting rhythm.

She dropped her head to her chin and closed her eyes. *Lord, he sounds so hopeful. I don't feel hopeful. Forgive me.*

The two stayed on their knees for another half hour before rising to their feet and leaving the chapel. As they walked back toward the hotel, Vivian asked the question circling in her mind. "Alistair, do you really think we will find Ginny?"

"I know if the Lord wants us to, we will."

Vivian scrunched her eyebrows as her boots stopped abruptly on the sidewalk. "But why wouldn't He want us to find her?" She said to his back.

Alistair turned. His cheeks were drawn, the creases at the corners of his eyes more pronounced. "Vivian, I don't know anything for sure." He swiped a hand across his forehead and down the side of his face. "But the Lord kept us both safe on the way to Dawson City, and we should do our best to find her."

The next day's search began with a change of plans as they'd decided over breakfast to start with the hospital before they tackled the saloons. Vivian and Alistair wandered their way to the far side of Dawson City and over to a two-story wood building pushed up against the side of a hill. The beams on one half of the unfinished roof were exposed to the breeze of the summer day. Upon entering the hospital, they enquired of a nun regarding Ginny. She directed them down the hallway to Father Thomas, founder of the hospital.

Cot upon cot lined the narrow hall. Men in varying degrees of emaciation from either typhoid or malaria followed their progress with bloodshot eyes. Alistair handed Vivian a handkerchief, and she lifted it to her nose. It didn't even begin to mask the smell.

At the door to the second ward they found the harried priest and questioned him about Ginny. As they followed him around, he whisked from bed to bed to offer a drink of water or a cold cloth to a patient. "I'm sorry," he said, "I cannot help you. We do not have any women here at the moment. They are rarely admitted as they tend to look after their own."

What was he implying by, "their own"? Her stomach rolled. Ginny was not a prostitute.

"I wish you well in your search," the priest said, his kind eyes full of sympathy. "We will certainly inform you if your sister is admitted. Please leave her name with the nurse you met on your way in. And if you'll excuse me, as you can see, I have many patients to tend to." His bent over frame scurried away before either of them replied.

"Alistair, please, I need to leave." Alistair's palm, warm against the small of her back, directed her between the cots and out the front door of the hospital. Vivian sucked in a huge breath. "I'm sorry. The smell—it was . . . I'm so glad Ginny wasn't there, even if it means we have to keep looking."

"I guess it is a good thing we didn't find her here. I would like to come back and help some day. That man is being run off his feet. But first we need to find your sister. Let's head back to Front Street and check in some of the saloons."

* * *

Vivian's feet were lead blocks as they entered the last saloon on the street facing the river. The crush of rowdy men in each establishment made it difficult to reach the bar. Once again, the appearance of a woman made quite a stir. Both Vivian and Alistair ignored the customers' crude comments as they pressed on to speak to the bartender.

The rotund man behind the bar with a wide smile and three gold teeth spoke to Vivian first. "If you're looking for work, I have all the waitresses I need." He continued to wipe the wooden bar with a damp cloth.

She didn't care if the man wanted to hire a waitress or not. The last four saloons had made the same comment. It was about time for someone to give more than a flippant remark. She needed to find her sister, and she needed to find her now. She'd had enough of the crowds, the comments, and the mud that stuck to her skirt and boots weighing her down like cement. "I'm not looking for work. I'm not looking for a handout. I'm looking for my sister. This is her photograph." Vivian's arm snapped out with the dog-eared photo coming within inches of the man's face.

After a moment, the man moved his head to the side to peer at her around the photo and raised an eyebrow. Vivian dropped her arm. Her chest warmed as the bartender skimmed over her from dirty boots to lopsided hat.

"Looks a lot like you, but I still haven't seen her." He dropped his eyes to his task. She was dismissed.

"Are you sure, sir? She was probably looking for work."

"Ma'am, I haven't seen your sister, and it's time for you to vacate my premises." He lifted a tall glass to a spigot and filled it with a sudsy liquid for a patron who'd stepped up to the bar.

"Vivian, let's go." Alistair grasped her elbow, and she resisted his pull toward the door.

The bartender knew something. Why else would he be trying to get rid of them? All the others had offered her a drink on the house. A woman customer was sure to increase business in this town. Vivian tugged her arm from Alistair's grip and straightened her shoulders. "I think you have. I think you have seen my sister. Her name's Ginny."

The man's eyes could bore through wood. "I said, miss, I haven't seen her, and I've also asked you to leave."

"Vivian, please, you're over tired; let the man do his job."

"I'm not leaving until this man tells me where he's seen my sister." As her voice rose, heads turned to stare, and men's eyes rose over the rims of their glasses.

The bartender's hand stilled. He returned Vivian's glare. "All right, little lady, have it your way. Have you tried the cribs?"

Silence spread through the bar at the man's words.

"I don't understand. What do you mean by 'the cribs'?"

"That's all I'm saying. It's time for you and your friend to leave. Larry, see these two out, would you?" A bulk of a man leaning against the wall sauntered over to Vivian and Alistair.

"That won't be necessary, sir. We're leaving," Alistair said holding firmly to Vivian's elbow and turning them in unison toward the door.

"Alistair," she tugged her arm, but he held firm. "I have more questions."

"Vivian, we are leaving." Alistair pushed her through the swinging saloon doors and out onto the street.

"What are you doing?" she asked. She rubbed the spot above her elbow where his fingers had dug into the flesh. She'd have two finger-shaped bruises by tonight. "You are being inappropriate. I'm going right back in there to talk to that man and find out what he means." Her hand extended toward the swinging door. Alistair wrapped his fingers around her arm and pulled her back.

"Dr. Williams, I insist that you refrain from putting your hands on me." The man had a strong grip. "If this is how you are going to act, I think it might be time we parted ways. Now let go of me." Alistair's bottom jaw thrust forward as he held fast onto her arm. Vivian pulled at his fingers attempting to pry them off. "What has gotten into you? Let me go this minute!"

"No." Alistair said.

"What do you mean, no?"

"I know what the bartender's referring to. Those men I chased down yesterday told me about the cribs. I'll let you go if you promise to hear me out."

"Fine. Why didn't you say so in the first place?"

Alistair released her arm as bedraggled miners gathered on the sidewalk around the feuding pair. "Miss Connor, let's retire to the café where we can speak privately on the matter."

Anger welled up in her chest. Why was he being so difficult? If someone had seen Ginny, it meant she was in town. The search could soon be over. "You had better start talking right here and right now, or I will go in and get my answers from that man."

"The cribs are where the cheap prostitutes are."

"What?" No. Ginny wouldn't. She would never sell herself. It couldn't be. *He's wrong; I know he's wrong. Her body swayed.*

"I'm sorry. She must be desperate; she'll need our help."

Her stomach heaved, and a wave of darkness moved toward the center of her vision.

"Miss Connor? Miss Connor?"

The voice was so far away. Darkness enveloped her.

* * *

Vivian raised a hand to her mouth, and her foot slipped off the edge of the narrow boardwalk as they rounded the corner behind the street of ornate dance halls. She swallowed. "Alistair, where are we?"

Before them stretched a dilapidated and mud-encrusted board-walk flanked on either side by tiny, decrepit wooden shacks. Several doors hung open, and women clothed in shapeless dresses leaned against the doorways. Puffs of smoke curled from cigarettes pinched between their fingers.

"I can't. I can't go any farther. I'm telling you, I know my sister, and she's not here."

Alistair reached for her elbow. "I know it's difficult, but remember what we prayed. The Lord will give you the strength to find her."

"But how could she have ended up here? Where's Logan? Why didn't she contact us? We would have sent money."

"The only one who knows the answers to those questions is Ginny herself. When we find her, she can tell you. Come along."

Her boots scuffing on the rough planks, Vivian followed Alistair further down the walk. He stopped in front of one of the shacks. A young girl with a rat's nest of blonde hair eyed him from the doorway. A sack-like dress hung from her thin form. She gave a half smile and shifted her weight to her other hip.

Vivian stepped around Alistair, smiled, and then walked toward the girl. Several women's faces peered at her from the filthy window beside the door.

"You won't be getting anything out of that one if it's information you're looking for."

Vivian rotated toward the raspy voice.

A tall, shapely woman twisted one of her copper curls around a finger as she leaned against a doorway on the other side of the board-walk. "At least, I assume it's information you want. Most men don't bring their women down here for a good time." She raised a painted eyebrow as she drew her eyes slowly from Alistair's feet to his head.

His face flushed, and the tips of his ears turned bright as cherries. He cleared his throat. "We're looking for someone; we were told she might be here."

"Well I'm about the only soul around who can speak English, and I wouldn't be here either if I hadn't broken my leg. Who needs a dance hall girl who can't dance?" She tossed her head back in laughter and slapped the door frame with an open palm.

Vivian flinched at the grating guffaw. Should they laugh, too, and gain her approval? It wasn't even funny.

The woman righted her head and wiped her eyes with her sleeve. "Most of these girls know only enough of the language to ply their trade, if you get my meaning. Who are you looking for?"

"Her name's Ginny and—"

"Darlin', most of us don't use our real names. What does she look like?"

"Like me, I guess, only her hair is black, and her eyes are blue. She's a few years younger than I am."

"Now that you mention it, I can see the resemblance."

Vivian drew in a quick breath. The woman had seen Ginny.

"Try the last shanty on the left kind of set off by itself. Don't expect too much, though. It's the infirmary, but I've never seen a woman come out of there alive."

Vivian ran down the boardwalk with Alistair's footsteps rhythmically thumping behind her. When she stopped in front of the shack door, her breaths were coming in heaves. She bent over and put her hands on her knees.

"Vivian, wait here. Let me go in first."

She answered between gulps of air. "She's . . . my . . . sister."

"We don't know what we'll find. I'm a doctor, remember?"

As though being prompted, a putrid smell emanating from the run down shanty wafted across her nostrils. Vivian stood up and pressed her shoulders back. "I don't care. I'm going in with you."

Alistair reached out his hand to the door. It squeaked on its hinges as he opened it slowly. He stopped midway and fetched two handkerchiefs from his inside pocket. Covering his nose with one, he handed Vivian the other. She held the handkerchief over her nose as she fell in behind Alistair, and they entered the shadowed room.

A small form wrapped in a tattered blanket lay on a narrow cot against the far wall. Rags lay in small heaps on the floor. The stench caught in Vivian's throat.

Alistair's foot nudged one of the piles, and a rat scurried across the floor into a gnawed hole in the corner of the room.

Don't scream, don't scream, don't turn around and run.

Alistair moved toward the bed. Vivian held on to the hem of his jacket and followed. A tangled knot of black hair lay against the filthy pillow. He placed his hand on the thin shoulder and gently turned the woman toward him. She looked at them with glassy eyes.

No, no, no. It can't be. It's not Ginny. The hand holding the handkerchief against her mouth shook.

The woman groaned and turned back toward the wall. "Go away. Let me die."

"Alistair," her stomach pitched, "it's her."

Alistair reached his arm around Vivian's shoulder.

God, what happened? How could this emaciated figure be Ginny? She'd left Brentwood less than two months ago. Vivian reached a shaking hand to Ginny's forehead and ran her fingers over the matted hair. Several strands pulled away and fell to the floor. She swallowed the sob in her throat and twisted in Alistair's arms. There was no air in the room to breathe.

Alistair held her tight. His eyes met hers, and then he turned her around. She closed her eyes and clamped her bottom lip between her teeth. *Lord, help me.* Vivian dropped to her knees beside the bed. Her fingers brushed across the blanket on Ginny's back. Every bone protruded. "Ginny, we've found you. The Lord has helped us find you."

"I said go away." The words were barely audible.

Vivian leaned forward and wrapped her arms around her sister. She was so tiny, almost nothing. "Ginny . . . I love you."

Ginny's shoulders shook in Vivian's arms as heart wrenching sobs filled the room.

CHAPTER 19

VIVIAN STEPPED OUT OF THE shanty and waved to Mona, the tall redhead they'd met on the first day in Paradise Alley.

"How is she today, Vivian?"

"Every day she's a little better; Alistair thinks we should be able to move her to my hotel room tomorrow or maybe the next day."

"Glad to hear that. That girl's lucky you showed up when you did."

If only Ginny felt the same way. She'd been silent and wouldn't talk to Vivian or even acknowledge her presence in the room.

After an examination, Alistair had determined Ginny was suffering from a severe case of Typhoid. He'd said it would turn around quickly if she continued to take the horse pills he'd prescribed. It would probably be months before she fully regained her strength. So far Ginny had refused to be moved. They'd cleaned out the shanty and thoroughly sanitized it the first afternoon. Vivian had wiped away weeks of grime from her sister's body and given her a fresh nightgown and bedding.

Alistair kept the night vigil, and Vivian cared for Ginny during the day. The hours stretched on forever in the silence. When would Ginny finally open up and confide in her? Ginny had told Alistair that Logan had left her penniless shortly after arriving in Dawson. Vivian knew little else.

The family had sent a reply of thanksgiving in response to the telegram Vivian had sent informing them she and Alistair had found Ginny. Other news from home had not been good. Father's health was not improving, and Dr. Mason didn't know how much longer he would live.

The highlight of each day was meeting with Alistair in the church in the early evening to talk about Ginny's condition and to pray for her. Alistair was so caring and kind as he helped Ginny to recuperate. The depths she'd sunk to were obvious. Most men would have walked away, and perhaps Alistair should have. Ginny didn't deserve his loyalty after the way she'd treated him.

Vivian walked the path between the shanties on her way to the church. The young girls watching her looked so hopeless as they stared at her from the doorways of their pathetic shacks. Did they all have families back home who loved them? Why would anyone choose this sort of life? She bent over to put the small paper sack of apples she'd bought earlier on one of the rough boards. One of the girls would retrieve it when her back was turned. Several attempts to give the women food from her hand had resulted in doors being closed in her face and icy stares through the windows.

Alistair was already kneeling at the altar when she arrived at the church. He was unaware of her presence as she tiptoed to the front and stood beside him on the wooden floor. His head was buried in his arms as he prayed, but the words were unintelligible. After several moments he lifted his head and swiped at his eyes. His face was damp. "Vivian."

"Yes, Alistair?"

"I've come to a decision."

"Yes?" Had he realized how hopeless Ginny was and was leaving for home? How would she care for Ginny alone?

"I'm going to ask Ginny to marry me, ask her officially I mean, right away."

"Marry you right away? Are you sure that's wise? What if she doesn't fully recuperate?" And what would become of poor Alistair if Ginny didn't change? Could he continue to love Ginny if she remained the self-centered person she'd always been?

"I know it seems hasty, but I love her. I will always love her. I can take better care of her as her husband."

"That's very noble of you, but you don't even know what all she's been through or what she's done," the words lodged in her throat, "with the men."

"I do; she's told me most of the story. Your sister's paid a very high price for her rebellion. But it doesn't matter. I still love her, and I know it's what the Lord wants me to do." He reached his hand into his pocket and pulled out the delicate, diamond ring.

Vivian stared at it as he rolled it around in his palm with his thumb.

"I've thought a lot about it and prayed about it, too. It seems like the right thing to do; it's what I want to do."

Vivian reached out, took the ring from his palm, and held it out between them. A slice of sunlight from the stained glass window hit the diamond and reflected warm rays into the room. "I know she'll love it; it's so beautiful. You're being very brave, Alistair."

"I don't really expect anyone else to understand. And I'm not sure how long it will take for Ginny to understand, either. After we're married we might stay in Dawson, although I know it would be difficult for your family."

"Stay here?" Vivian couldn't imagine remaining after all that had happened. "But I've come to take her back home. She can't stay here. You have to bring her home."

"I know you feel that way, Vivian, but I don't think Ginny does. She's not ready to face the family yet. I don't want to force her."

"I can't leave her here; I've come all this way." *There was no way Ginny would be staying in Dawson. She needs her family, and we need her. It's not too late; Father is still alive.* "My family's anxious for us to return. I'm going to go and see her right now. It's time that Ginny did more than ignore me."

Vivian ran from the church back to the shanty. She planted one foot firmly in front of the other as she opened the door and crossed the threshold. "Ginny, we need to talk."

Ginny was sitting up in bed staring at the wall with her hands clasped in her lap. Her cheeks had begun to fill out, and her skin was returning to a porcelain white instead of grey. Her eyes, however, when she finally made contact, were cold and resentful. "Back again so soon? You just left. No matter. I'm tired, and I need to rest." She rolled over and scooted down into the grey woollen blanket.

Vivian knelt on the floor beside the bed and put her arm on Ginny's shoulder. "Why won't you talk to me?"

"I said I'm tired; could you let me rest?"

"We have to talk. Alistair says you're not ready to come home and face the family. But I don't understand. We all love you, and I've searched for you for weeks to bring you home."

"No doubt so you can parade me around as an example of the wages of sin."

The barb hit its mark, and Vivian gasped. "How can you say such a thing? You know it's not true."

"It is true; you've always been the good daughter." Ginny turned over in the bed and sat up. Her eyes snapped as she fixed them on Vivian. "And you've always taken every opportunity to point out my weaknesses."

"Don't be ridiculous." There was no need to point out Ginny's weaknesses. They spoke loudly all on their own. "Do you honestly think I came all the way here to find you because I want to show you up?" Ginny was not thinking straight; perhaps the illness had affected her mind. "I love you. I want you to be safe."

"Well, I didn't ask for your help. You should have left well enough alone. I would have been dead by now, and no one would be the worse off."

"Ginny, don't say that."

"I will say it. You would all be better off without me. Do you have any idea, Miss Perfect, how awful I've been? I've compromised myself at every turn. If there was something to be gained by misbehavior, I was willing."

"But it can all be forgiven; you only have to ask."

"Ask whom? I've walked away from my family, from God, and from someone who genuinely cared about me." A tiny drop appeared at the corner of Ginny's eye, and her voice wavered. "Could you please leave me alone?" She clenched the blanket up in her fists and pushed it into her eyes.

"Is that why you won't talk to me? Do you think I don't love you enough to forgive you? Do you think God doesn't love you enough to forgive you?" *Lord, what have I done? She really doesn't know I love her. I've been such a hypocrite. And it could have been different. It could have been me languishing in this wretched excuse for a shelter. If Ben hadn't searched or if he'd given up, it would have been me. I was so stubborn. I wanted my own way. Lord, I'm so sorry.*

Vivian sat up on the edge of the bed and put her arms around Ginny's bony shoulders. "It doesn't matter where you've gone and what you've done. God has promised to forgive, always. Though your sins be as scarlet, they shall be as white as snow." She laid her cheek against her sister's silky hair. "You know that."

A muffled reply came from within the blankets, "I don't deserve it."

Vivian tightened her embrace. "You're right, we don't; neither of us deserve it." And she rocked her sister back and forth, stroking her back as they wept together.

"God's grace is a gift. He gives it to us because He loves us and not because we've earned it. We could never earn it. Ginny, please, I need you to understand."

Ginny's sobs shook her whole body as Vivian held her.

"Could I pray for you?" Vivian whispered.

Ginny nodded.

"Dear Jesus, thank You for helping me find my sister. She's hurting right now, Lord, and she needs Your comfort. She needs to know You still care. Give her Your assurance, Lord. Let her know she can never run beyond Your forgiveness."

"Jesus," Ginny said in a broken voice, "please forgive me. Help my family to forgive me." And then she wrapped her arms around Vivian like she was hanging on for her life.

* * *

Dawson City lay snugged along the shore of the Yukon River. He'd actually made it after weeks of toil he'd never done the likes of his entire life. Every muscle still groaned in the mornings, and it had been over a week since Ben's last ascent over the Chilkoot. If the pass hadn't been enough to almost kill a man, helping to build a boat on the shores of Lake Lindeman was a close second. Lucky enough he'd met up with two brothers sorely in need of some help to finish their rough-sawn craft, or he'd have never made it across the lake. The rapids upriver were something else, too; it was a wonder anyone ever made it to this forsaken town. Although, judging by the buildings lining the streets, it was hard to believe he was in the middle of the Northern wilderness. They looked like the ones he could find in any city down South.

Ben walked down the gangplank of the sternwheeler and aimed his boots toward the nearest hotel. After finding a room for the night and a well-earned bath and shave, he fell into an exhausted sleep. The noonday sun shining through the window woke him the next day. "Ugh." He hadn't meant to sleep so long. He wouldn't be getting an early start in the search for Vivian and Ginny. He threw on his clothes and splashed cold water from the basin on his face. Wiping it with his sleeve, he left the room and headed for the restaurant on the main floor of the hotel.

The tables were crowded with men wearing tattered wool shirts and trousers, crusty hats, and beards that hadn't seen a razor in many a day. He ran a hand over his clean shaven chin and sat at a stool along the polished bar.

"You just come into town, son?" A grizzled miner to his right spoke through the steak he was gnawing on.

"I guess I'm kind of obvious. If I had known there was an official outfit, I wouldn't have gotten so cleaned up."

The fellow chuckled and reached out a greasy hand to shake Ben's. "The name's Davey, Davey Thorpe. Pleased to make your acquaintance."

Ben returned the fellow's strong grip. "Ben McCormack, it's nice to meet you."

"You here to strike it rich?"

"Nope." Although if Vivian would have him, he'd be the richest man alive.

"Didn't think so. You don't have that glazed look in your eye the rest of us fools do. Whadya here for then?"

"I'm here to find my girl and see if she'll marry me."

A young man, coffee pot in hand, turned a mug right side up on the counter in front of Ben with a thump. Sloshing coffee over the side as he poured, he asked, "What'll be, sir?"

"I'll have three eggs and some salt pork with two biscuits on the side."

"Coming right up."

The miner chuckled once more. "Do you have any idea how much that order is going to cost you?"

The man was being forward. What business was it of his? "I got some idea of what things cost."

"Well maybe not here, son. That will be about twelve dollars. Unless you're paying in gold—then it'll be more."

Twelve dollars? Back home it was close to the cost of a farm wagon. Ben loosened his collar. "I guess I should have asked. I never thought . . ."

Davey reached inside his coat pocket and retrieved a fist sized leather pouch. After unravelling a leather thong from the top, he removed a thumb nail-sized gold nugget and sat it on the counter. "Consider your breakfast on me. But after this you better find some-where cheaper to eat unless you got a pocketful of gold. Now, what's your girl doing up here? It's kind of a rough town for women."

"Thanks for the breakfast, sir, I appreciate it. The girl I'm hoping to marry came to Dawson to find her sister. I have no idea if she's been successful or not."

"And you let her come up here alone to this wild place? In that case, you better not waste any time trying to locate her. There're very few women who come up here innocent and way fewer that go home that way." Davey stood and wiped his hand on his trousers before giving Ben a hearty slap on the back. "I wish you luck. It's time for me to get back to my claim." He sauntered away.

The eggs were rubber in Ben's mouth as he mulled over Davey's words. He never should have let Vivian come up to Dawson without a man's protection, Audrey or no Audrey. His pulse accelerated remem-bering the girl's name. He'd never be duped again, that's for sure. But it'd probably be best to put his anger to work to find Vivian before she came to any more harm.

He left the restaurant and headed to the next hotel to inquire if she might be registered there.

* * *

Ben removed his cowboy hat and wiped his brow. The afternoon had brought nothing but disappointment as he'd trudged from estab-lishment to establishment inquiring into Vivian's whereabouts. If he hadn't stood out like a sore thumb, he probably wouldn't have been approached by every disappointed soul looking to head home. He'd been offered every contraption you could think of for extracting gold at a "real good price" and everything else a fellow could think of, too. But if he heard one more sob story about being down to the last dime, there's no telling what he might do. He needed some peace and quiet. A small, white church with a narrow steeple sat on the next corner. It would be as good a place as any other to ask about the girls. If they didn't know anything, he could spend some time in prayer.

After stepping into the small entry, his feet paused as he recognized the form of the woman standing at the altar. Vivian? Her arms encircled the narrow shoulders of the man standing next to her. As she turned to face the man, her eyes shimmered with dampness, but her smile blazed across the room. The couple disengaged and clasped hands. Alistair? What was he doing here? He'd never said he had plans to come up North. But then again, the day they'd left home Alistair had been at the train station, and Vivian had never said one word about it. He had been duped again. Vivian was like Audrey—a figment of something he wanted to be true. He should have known better, but maybe he deserved her lack of disclosure.

If only she'd told him her affections lay with Alistair, he wouldn't have wasted almost two months trying to get to Dawson City. His heart weighed a thousand pounds as he turned to leave the church before he was noticed. There was no way he was giving Alistair the chance to gloat. And if he left on the earliest boat in the morning, at least he'd have some pride left—if nothing else.

* * *

Vivian's eye caught a movement at the back of the church and she turned toward a figure in the shadows. It looked like Ben. "Ben? Ben, is that you?" She ran toward him and jumped up. Throwing her arms around his neck, she buried her face in his collar. "I can't believe it."

Ben stepped back to gain a footing and wrapped his arms around her.

"I can't believe it's really you; I've missed you so much." Vivian said as she tightened her grip on his neck. Who cared what Alistair thought? Ben was here in the flesh, but only then did Vivian remember he had a wife. "I'm so sorry. I don't know what came over me." She squirmed out of his embrace. He seemed reluctant to put her down. "Where's Audrey?" she asked as she straightened the front of her dress and smoothed her hair. "What your wife would think of me if—"

"There's no wife."

"No wife? What happened?" She wanted to extend her fingers across the gap between them and erase the pained look on his face.

"She wasn't real, Vivian. It's a long story, but I knew in my heart she was never the one for me. I was too stubborn to admit it." Ben reached out and clasped her hand. His fingertips slid over hers as he turned for the door. "I wish you all the best."

The tingle of his touch travelled up the hairs on her arm. "You're leaving?" He must have just arrived. Why was he leaving so soon? "Ben?" Her fingers brushed the soft muslin on his shoulder, and he stepped away. He still didn't care, even without Audrey. *Lord, why?*

"I'm leaving first thing in the morning."

Her voice quaked as she replied. "I don't understand. You haven't even asked about Ginny."

He paused and turned back to face her. "How is she, then? Have you and Alistair rescued the poor girl?"

Was he mocking her? "We have. We've found her, and she's recuperating well."

"I'm glad you've found her. I assume she's not with Logan anymore."

Lord, I love him so much. "No, she's not with Logan. He left her when they reached Dawson. She's recovering from typhoid and getting stronger every day. We think she's going to be all right."

"I'm happy to hear that." He tipped his hat. "I'll be going now," he said and stepped through the door.

"Ben, please, can't we talk?"

He continued down the walk as he said over his shoulder, "I'm not up for any more double dealing. Take care."

That was undeserved. She hadn't been the one playing games. Nor had she been the one leading him to believe there was something between them when there apparently hadn't been. How dare he accuse her? She stepped through the open door and called to his back, "Mr. McCormack, you owe me an apology."

"An apology?" His boots stuck to the walk. He turned slowly, jaw clenched, his eyes a dark pool. "Pardon? If you think for one minute I'm going to apologize for believing you were something you're not," he punched the air with a pointed finger, "you've got another thing coming."

"What do you mean I'm something I'm not?"

He looked like he wanted to throttle her. "What is Alistair doing here? You never said he was coming."

It was like an accusation, but how could she have known? "I didn't know. He's here for Ginny."

"He's here for Ginny? Explain that right now."

"They are to be married when she's well enough. They might not even come back—"

Ben stepped forward quickly and dropped to one knee.

"What are you doing?"

His warm hands engulfed her own.

"Ben?"

"Vivian, before one more moment of our lives is wasted, I want you to know I love you with all of my heart."

The air was trapped in her lungs. He loved her?

"You'll never know the agony I felt trying to reach Dawson so I could be sure you were safe. I'm sorry I've been such an idiot by chasing the dream of a girl who didn't exist when the very first moment I met you I knew you were the one meant for me." He scrambled in his trousers' pocket and pulled out a ring with a small gold nugget. Placing it on her finger, he asked, "Miss Connor, would you do me the honor of becoming my wife?"

Vivian looked at the beautiful token of his love. It would change her life forever. "I can't think of anything I would love more, yes."

Ben rose to his feet and folded her into his embrace.

EPILOGUE

VIVIAN SMILED UP AT BEN on the front steps of the little country church a mile down from the couple's farmhouse. Her dress was a long, white, satin gown with a shirred yoke and pleated bodice. Aunt Margaret had done a lovely job on the high, ruffled neckline and cuffs, too. At Ben's request, she also wore a wide, gold ribbon at the waistline. It was to remind her he said, "Silver and gold have I none; but such as I have, give I thee."

The groom bent down and whispered, his lips brushing her earlobe, "I love you, Mrs. McCormack."

The words filled up her heart.

The day had been unusually warm for October, and the colored leaves made a beautiful backdrop to the long tables with white tablecloths. They were set out along the maple trees edging the church property. Soon they would be laden with food brought by all the friends and relatives who had gathered after harvest to observe their vows and wish them well.

Thankfully, Father's health had stabilized, and he was able to attend. Although he couldn't conduct the service, he'd said he was pleased to see his daughter marry such a fine young man.

The pastor's melodic voice rang out, "I would like to introduce, Mr. and Mrs. Ben McCormack."

Ben turned and kissed Vivian's upturned lips as rice flew at them from every direction.

As Vivian and Ben descended the wooden stairs, Sarah and Jeremy pushed to the forefront and stepped in to hug the newlyweds.

"Vivian, we are going to miss you all over again," Sarah said as she sniffled and hid her face in the folds of Vivian's dress.

Vivian crouched down after handing her nosegay of dried roses and baby's breath to her mother. "Sarah, you don't have to be upset. You can come out and visit us at the farm any time you want."

"We can?" The two chimed together.

"You sure can," Ben said. "I can use some strong arms around the place." Jeremy giggled as Ben squeezed his bicep.

On the next step, Ginny removed her hand from her rounding stomach and leaned in to hug Vivian. "Thank you for not giving up on me. I wish you both everlasting joy." Tears gathered in Vivian's eyes as she returned Ginny's hug.

Alistair reached out to shake Ben's hand. "Welcome to the family, brother-in-law. Six months ago who would have thought you and I would have been related?"

Ben and Vivian descended the rest of the stairs and continued to greet and visit their other guests until it was time for the luncheon to be served. The whole crowd whooped as Ben lifted Vivian up and carried her over to their awaiting table.

"I don't suppose it would do any good for me to ask you to put me down?"

"Never again, Vivian. Never again."

For more information about

Lisa J. Flickinger
and
All That Glitters
please visit:

www.lisajflickinger.com
lisaj.flickinger@gmail.com
Facebook Page: Lisa J. Flickinger

For more information about
AE BOOKS
please visit:

www.ambassador-international.com
@AmbassadorIntl
www.facebook.com/AmbassadorIntl